What read
The Moth

"Just finished reading Silver Lining of The Glendale Series!! During the series I felt like I was part of the family. I would laugh with them, cry with them and rejoice with each victory!! I felt myself drawn closer to the Lord in each book!! I was sad the series came to an end!! I highly recommend that all read this series!! It is life changing!!"

-Pam D.

"I've read the entire Glendale series in 2 weeks. Wow!! From laughing to crying I completely enjoyed every single book!! Thanks for the awesome series."

-Kimberly C.

"This series had a profound effect on my life. It made me realize some truths that were hidden in my heart and revealed where healing was needed. I highly recommend it to everyone."

-Theresa G.

"It's been hard to find books that capture my attention, but after reading the first Glendale series books, the Mothers of Glendale were a great continuation. Great insight and wisdom in these books. The author is a wonderful writer!"

-Mirpags

"Ann Goering is a young mother and a fresh new author. She can't keep them coming fast enough for me. Very entertaining and clean. :)"

-Rhonda T.

"I was so sad to complete The Glendale Series but reading One Desire (Mothers of Glendale) I was just as moved. I can't wait for the next book in this series to come out. They are like family to me."

-Thia

"Mrs. Goering never disappoints. She brings real life issues to the surface yet keeping the spotlight on Jesus. Love her work."

-Kayla M.

"This book shows how temptation can happen to anyone. I love how it ends. I recommend this book to help us all stay on guard!"
-Renee H., *Gray Area*

"This is the book that brought me to my knees. I have never been so convicted as I was while reading this book."
Lindsey W., *Gray Area*

"Very good book and I would recommend it to anyone that likes romance novels. I read for relaxation and it fit the bill."
-Chris, *Gray Area*

"This is a very good book! Love the first series and I love the second! Real life situations and love how God comes through for the families!"
-Ashley N., *Gray Area*

"Just finished reading Silver Lining. This is by far the best book I have ever read. Thank you so much for The Glendale Series."
-Christine A., *Silver Lining*

"I have never read a book that touched the very depths of my heart and showed the love of God and his mercy so much. Thanks GOD for devoted Christian writers such as Ann Goering."
-Rosanna T., *Silver Lining*

"I have absolutely loved this series and I am very sad to see it come to an end. I happened upon this series purely by accident. In each book I have read I was immediately pulled in and Silver Lining was no exception. I lived, breathed, ate and drank this book. While at work I thought of this book. Thought of ALL the books in this series. AMAZING! ABSOLUTELY AMAZING! Highly recommended."
-Melissa, *Silver Lining*

"Goering has written a beautiful ending to a wonderful Christian Series. The novel and series are timeless, revitalizing, and full of heart. Goering praises and glorifies the Lord in her words and characters. Wonderful book. It is a must read."
-KHBU, *Silver Lining*

THE GLENDALE NOVELS

The Glendale Series

Glendale
A New Day
Promising Forever

Mothers of Glendale

One Desire
Gray Area
Silver Lining

Ann GOERING

SILVER LINING
Mothers of Glendale

COVERED PORCH PUBLISHING

Silver Lining

Copyright © 2013 by Ann Goering. All rights reserved.

Cover design copyright © 2013 by Ann Goering. All rights reserved.

Edited by Eileen Fronterhouse

ISBN-10: 0989086658
ISBN-13: 978-0-9890866-5-3

Library of Congress Control Number: 2013904218

www.coveredporchpublishing.com

www.anngoering.com

Requests for information should be addressed to:
Covered Porch Publishing, Ann Goering, PO Box 1827, Hollister, MO 65673

Scripture quotations are taken from the Holy Bible, New International Version®, NIV® Copyright © 1973, 1978, 1984 by Biblica, Inc.® Used by permission. All rights reserved worldwide.

Scripture quotations are taken from the New King James Version®. Copyright © 1982 by Thomas Nelson, Inc. Used by permission. All rights reserved worldwide.

Scripture quotations are taken from the Holy Bible. New Living Translation copyright© 1996, 2004, 2007 by Tyndale House Foundation. Used by permission of Tyndale House Publishers Inc., Carol Stream, Illinois 60188. All rights reserved.

This book is a work of fiction. Names, characters, places, and incidents are fictitious and a product of the author's imagination. Any resemblances to actual people or events are coincidental.

Printed in the United States of America

17 16 15 14 13 A 7 6 5 4 3 2 1

This book is dedicated to the God of glory, who is always victorious;

My husband, who has taught me that forever would not be long enough;

My editor, Eileen, who has demonstrated how to love well and face sickness and death with confidence in Jesus – I'm so glad you received your miracle;

And to faith, which sustains.

One

Hannah Colby dropped onto a straw bale, thoroughly exhausted, but happy. She watched as her husband, Chris, was convinced by their two oldest grandsons to go down the slide with the burlap sacks just one more time. Shooting her a grin over his shoulder, he headed up the straw bale stairs once again, being pulled along by the boys.

Hannah smiled lovingly at her grandsons whose hair was the same color as the straw, then scanned the playing children for her other grandkids. She found Kimberly's youngest two, Clinton and Caiden, playing with toy tractors in the cornbox with Kaitlynn's two boys, Adam and Austin. She had brought little Ava, who wasn't quite two, back to the straw bale with her. Now she pulled her up into her lap and snuggled her in close. Ava's blonde, baby-soft hair tickled her face, and Hannah pressed a kiss against the little one's head.

Bringing the grandchildren to the pumpkin patch had been a good idea. It wasn't often that Kim and Kaitlynn were home with their families at the same time. When Chris suggested giving their daughters and their husbands a date day, while he and Hannah spent some quality time with the kids, she had quickly agreed. It had been a wonderful chance for the cousins to play, as well as a time for Chris and Hannah to spend a few precious hours laughing and playing with their grandchildren.

Earlier in the day, they had all stepped into burlap sacks and gone down the tall slide, played in the sandbox full of dried corn kernels, picked out their pumpkins from the patch, gone through the petting zoo, learned to milk a cow, and enjoyed a snack of caramel apples, popcorn and apple cider. Ava's face still held remnants of the caramel, and Hannah dug in the diaper bag Kaitlynn had sent to find a wipe to clean the little one's face with. Finding it, she scrubbed at the caramel, talking to Ava all the while to avoid a protest, until Ava's sweet little face was clean. Kissing her forehead, Hannah settled her on her lap more firmly and wrapped her arms around her, drawing her back farther, cuddling her close.

Hannah tipped her face up to the sun and smiled. The weather had not yet turned cold. In fact, they were having something of an Indian summer. Still, there was a slight chill in the breeze that had picked up as the afternoon wore on, and Ava seemed happy to snuggle into the warmth of Hannah's embrace. Hannah glanced up to keep tabs on the little boys, then watched Chris and the older boys race down the wide metal slide. When she glanced back down at her granddaughter, she found that she was sound asleep. Hannah smiled, sending a prayer of thanksgiving up to heaven. Her grandchildren, her husband, her children and her family were the sweetest gifts she had ever been given, next to salvation, of course. And here she was spending a whole day with the simple purpose of enjoying them.

Carson and Samuel raced ahead of Chris to the cornbox, where they began talking to the younger boys in animated terms while gesturing to the pedal tractors across the barnyard. She watched Austin and Caiden, who were the youngest boys in the group at almost four, take off for the tractors. Kim's Clinton, who was six, and Kaitlynn's Adam, who was seven, continued to dig in the corn for a few more seconds, taking longer to be convinced to leave their play. Finally they did, and Chris got to the cornbox just in time to jog after the boys as they all made their way to the tractors.

Hannah chuckled. Their grandsons could definitely keep them busy. They were all good boys, but when there were six boy cousins within six and a half years of each other, there was bound to be mischief. When Joe's three kids, Kelsi and Kamryn, eight-year-old twins, and Joshua, who was the youngest boy of the family at two and a half, joined the gang at Christmas, there would likely be even more activity. She couldn't wait.

Hannah stiffened as a sharp pain moved through her pelvis. If she were younger and hadn't gone through the big change several years back, she would think her body was gearing up for her monthly cycle. She had been experiencing low-grade cramps for most of the afternoon. Taking a deep breath as the pain subsided, she repositioned. It was likely all the activity that had caused the pains. She had experienced brief occurrences of the cramps off and on for the past few years. Seeing Adam jump off his tractor and run around with his fists outstretched in the air in jubilation, his shouts of victory audible from her spot on the straw bale, she forgot about the mild pain in her lower abdomen. Her attention shifted back to her grandchildren.

Ava sighed in her sleep, and Hannah brushed the blonde hair back from her face. The little girl looked so much like Kaitlynn had as a baby...and Kara, for that matter. There was no denying that each of her children and grandchildren descended from the Colby line. They all had the same green eyes, the same smile and the same chin, even on to this next generation.

Hannah's thoughts turned to her youngest daughter, Kara, who was happily settled in the area with her husband, Justin. They were coming over for dinner later to see the girls and their families while they were all in town.

Hannah ran her fingertips over Ava's face and thought of Kara. The young couple had celebrated their five year wedding anniversary last summer, and yet there were no babies. Hannah watched Kara with her nieces and nephews and knew how much she loved children, yet they went childless. For the past five years, Hannah had told herself that she wouldn't be a meddling mother, but more and more lately she had been thinking of asking Kara about it. Hannah wasn't sure if the lack of children was something the couple had planned, or if they were having a problem conceiving. If it was the first, Hannah wanted to reason with them that they weren't getting any younger. If it was the latter, she wanted to know in hopes of somehow being able to help or comfort her daughter.

She had never experienced difficulties becoming pregnant herself, but she had many friends who had struggled to conceive and knew of the frustration and pain it could cause. If Kara was having problems, she wanted to know. If nothing else, she could be a listening ear, a shoulder to cry on, and an aide in finding help.

"Grandma! I won the tractor race!" Adam exclaimed, running up to her, a cloud of dust being kicked up by his fast-moving little feet.

"I know! I was watching. Congratulations!" she told him, waving the dust away from her face with her hand.

"Sammy said he won, but Grandpa said I won by a fraction of an inch. I don't know what that means, but I know Grandpa's right. He's always right, isn't he, Grandma?"

Hannah smiled as she tucked her shoulder-length brown hair behind her ear to stop the wind from blowing it in her face. "Yes, he is."

"Well, he said you've learned that over the years, and I just thought I would check," Adam rambled on. Hannah shot Chris, who was pushing Austin's tractor to make him go faster, an amused look. "Did you think I won, too, Grandma?"

"Definitely," Hannah assured.

Adam bobbed his head. "I knew it. I'm going to go tell Sammy that you said I won, too." Adam was running back to the group of boys before Hannah could say anything else. She watched as he relayed the information to his cousin, and as Samuel made a face at him. She chuckled.

When she and Chris were raising their own family,

they had one son amidst four daughters. Their kids had their wild moments, and Chris had always been intentional about getting Joe outside to throw around a ball, go fishing, or move dirt in his toy dump trucks. But the majority of the play and fights in their household revolved around tea parties, baby dolls and Barbies. Having so many grandsons was a completely different story. She had not been aware of the energy level or the competitiveness that half a dozen boys brought to a family. While it could be a little exhausting at times, she loved it.

With all of the boys settled on a tractor, pedaling like mad to the next appointed finish line, Chris meandered back to join her. In his jeans and button-up green and white plaid shirt, her handsome husband could still bring butterflies to her stomach with his charming grin and characteristic wink. When he sat down next to her, letting his arm settle loosely around her shoulders, she snuggled into his side with a happy sigh.

Life was good.

"I think they'll stay busy on those for awhile," Chris told her, his deep voice rich and amused. "Is this one sleeping?"

Hannah pulled back a little to allow Chris to see Ava's peaceful face. "She's getting a good little nap in. It won't be as long as normal, but at least it's something...hopefully it will be enough to get her through until bedtime."

"I think bedtime might have to come a little early for all of them tonight. I'm guessing the whole lot of 'em will be worn out," Chris told her, grinning.

"We could put all the kids to bed and play cards," Hannah pointed out. They had always been a family that played a lot of games, but when all of the kids started having babies, it grew a little trickier for a few years. It was just now getting to the point that the kids were old enough to entertain themselves while the adults played cards. An early bedtime would ensure them the opportunity.

They settled into a comfortable silence, and Hannah rested her head on Chris' shoulder. With him serving as a wind block and his heat soaking into her, she grew drowsy. Fighting the urge to take a quick nap, she looked up at him and took in his strong jawline, masculine chin, tanned skin and green eyes. His chocolate-colored hair was becoming speckled with gray, and she liked how it looked. Her dashing husband was aging well. His appearance somehow reflected the wisdom he had come to possess. He felt her attention and glanced down at her, a smug smile on his face. He kissed the tip of her nose.

"This was a good idea to come here today," she told him, smiling. "It's been a fun day." She paused. "But then again, I suspect you knew I would agree that it was a right decision to come...after all, according to Adam, you're always right, and I've come to learn that over the years," she continued, teasing him.

Chris laughed and his grin was sheepish. "I wondered if he would repeat that to you."

"Hm. Yes, he did," Hannah answered, her eyes full of merriment.

"Let me explain that," Chris said, snuggling her in closer.

"Be my guest."

"Well, the boys were all racing to the tree. Samuel thought he won, and Adam thought he won. The boys made me the judge, and I said Adam won fair and square. Samuel didn't agree and thought we should call you in for a second opinion."

"And you told them I'd learned you were always right to avoid further argument," Hannah finished, amused. Chris shrugged, grinning again. "Well, I'll do my best to remember what I've learned."

"Do that."

Hannah chuckled. They fell quiet again, both of them still smiling. A couple of decades earlier, Hannah may have taken offense at Chris' smug statement to the boys, but not after thirty-four years of marriage. By now she knew his heart and how he had meant his comment...and how he hadn't.

"Well, that didn't last long," Hannah observed as the boys all suddenly jumped off their tractors and raced across the barnyard on foot. Chris reluctantly stood as they disappeared behind a shed.

"Looks like they're headed back to the pumpkin patch," he told her. "I'd better go see what mischief they have up their sleeves now. What do you say about leaving in twenty?"

It had been a fun day, but a full one. It would be nice to get out of the sun and wind, and she needed to get home to start dinner. "Perfect." She reached out and swatted his behind as he left, enjoying the fact that it was still as shapely as it was when they met in college.

Hannah waited on the straw bale until she saw Chris and the boys come around the corner of the shed, their arms full of the pumpkins they had picked earlier in the day. Chris nodded toward their SUV, and Hannah stood, lifting Ava in her arms, getting his message that he was ready to go. Hannah bent to grab the diaper bag, and Ava woke. Pressing a kiss against the little girl's forehead, she set her on her feet, keeping hold of her hand, so that Ava could walk to the car.

Later, once Ava, Austin and Caiden were buckled into their car seats and Adam, Carson, Samuel and Clinton were double-buckled in the third row, they started home. It was a short drive, and Chris and Hannah took the opportunity to discuss the day in hushed tones as the little ones dozed in their car seats and the bigger boys had their own conversation in the back.

Once home, the kids piled out of the car, running inside to tell their parents about their day. Hannah settled Ava on her hip, looped the diaper bag strap over her arm and accepted the pumpkin that Chris gave her, squeezing it between her free arm and her stomach.

Kaitlynn met her at the front door. "Hey Mom! Oh, here, let me take the baby." Kaitlynn took Ava, giving Hannah both arms to carry the pumpkin.

"There are more of these out there," Hannah told her, heading for the kitchen where she could put it down on the counter.

"Jake, Greg, do you guys want to help Dad carry in pumpkins?" Kaitlynn called. Both men emerged from the living room, Jake with Austin and Caiden sitting on his feet, their arms and legs wrapped around his calves. Hannah laughed as Jake went out the front door to carry pumpkins, the boys still in tow.

She set her heavy pumpkin down on the kitchen counter and turned to the sink to wash her hands.

"How was your day?" Kaitlynn asked, settling on a stool at the breakfast bar facing Hannah, setting Ava on the counter in front of her.

"It was wonderful! The weather was perfect, and the kids had a blast."

"I can see that," Kaitlynn agreed with a smile. "The boys haven't stopped chattering since they walked in the door. Adam seems quite proud of his win on the pedal tractors."

"You heard about that already, did you?"

"Oh, you bet. He never misses an opportunity to brag about a victory!" Kaitlynn told her, her eyes laughing.

Hannah chuckled. "Yes, he was quite proud of himself." She paused. "Did you guys have a good day?"

"Yes!" Kaitlynn popped a candy covered chocolate into her mouth from the candy dish on the counter. "Jake and I had lunch together, did some Christmas shopping for the kids, then met Kimmy and Greg for a matinee. It was such a treat to have a whole day with just adults and to have some time for the two of us. That certainly doesn't happen often. So, thank you!"

Hannah smiled. "I remember those days. Trust me, even though it doesn't feel like it now, it passes much too quickly. Then all you have is time for just the two of you. Don't get me wrong – your father and I love spending our days together, we both just miss when you guys were all young and at home."

Kaitlynn's smile was sad. "I miss that sometimes, too, Mom."

"But if you lived closer, we could watch the kids more often and you two could have a date night every week," Hannah continued, unable to resist putting in a plug for them moving back to Glendale. She wanted grandkids close by. She wanted to go to ball games, babysit for entire weekends, attend school functions, and see her grandchildren throughout the week. Kaitlynn sent her an amused grin.

"Mom, what are you thinking for dinner?" Kimmy asked, entering the kitchen.

"Hi, Honey! Did you have a good day?" Hannah asked, turning to accept Kimberly's hug.

"Yes, it was wonderful! Thank you for keeping the boys."

"You are most welcome. We had a blast," Hannah told her. "I was thinking I would make tator tot casserole and steamed carrots. I made a spice cake with cream cheese frosting this morning before we left, so we can have that for dessert."

"Yum! Is that what smelled so good down here this morning? I was wondering," Kaitlynn said, handing a piece of candy to Ava and putting a couple more in her own mouth.

"That sounds great," Kimmy started, "but Greg and I were talking about it, and we would like to treat everyone to pizza, if that's okay. You've been out all day with the kids; you don't need to come home and make dinner for everyone, too. Why don't we call in pizzas and have Kara pick them up on her way over? Then we won't have to worry about making and cleaning up a meal."

"We could still have cake for dessert," Kaitlynn pointed out.

"That sounds great," Hannah admitted. She had been prepared to make a big meal for everyone, but truth be told, she felt tired after their day at the pumpkin patch, and it sounded wonderful to have pizza brought in. If she had thought of the idea herself, she would have suggested it. "Your dad and I were hoping we could all play some cards tonight. Pizza makes that even more likely."

"So true," Kaitlynn said, reaching for another piece of candy.

"That would be fun! Let's do that. So, what kind of pizzas should I order?" Kimberly asked.

"Pepperoni for the kids," Kaitlynn volunteered.

"Supreme for the men," Hannah added.

"And Canadian bacon, mushroom, black olive for the four of us girls," Kimmy finished. Hannah and Kaitlynn both quickly agreed. "We could be terrible and get two pizzas for us girls, like we will for the guys," Kimberly suggested, looking sheepish. "I'm starving!"

"I'm on board! Every once in awhile you have to live a little...and sometimes that means eating more than two pieces of pizza," Kaitlynn offered.

Hannah laughed, enjoying having her two oldest girls home. "I'm game!" She patted her stomach and laughed. "I probably shouldn't be, but I am."

"Whatever! You're looking thinner than you have in a long time, Mom!" Kimmy pointed out.

"Well, that's certainly not true," Hannah protested, waving away Kimberly's observation.

"No, I noticed that too," Kaitlynn agreed. "Have you been dieting?"

"You girls are silly. I haven't been doing anything to lose weight...although I probably should be."

"Well, I still think you look thinner," Kimmy told her, and Kaitlynn nodded in agreement.

Kimberly pulled out the phone book and leafed through it until she found the number of the pizza joint in Glendale.

"You wouldn't have had to find it. I could have told it to you," Kaitlynn told her sister. "I still have it memorized."

"Why does that not surprise me?" Kimmy asked, rolling her eyes good-naturedly. It was a well-known fact that the eldest Colby daughter had a memory like a steel trap. Nothing escaped her. Not a phone number, not an address, not a family memory, not even what someone was wearing in a memory.

Kaitlynn shrugged. "Just saying."

"Can you call Kara and ask her to stop and pick up the pizzas while I order? I'll pay her back when she gets here." Kimberly asked Kaitlynn. "I don't want to wait too long to tell them the plan and have them show up without the pizzas."

"Sure. Mom, can you watch her? My phone is up in my room charging."

Hannah reached for Ava, who leaned into her arms, and Kaitlynn headed for her phone. Hannah sank down onto a chair at the table, settling Ava in her lap. She ran her hand through the baby girl's hair while Kaitlynn and Kimmy made their phone calls, simply enjoying having her kids home again. She was glad Kara and Justin were coming over and wished Joe and Jessi could, too. She was never happier than when all of her kids and their families were home.

With a sudden wave of sadness, her thoughts brought up a harsh reality that time had begun to ease. *All* of her children would never be home together again, not this side of heaven.

It had been a long time since they had lost their daughter, Kelsi Kamryn, to leukemia, but the longing she felt for her child had never diminished. Time had taken the sting out of Kelsi's death, but Hannah doubted that the overwhelming bittersweet longing she felt for the freckle-faced blonde would ever fade.

Now, with Kaitlynn upstairs, Kimmy on the phone and Kara on her way over, Hannah thought of her third born. She would be twenty-nine – right in between Kimmy and Joe in age. She would likely have a husband and children of her own by now, had she lived.

Hannah closed her eyes briefly and pictured how she might have looked. It wasn't hard. She would probably look a lot like Kaitlynn and Kara. She had always favored them. Kimberly was the only one of the girls who looked different. She had her daddy's dark hair and Hannah's face shape. Kelsi had looked like the other girls. Hannah could picture her now.

Sadness welled up within her, and she took a deep breath, pushing it back down. They had been given five beautiful years with Kelsi. She would be thankful for that.

Kaitlynn came back into the kitchen. "Kara was ready to walk out the door. They'll wait for the pizza and then be over."

"They should be here in about twenty-five minutes, then," Kimmy said, just hanging up from ordering their dinner.

Caiden and Austin ran into the kitchen, capes flying from their backs and foam swords in their hands. "We are superheroes, here to save the day!" Caiden announced, striking a manly pose.

"Superheroes!" Austin echoed. "My is a real superhero! Did you know that, Nama? My is! A *real* superhero!"

Hannah's eyes lit up in merriment at the almost four-year-old in front of her. "A *real* superhero?" she asked. He nodded, his dimples showing. "Wow, Austin. That's pretty cool. What's your superpower?"

"My is super strong! My can lift cars with my bare

hands! See watch!" Austin braced his legs and lifted an imaginary car above his head, grunting and making faces as he did.

Hannah laughed, clapping her hands in delight. "You sure are strong!"

"Yeah," he agreed, throwing the car aside.

"Oh yeah? Well, I can fly and get the bad guys!" Caiden interjected, determined not to let his cousin get all the attention.

"Wow, Caiden! That's very superhero-ish, too. I've always wanted to be able to fly," Hannah told him, her expression serious, unwilling to hurt their feelings or deter their little-boy imaginations.

"Well, I'll teach ya sometime," Caiden promised.

"Why don't you superheroes fly on out of here and tell your dads that we'll eat in about half an hour," Kimberly told the boys.

Their super-mission clear, the little boys were gone with flapping capes and extended swords.

"Huper, huper, huper!" Ava exclaimed, clapping her hands and squirming to get off of Hannah's lap. Hannah set her on the ground and gave the little girl's bottom a pat as Ava set off to chase her brother and cousin.

"We need more girls in the family," Kaitlynn said, watching her daughter go.

"We do. Poor Ava," Kimmy agreed. "I tried. I feel for her, I do, but I'm not trying anymore. Four boys is barely manageable chaos. I can't imagine five."

Hannah and Kaitlynn laughed. "But maybe you would have a little girl next time," Kait pointed out.

"Don't even say that," Kimmy warned. "Talk like that is what led to Clinton…and then Caiden. Nope, we're destined to have all boys, and four is the perfect number."

"If only Kelsi and Kamryn were closer," Hannah observed. "Then Ava would have girls to play dollies and dress-up with."

"True. I don't see them moving anytime soon, though. And from August to January, they're pretty much stuck in Minnesota on the weekends, which is the only time we can come back," Kaitlynn said.

"Well, maybe Kara will have a little girl for Ava to play with," Kimmy offered.

"Has she said anything to either of you girls about having kids?" Hannah asked, glad the topic had come up. Hoping not to seem too eager, she pushed herself up off the chair and went around the island to get plastic cups out for dinner.

Both girls shook their heads. "I've wondered, though. How many years have they been married now?" Kimmy asked.

"It was five this summer," Hannah answered.

"That's right. Adam had just turned two and Clinton was still one at their wedding," Kaitlynn agreed.

"Hm. You would think they would be starting a family sometime soon," Kimmy said, pulling several two liters of soda out of the fridge.

"I thought they would have already," Kaitlynn agreed.

"Me too," Hannah added. Again, she wondered at her daughter's reasoning. She watched her with her nieces and nephews, and she knew that Kara longed for children of her own. She could see it in her eyes. She had hoped that Kara had confided in one of her sisters, but they both seemed as perplexed as she was. Hannah made a mental note to ask Jessi about it next time she called. If anyone would know, it would be Jessi.

For a moment, she wondered if she should just ask Kara rather than trying to sneak around to find out, but once again, decided against it. If they had been trying, but couldn't get pregnant, it could be a sore subject. Hannah's biggest fear was that Kara couldn't have children at all.

There had been complications when Kara was born. She was one sick little baby. The doctors made lots of predictions about Kara's future then, but so far she had proven them wrong. Doctors said she wouldn't live; she did. Doctors said she would never walk; she did. They said she would never be able to talk, write or live a normal life; she accomplished all of those things. Those victories gave Hannah confidence that the doctors would be proven wrong in every case. Except Kara still didn't have children...the one remaining prognosis Hannah had spent the last twenty-five years praying the doctors were wrong about also.

The conversation moved on, and Hannah chatted easily with her two oldest girls as they poured drinks and set out paper plates. When Justin and Kara arrived with the pizzas, the men and boys came flooding into the kitchen, following the smell of food. The early evening passed in a blur of pizza, soda, laughter, children, and conversation. When they were done with dinner, Kaitlynn and Kimberly announced that it was bedtime, which met with fewer groans and protests than normal.

"I think you guys wore these kids out today," Jake exclaimed, chuckling as he stood from the table, watching his droopy-eyed sons come around the table to give goodnight hugs.

"I think it was mutual," Chris responded, yawning. Everyone laughed. Hannah gathered her grandsons into her arms, covering their pizza sauce-smeared faces with kisses. They moved on to give their grandpa hugs, and she hugged and kissed little Ava, then Clinton and Caiden. At ten and nine, Carson and Samuel thought they were too old for goodnight hugs and simply headed upstairs to bed, already discussing which movie they would watch until they fell asleep. Getting up from her chair, Hannah chased them down before they made it to the stairway, and with sheepish grins, they gave her goodnight hugs before she let them escape to the safety of Joe's old room. As she turned to go back to the table, she found Kara coming through the kitchen archway, her face serious.

Concerned by her daughter's expression, Hannah held out her hand to her youngest. Kara stepped close, putting her head close to Hannah's. "Mom...don't worry, I don't think anyone else noticed, it's not much, but," Kara let her sentence trail off rather than finishing it.

Hannah searched her daughter's face, clueless. "What's not much?"

Kara gestured to Hannah's jeans, looking both concerned and embarrassed. "Mom, you're bleeding."

Two

Hannah ran from the living room to the kitchen to answer the ringing telephone. She hardly ever sat down during the day, but after the big weekend with all the kids, she felt worn out. Jake and Kaitlynn had been the last to leave, and she had driven them to the airport just the morning before. After that, she stopped by the grocery store, went to see her doctor about her incident over the weekend, and stopped by the church to drop off some groceries for the church dinner Wednesday night. She had coffee with a friend and arrived home just in time to make dinner, then go back to the church with Chris for an elders' meeting.

Chris had been an elder at the church for the past fifteen years, and she appreciated that he wanted her to accompany him to the meetings. Her husband treasured her opinion and insight. Being reminded of that every Monday night was a gift. Last night was one of the first times she had seriously considered staying home from the meeting. She was absolutely exhausted. Thus, when she turned on the television that morning to flip to the Christian music station and saw that one of her favorite home decorating shows was on, it didn't take long for her to snuggle up on the couch with her favorite throw.

Now, she felt guilty as she snagged the phone off the kitchen counter. What was a woman her age doing watching television during the day? She had sheets to wash, a house to clean, and her checkbook to balance.

"Hello?" she answered.

"Hello. Mrs. Colby?"

"Yes."

"This is Rita from Dr. Thorlo's office."

"I thought it sounded like your voice!" She had known Rita for years and had enjoyed visiting with her the day before at the clinic. "How are you today?"

"I'm good. How are you doing, Hannah?"

"Very well, thanks."

"Dr. Thorlo asked me to give you a call to let you know that he got your test results back. He would like to schedule a time in the next day or two for you to come in to go over them."

For a moment, Hannah's heart jumped and alarm coursed through her. Being called in to go over the results of medical testing couldn't be a good thing. Then she remembered that Dr. Thorlo had said he would have her come in to go over the results, regardless of what they said. Her shoulders relaxed, and she let out the breath she had caught. "Of course. I could come in this afternoon or tomorrow morning."

"Dr. Thorlo asked that Chris come with you."

Again, Hannah felt alarmed. This time nothing came to ease her mind. Of course, Dr. Thorlo and her husband were friends. They had golfed together on a few occasions and always enjoyed conversation when their paths crossed, but she doubted that was reason enough to ask for Chris to accompany her to the appointment. Was there bad news waiting for her at Dr. Thorlo's? Or was there another explanation? "In that case, does he have any time available this afternoon?" Hannah asked, forcing her voice to remain steady. Chris had a house closing in the morning.

"How about five o'clock?" Rita suggested.

"I thought his last appointment of the day was at four thirty," Hannah said.

"He said he could make an exception if needed, to accommodate your schedule."

"I don't know if I like the sound of that," Hannah said, forcing her voice to remain light. She hoped Rita would give her an explanation that would put her mind at ease.

"We'll see you at five, then," Rita said.

"Okay. Goodbye," Hannah answered. Rita hung up. Hannah stood with her hip against the kitchen counter and stared out the sliding glass doors at the sprawling patio. The patio ended at green grass that served as a fresh carpet stretching all the way to the edge of the heavy forest. Hannah stared off into the thick trees as she processed the phone call.

Why did Dr. Thorlo want her to come in to discuss the results of the tests he had run? When he did the pelvic exam, Pap smear and endometrial biopsy, he said they were routine tests for any woman who experienced vaginal bleeding after menopause. She hadn't thought anything of it. He explained that some women simply had spotting or even periods after menopause, and it didn't mean anything was wrong. They were simply going to eliminate possibilities, is what he had said. She didn't know what those possibilities were, but she was quite certain she didn't want to find out. Now, she was filled with dread as she thought of her upcoming appointment with him.

"For You have not given me a spirit of fear, but of power and of love and of a sound mind," Hannah whispered to herself, quoting the passage she had learned to love over the span of her lifetime. Fear had been her constant companion from a very young age, always trying to wreak havoc on her heart and mind. However, through praying for and receiving peace and speaking the truth of the Word, she had found more and more victory over it with each passing year. Now she took a stand against it again, refusing to let it raise its ugly head. She repeated the verse over and over as she dialed a familiar number.

"Hey, Pretty Lady."

Her husband's cheerful greeting brought a smile to her face and reassurance to her heart. "Hi."

"How's your morning going?"

"I curled up with a blanket and watched a dingy dining

room be transformed into a beautiful, elegant place to enjoy family dinners."

Chris chuckled. "So, what color are we going to paint our dining room?"

He knew her well. "A charcoal gray."

He chuckled again. "Well, I'm glad you took time to rest this morning."

"I should have cleaned the house."

"The house will wait." His voice was warm and loving, and the shadows of fear that had been clouding her heart were chased away. Still, she needed to tell him of her doctor's appointment at five. It may come as a bit of a surprise, as she hadn't told him she stopped by the doctor's office the day before. She simply hadn't been worried about it.

"I went to the doctor yesterday. He ran some tests, and told me he would have me come back in to discuss the results. The results are back, and Rita called to ask if we could come in during the next couple of days. I made an appointment for five o'clock tonight since you're closing on the house on Elm in the morning."

Chris was quiet for a moment. "What kind of tests?" He sounded confused.

"Routine tests. Remember my little issue Saturday night? I went in to get that checked. He ran tests, but said it was probably nothing."

"Oh right. Makes sense. Alright, I'll plan on five o'clock then."

"Do you want to meet there?" Hannah asked.

"Oh, I can wrap up here in time to come home and get you," Chris answered casually. He was at his office in town making preparations for the house closing the next morning and getting a new listing ready to go on the market. She appreciated the fact that she came first, even if he was busy. "I'll plan on being home around four thirty. Does that work?" he finished.

"I'll be waiting," she promised.

"Are there any of those monster cookies left?"

Hannah smiled. "I'll make a new batch." She wasn't sure who loved her cookies more – her husband or her grandkids. Needless to say, over the past weekend they had disappeared fast.

"Oh, you don't have to do that," he protested, though she knew it was half-hearted.

"I know I don't have to," she told him with a smile. "I'll let you get back to your work."

"Yeah, I'd better. I'll see you this afternoon."

"Alright. Love you," she told him.

"Love you, too," he answered before hanging up. She looked around her kitchen. The dishes from dinner the night before were still in the sink, and the tile floor desperately needed swept. She knew that sheets from four beds needed stripped and washed, then the beds remade. The bathrooms should be cleaned, and the living room needed to be vacuumed and put back in order. Kait had helped her clean up Sunday evening, but somehow in the span of the next morning before leaving, it looked like a whirlwind had gone through the house again.

Hannah looked around her dirty house and made a face. She would gladly do housework if it meant having her kids home, but there was no doubt that the family time was much more enjoyable than cleaning up.

She suppressed a yawn with her hand and shifted, trying to ease the pain in her lower abdomen. She sure thought she had left cramps behind when she went through the big change. She remembered Dr. Thorlo saying some women never got over menopause symptoms. She certainly wasn't going to accept that.

Deciding to enjoy the only enjoyable part of a monthly cycle, she opened a nearby cupboard and removed several coffee mugs to uncover a stash of chocolate she had kept full for decades. Selecting a chocolate bar and making herself a cup of coffee, she made her way back out to the living room. Regardless of the things she should be doing, she set her coffee on the end table and laid down on the couch, pulling her blanket across her once again, opening her chocolate bar. She pushed play on the television and resumed her show.

Glancing from the television to the dining room that was visible through a large arched doorway, she smiled. She liked the idea of painting it charcoal gray. She was glad Chris had suggested it. She really had no plans to repaint until he said something, and she knew it was his way of saying she could if she wanted to. A dark gray on the walls, bright white trim, and a new crystal chandelier would make the room more modern. Happy with her decision, she smiled and ate her candy bar slowly, enjoying the smooth taste of the milk chocolate.

One show led into the next, and she stayed for it, too. After watching a third episode, she shut off the television and pushed herself to her feet. She had spent enough time being lazy. She had things to do.

She baked cookies and washed dishes. She swept the tile floors and scrubbed the kitchen table. Satisfied that her kitchen was in order, she glanced at the clock and found that it was after one. She didn't feel hungry, but made herself a sandwich anyway, knowing she should eat. After the girls mentioned that she looked thinner, she weighed herself and found that she had lost fifteen pounds. While she hadn't been dieting, she hadn't felt as hungry lately. Even though it was nice to have a little extra room in her clothes, she wanted to make sure she was getting proper nutrition. She sat down at the breakfast bar with her sandwich, a cup of yogurt and a glass of milk. She would be turning fifty-five in the spring, and it was time to make sure she was getting plenty of calcium. In thirty years, she would be glad she had.

After lunch, she climbed the stairs to the second floor and stripped sheets. As she collected sheets from the bed

Adam and Austin had slept in, a toy superhero fell onto the floor. Picking it up, she smiled. 'My is a real superhero! Did you know that, Nama? My is! A *real* superhero,' she remembered Austin saying. She chuckled and took the superhero into the upstairs living room where an ottoman with a hinged lid had been converted into a toy box. She opened the lid and dropped the figurine inside, before going back after her sheets.

Later that afternoon, when she checked her cell phone after getting out of the shower, she found a text message from Kara asking if she could come over later. Justin was going out of town for business, and she wanted to come spend the evening with them.

'That sounds wonderful, Honey!' Hannah texted back. 'I have to run into town this afternoon, but should be home by six.'

Hannah felt her excitement build when Kara texted back that she would come over after she got off work.

Hannah enjoyed each of her girls, but she undoubtedly spent the most time with Kara. She was the only one of their children who still lived in the area, and she came over often. Additionally, she was Hannah's baby. With the exception of Kaitlynn, Kara was the only child Hannah had at home all by herself. After Joe graduated from high school, Kara was home a full two years with all of the other Colby kids away at school, married, or off on their own. When Kara graduated and went to college, Hannah missed her in a way that she hadn't the others; after Kara left, she and Chris experienced having an empty nest. She enjoyed the additional time she had with her husband, but she missed the house being full of conversation and laughter. She missed the youth and energy that her children had brought to the home; the friendship they offered and the way they had kept her plugged in to the community.

In the seven years Kara had been gone, Chris and Hannah had rebuilt a life, just the two of them. She found new ways to be involved in the community. She grew accustomed to the quietness of their home. She learned to depend on her husband's friendship, as well as the friendship of other women. She took up her old hobby of painting and took classes to improve her skills. She had even begun to bring in a small income by selling her work in a few local galleries.

After Kara moved out, Hannah went through a few hard months when life felt empty and dull. Now, life felt good again. She enjoyed seeing Kara throughout the week and on Sundays, enjoyed when the others came home to visit, and enjoyed taking trips to visit all of them. But when it was just her and Chris and the simple lifestyle they had formed as empty nesters, she enjoyed that, too.

Still, as she put on her makeup, she found herself being excited for a night with her daughter. She would throw something in the slow cooker before she left for the doctor so dinner would be ready when they got home. She was glad she had made more cookies. She would make a pot of tea later for her and Kara to enjoy with their treat. Chris would have milk. Maybe they would put in a movie or play a game of Monopoly.

She was hopeful that she would get a chance to talk to Kara about how life was and how she was doing. She had seen her daughter often enough over the past couple of months, but didn't feel like they had really had a chance to have a real conversation. There were always other people around or things to be done.

By the time Chris walked through the front door, she had almost forgotten about the upcoming appointment with Dr. Thorlo. Kara's impending visit had been a welcome distraction.

"Hi, Sweetheart," Chris said, walking into the kitchen. "Sorry, I'm a little late. Are you ready?"

Hannah glanced at the clock after returning his light kiss. It was twenty till five. "Yes, I am." She slipped her apron off over her head and laid it on the counter. "We're having chicken and stuffing for dinner. It should be ready by the time we get back."

"I know. I could smell it as soon as I walked in the door. It smells wonderful!"

"And I cut up veggies for a salad that I'll toss as soon as we get home. Everything should be ready."

"Sounds great," Chris said, following her into the entry, where she pulled on her denim jacket and stepped into her brown clogs.

"Kara's coming over tonight," Hannah told him on her way out to his pickup.

"Is she?" His face lit up as she knew it would.

She nodded. "Around six. Justin is out of town tonight."

"Well, I'm glad she decided to come over. On Saturday, she promised me a game of Monopoly the next time she came. Think I'll cash in on that tonight." Chris seemed pleased, just as Hannah knew he would be. After watching him be a parent for thirty-three years, one thing she knew about Chris Colby was that he was a good father and a good man. She was proud of him.

He told her about his day on their way into town and the new house he was in the process of listing. He asked when she wanted to paint the dining room, and they made plans to make it their Saturday project. The short trip into town went quickly, and they walked into the doctor's office three minutes early.

Rita greeted them warmly and proceeded to lead them into Dr. Thorlo's office – not his examining room, but his office. Hannah looked around curiously as she sat down in one of the two chairs on the near side of his desk. Rita left them, saying she would tell Dr. Thorlo they were there, and that he would be in shortly.

Hannah looked around the room. It was relatively small, but nice. A picture of his family sat on his desk. Certifications hung on his wall. Thick books lined his shelves. A coffee mug sat beside his computer screen. A small pond with a fountain was visible through the large window. Pictures of newborns covered his bulletin board, along with several thank you notes that were pinned up amongst them.

"He's delivered all five of our children, and I've never been in this room," she told Chris, turning to look at him.

He reached for her hand and shot her a reassuring smile. "It's going to be fine. There's no need to meet in an examining room if we're just going over test results."

His reasoning made sense. It always did.

Hannah had just opened her mouth to answer when Dr. Thorlo came into the room. A smile filling his face, he shook both of their hands. Taking a seat behind his desk, he got straight to the point, as was his normal style. "I asked you to come in today to go over the results of some tests I ran. As you know, Hannah, you came in yesterday because you had experienced vaginal bleeding over the weekend. I started with a pelvic exam. Now during that exam, questions were raised."

"What kind of questions?" Hannah asked. He hadn't mentioned anything about questions the day before.

"Questions that led me to do additional testing. Your uterus felt a little different than I would expect it to. That's why I decided to do a Pap smear and an endometrial biopsy. The Pap smear came back fine."

Hannah nodded, both thankful and relieved. She had heard so many stories of cervical cancer that she always felt immense relief when a Pap smear came back normal. It had been the first thing she thought of earlier when Rita had asked her to come in. Now, she felt herself relax deep within. Everything was fine. Dr. Thorlo asked them to come in simply to share the negative test results and perhaps give them ideas on how to keep her body in balance post-menopause.

"However, I also did an endometrial biopsy, and," Dr.

Thorlo paused. "That didn't come back good."

Hannah's relief shattered. "What do you mean?" she asked.

"What's an endometrial biopsy?" Chris asked at the same time, shifting in his chair while keeping a firm hold on Hannah's hand.

"An endometrial biopsy is when I extract cells from the endometrium – the lining of the uterus – to be studied under a microscope to check for abnormalities in the cells," Dr. Thorlo explained. Chris nodded, understanding. Dr. Thorlo paused and looked from Chris to Hannah, back to Chris, then back to Hannah. She felt her pulse begin to race. "Hannah, I found a lot of abnormalities in the cells I collected."

"What's that mean?" Chris asked.

Dr. Thorlo folded his hands loosely on his desk. "I hate to tell you this, I really do, but Hannah, you have endometrial cancer, specifically clear-cell carcinoma."

Chris and Hannah both stared at him, both speechless, both shocked. He continued. "Endometrial cancer is the most common kind of uterine cancer, however clear-cell carcinoma is a much less common form of endometrial cancer. I'm referring you to a gynecologic oncologist. Tests need to be run to see how far the cancer has spread and you need to begin treatment right away."

Three

Hannah hadn't taken a breath since the doctor said the unthinkable.

She had cancer? *Cancer?* Had he really just said that?

She knew he continued talking, but she hadn't heard anything past the dreaded word. Her head was spinning. His voice had faded. Fear and disbelief waged war on her. Had she heard him right? Was he sure? What did that mean? Was it some kind of terrible joke?

"Are you sure, doctor?" Chris asked, putting words to her own thoughts, his voice strained, bringing her back to the room and the conversation going on around her.

Dr. Thorlo nodded. "I'm certain."

"You can't treat this? Here? In your office? Do we really have to go to a specialist?" Chris asked.

He was asking all the questions that were overloading Hannah's brain. A specialist seemed scary and extreme. Surely Dr. Thorlo could treat it. When a woman in their church, Susy Reynolds, had been diagnosed with breast cancer two years ago, Dr. Thorlo was able to treat her himself. Why had he treated Susy, but was referring Hannah to a specialist?

Dr. Thorlo pressed his lips together. "I can treat endometrial cancer in its early stages, mostly by conducting hysterectomies."

Chris nodded, looking relieved. "Then do it. Take it out."

Hannah's head snapped around as she stared at her husband. Take it out? Take out her womanly organs? Surely there was another way.

Dr. Thorlo didn't answer right away. Finally, he gave a

slight shrug of his shoulders. "I can take the uterus out, and I probably will, but it likely won't be enough. Endometrial cancer is differentiated by types, grades and stages. First of all, there are two types – type one and type two – based on outlook and causes. Type one is thought to be caused by excess estrogen. They are normally slow-moving. We're not quite sure what causes type two cancers, but they are much more likely to spread outside the uterus. Unfortunately, with type two cancers there is commonly a much poorer outlook and treatment needs to be aggressive. Clear-cell carcinoma, the type of cancer Hannah has, is a type two cancer."

"The second scale endometrial cancer is measured on is by grades," Dr. Thorlo continued. "The lower the grade, the more the cancer tissue forms glands that look similar to normal, healthy endometrium. Less than half of the cancerous tissue in Hannah's endometrium is forming normal glands, signifying that it is a grade three cancer...which tends to be more aggressive."

Hannah's head was spinning. It all sounded like Latin to her.

"Lastly, it's described by stages. Stages refer to how far the cancer has spread to surrounding organs. We don't know which stage you're at yet, Hannah, and we need to do more tests to determine that. However, clear-cell carcinoma is more aggressive than most endometrial cancers. It tends to grow quickly, and most often it has spread outside the uterus by the time it's diagnosed." The doctor paused. "Because of that, I feel like I need to refer you on to someone who can do more than just a hysterectomy."

Hannah was having a hard time making sense of what the doctor was saying. The one thing that stood out was her prognosis. "Dr. Thorlo...are you...are you saying I'm dying?" she asked, her voice sounding small and weak.

Chris cleared his throat and looked down, rubbing the back of his neck with one hand, while squeezing hers tightly with the other.

"No. I'm not saying that, Hannah. I'm saying the outlook isn't good, but there is definitely still hope. There are treatment options. And we will treat this. I'm referring you to a very, very good gynecologic oncologist. We'll run more tests to find out if the cancer has spread, and if so, how far. Then, we'll formulate a plan of treatment. You can beat this; thousands of people have. I am not giving you a death sentence. We'll begin treatment and see how the cancer responds."

"That's right. What are the statistics? Surely there are statistics," Chris asked, taking a deep breath, searching for hope.

"It's hard to give a number as I'm not certain if the cancer has spread and which stage it is at. I'm guessing that you likely have a stage two or three cancer, though, Hannah, based on the information we do have available to us at this time. You're likely looking at a thirty to forty-five percent five-year survival rate."

Hannah felt as if the wind was knocked out of her. "Thirty to forty-five percent?" she echoed in a whisper. Best case scenario, there was only a forty-five percent chance that she would be sitting beside her husband in five years? There was only a forty-five percent chance that she would make it to her sixtieth birthday? There was only a forty-five percent chance that she would see Kara turn thirty?

"Hannah, if you lined up one hundred women with the kind of cancer you have, thirty to forty-five of them would be alive in five years. You could be among those forty-five," Dr. Thorlo encouraged.

She felt small and scared. Those numbers didn't feel reassuring.

"Hannah," Chris said, getting her attention. She turned toward him, near tears. His gaze was steady, his face peaceful. "You *will* be among those forty-five. We will get through this, Love. You and me. We're going to fight this cancer, and you are going to win, alright?"

Tears welled up in her eyes. She had nothing to cling to other than his words. They were a lifeline in what felt like an ocean of uncertainty that was threatening to consume her. She nodded, not trusting herself to speak, and clung tightly to his hand.

"That's right. Stay positive. Believe that you can beat this. Pray." Dr. Thorlo's face was etched with concern. "We're going to treat this very aggressively. I already have a call in to the oncologist I was telling you about. She is very good at what she does. She knows what she is talking about. I've worked with her before and have been highly impressed. If anyone can help you, it's her." Hannah saw Dr. Thorlo cringe as he finished.

'Am I unhelpable?' she wanted to ask, but didn't. What could he possibly say? They had to begin treatment and see how the cancer responded before he could answer a question like that. That was all there was to do. There was nothing more he could know, nothing more he could say, nothing more he could encourage them with until they knew if it had spread, and how it was going to respond to treatment.

It had been over twenty years since Kelsi was diagnosed with leukemia and they had been immersed into the world of cancer, treatments, prognoses and oncologists, but now it felt fresh again. The fear it brought was stifling. Their family track record with cancer wasn't good.

"How did we not catch this before?" Hannah asked weakly.

"There is no routine test to find endometrial cancer. Most cases are found once symptoms begin to occur," Dr. Thorlo explained.

Hannah stared up at the ceiling for several moments before looking back at her doctor. "If I had come in earlier...told you about these symptoms earlier – the pain in my pelvis, the cramping, the weight loss – would you have caught the cancer earlier? Would we have been able to stop it before it got so bad?"

"Maybe. Maybe not," the doctor answered. "There is no blame, Hannah. This is no one's fault. You didn't realize your symptoms could be indicative of something ominous. And sometimes those symptoms aren't. As a result, you didn't tell me. I didn't realize you were having them. It simply is what it is. At this point all you can think about is getting well. Don't spend time or energy thinking about what could have been." He caught her eye. "I'm serious. Don't even go there. Focus on getting better...on what's ahead." He stood. Chris and Hannah followed suit. "I expect to hear back from the oncologist tomorrow. I'll give you a call when I do, and we'll go from there." He shook Chris' hand, clasping it for a long moment, then patted Hannah's shoulder. "I'm so sorry to give you this news, guys. Really, I am."

Hannah let Chris stumble through a goodbye, as she tried to wrap her mind around everything they had been told. They made their way out to the parking lot, both quiet. Chris opened the truck door for her, she stepped up onto the running board and sat down heavily in her seat. He closed the door and went around to get in his side. They both just sat there quietly for several minutes, staring out the windshield.

"You're going to get through this, Hannah. *We're* going to get through this," Chris finally said, taking a deep breath, his voice firm.

She nodded. It was the only thing she could do. She didn't know what to say. She didn't know if there was anything to say.

"Do you want to go home?" he asked, reaching for her hand again. She bobbed her head, and he put the truck in reverse.

The trip home was quiet. They spent the time processing internally, making sense of the information and emotions. Hannah felt crampy, and she wanted to reach down and scratch out her insides with her hands, knowing now that the pain was caused by a deep and dangerous disease that sought to claim her life.

She wanted it gone from her body, gone from her life, gone from her future. She wanted to unwind the last three days. She wanted to forget about cramping, bleeding and everything that had anything to do with endometrial cancer. She didn't want it to be true.

Still, the pain in her lower abdomen continued.

She had cancer. In her uterus. It was the very part of her body that had given her five of the greatest gifts of her life; now, it was trying to destroy her.

Her throat ached so badly she could barely swallow.

As they pulled into the driveway, she saw an SUV parked in front of the garage.

"Kara's here," Chris said simply, his words thick with emotion.

"I forgot she was coming," Hannah admitted. "Chris," she started, "we're going to have to tell the kids." With that realization came her first tears since having been told the news she had dreaded hearing for her entire life. They came swiftly and in great supply. Her tears turned to sobs.

"Hannah," Chris breathed brokenly. He stopped the truck and reached across the seat, gathering her into his arms and pulling her across the center console onto his lap. He held her tight and buried his face in her hair. Their tears mixed.

"I don't care what the numbers say or what the doctors say, you are going to beat this cancer," he told her fiercely. "And I'm going to be with you every step of the way. Our whole lives, no matter what has come our way, we've gotten through it together, haven't we? With Jesus, there is nothing we haven't been able to overcome! Why should that change now? Let the odds be stacked against us! We're going to defy them. You are going to see your grandchildren grow up," he told her, his voice wobbling. "You are going to grow old with me. We're going to retire together. We're going to watch our children and their families grow. We're going to take that trip to Hawaii we've always talked about. We're going to celebrate our fiftieth and sixtieth and seventieth wedding anniversary."

She clung to him, as she clung to his words. He held her a little longer, then pulled back. "We are going to get through this. Do you hear me? We're going to get through this."

She nodded, wishing she could shake off the fear and have his confidence. Taking a deep breath, she wiped her eyes. "Let's not tell the kids yet."

"They need to know," he protested.

"And they will...soon. Let's just wait until we have all the information and a treatment plan in place. I don't want to worry them before we can tell them what we're going to do to fix this."

"A family that prays together stays together," he reminded her, quoting something they had both said from the time they married.

"And I covet their prayers. But let's just give ourselves a couple of days to process this before we have to share it," she pleaded. She couldn't imagine telling them, seeing their faces, watching the tears collect in their eyes, seeing the hurt and fear on the faces she loved so much. She bit her lip and blinked back fresh tears. That surely would be the worst part of all.

He considered her face and then nodded, glancing out the window as he prepared to agree. He shut his mouth. "I think it's too late, Love."

Hannah looked up to follow his gaze. Kara was standing on the cement with tears running down her cheeks. Hannah dashed at her own tears, regretting that her daughter had seen her like this. She could tell by the tears on Kara's cheeks that her tender-hearted daughter had been standing there long enough to see them weeping together.

Knowing that her presence had been discovered, the young woman opened the heavy truck door. Reaching out her hand to Hannah and looking from one parent to the other, her eyes landed on Chris' face. "Daddy," she paused. "What's wrong?"

Whether or not they wanted to wait to tell the kids, here they were. An explanation had to be given. Hannah kept her eyes downcast, in too much emotional pain to bring herself to look at her husband or her daughter.

"Let's go inside," Chris suggested, his voice sounding much stronger than Hannah knew he felt. Kara stepped back, and Hannah climbed down from the seat of the truck. Kara looped her arm through hers as they walked toward the house. She didn't ask any more questions, and Hannah didn't offer any explanations.

Once in the house, Chris smoothed his hand over his mouth and chin, then gestured toward the living room. Pulling herself together, Hannah led Kara to the couch and sat down with her.

She was a mother. She had to be strong and help her children understand and deal with the diagnosis that she had only begun to comprehend herself. She had to be brave and strong because she wanted them to be brave and strong. How she dealt with the news they had been given would influence how they dealt with it.

Chris pulled a wing chair over and sat down in front of them. Kara took a deep breath and looked at them calmly, waiting for them to start, her eyes still moist.

Hannah appreciated that the young woman wasn't freaking out or asking questions. Kara obviously knew bad news was coming, but here she was, sitting calm and quiet, possessing the maturity it took to wait. Hannah was so proud of her. She reached over and took Kara's hand, holding it between both of hers.

"Kara, as you know, I went through menopause a number of years ago," Hannah started. "I should not have been bleeding like I was Saturday night. I went into Dr. Thorlo yesterday to have it checked out. He asked us to come into his office this afternoon to go over test results, and there he told us that I have endometrial cancer." Hannah sounded calm and strong, surprising even herself.

Kara absorbed the news gracefully, clutching Hannah's hand a little tighter. Their youngest looked to Chris, and he nodded, confirming what Hannah had said. She looked back to Hannah. "Has it spread?"

"They need to run more tests before they can say for certain," Hannah answered carefully.

Kara looked down at her hand, held in between Hannah's, and blinked several times. "When will they start treatment?"

"Dr. Thorlo has a call into a gynecologic oncologist," Hannah told her. "Once we go in to see her, and she runs more tests, we'll begin treatment."

"How will they treat it?"

"We don't know yet," Chris answered. "It sounds like it all depends on if it has spread yet and if so, how far. Hopefully a hysterectomy will be enough."

"If not, they'll likely look at chemo and radiation," Kara offered. "What is their prognosis?" The petite blonde's tone was professional. She sounded as if she were discussing the case of a patient rather than her mother. She was a therapist, not a doctor, yet she understood well the severity of the diagnosis.

"They can't give one yet," Chris answered. "They still have questions that need to be answered first."

Kara nodded, and her eyes fell for several long moments. A few solitary tears slid down her cheeks. Hannah braced for what came next, expecting more tears and questions. She took a deep breath, drawing herself up on the inside, preparing to comfort her daughter as she dealt with the news. She leaned over and wiped the tears from Kara's cheeks and pulled her into her embrace.

"The LORD is my shepherd, I lack nothing," Kara quoted quietly, surprising both of her parents. "He makes me lie down in green pastures, He leads me beside quiet waters, He refreshes my soul. He guides me along the right paths for His name's sake. Even though I walk through the darkest valley, I will fear no evil, for You are with me; Your rod and Your staff, they comfort me."

Hannah felt taken aback by Kara's response, but as the quiet words spilled from between her daughter's lips and sank into her troubled heart, she leaned her head against her daughter's and absorbed each and every word, wiping at her own eyes.

She saw Chris' face light up as a smile aimed at Kara filled his face. He nodded and reached out to squeeze her knee, picking up when she finished. "A thousand may fall at your side, and ten thousand at your right hand, but it shall not come near you," he said.

"But He was wounded for our transgressions, He was bruised for our iniquities; The chastisement for our peace was upon Him, And by His stripes we are *healed*," Kara continued.

Chris stood and left the room. When he returned, he carried his worn leather Bible. "Come to Me all you who are heavy laden, and I will give you rest," he read.

Hannah closed her eyes and simply let the familiar words wash over her. Tears ran down her face unchecked. She might have to come to terms with the fact that there was cancer in her body, she might have to deal with the fact that surgery, radiation and chemotherapy were going to be a reality in her near future, but there was a God who was bigger. A God who she had a history with, a history that gave her confidence in His character and in His plan for her. A God who was the same yesterday, today and forever. A God who had shown Himself faithful before her cancer diagnosis, and who she knew would show Himself faithful in the days ahead.

Over the last fifty-four years, she had come to love Him deeply. His character, His very nature, had compelled her. She knew that she was His beloved as well, and He loved well. Come what may, her life could not be taken away. It had already been hidden in Christ Jesus. Even should she die, she would live! That truth was cool balm to her heart.

They sat on the couch for a long time, Kara and Chris taking turns reading scripture, Kara holding her hand tightly. Hannah let the words soak over her, renewing her mind and stabilizing her emotions. When they finally stopped, Chris led the three of them in prayer.

They didn't think to eat dinner until after eight. Chris and Kara insisted that Hannah rest on the couch while they put the food on the table. Hannah was glad she had started their dinner cooking before they went to town.

After eating, Hannah and Kara settled on the couch together to watch a movie, while Chris found a spot in a nearby chair, his laptop open on his lap. Without having to look, Hannah knew her husband was finding out everything there was to know about the disease that was waging war against her body. It was simply who he was. He was one of those men who liked to know an opponent inside and out. That often took the form of extensive research. She knew she would have plenty of questions of her own and would eventually want to hear what he found out, but for now, she was content to let him do the research while she watched a movie with her daughter and pretended the cancer didn't exist.

Four

The next night, Chris and Hannah sat down on the couch together and called their children. Hannah asked Chris if he would be the one to share the news with their kids, and she sat and clung tightly to his hand as he did. She knew it was taking the easy way out, but she didn't know how to speak the words to her children. Mothers were supposed to love, nurture, and comfort, not inflict fear and pain.

Together, they did their best to reassure their children and their spouses, answer their questions and help them process the information. Each one of the kids responded differently.

Kaitlynn, their firstborn, was the first one they called. She asked every question imaginable, trying to wrap her head around the diagnosis logically. Chris told her everything about endometrial cancer, specifically clear-cell carcinoma, he had learned through his research and repeated the information the doctor gave them. Kaitlynn wanted to know what would be done next, the name of the oncologist, when their appointment with her was, the kind of tests that would be done, and the kind of treatments available.

She exhausted the information they knew about the disease and wanted to know more. She was determined that Hannah would beat cancer; that they would beat it as a family. She wanted to know what she could do to help. As much as Hannah appreciated Kaitlynn's concern and commitment to know as much as possible to help Hannah defy all odds, she felt exhausted by the questions by the time they hung up the phone. And they still had two other kids to call.

Kimberly started crying the moment Chris relayed the

news. It was Greg who asked enough questions to give them an idea about Hannah's condition. Kim's tears never dried. Hannah's heart hurt, listening to the quiet sounds of her daughter crying, the wobble in her voice, and the fear contained in the few questions that she asked. Hannah did her best to reassure and comfort her, but there was only so much comforting that could be done over the phone. Hannah found her own tears falling afresh, wishing she could be there to hug and hold her dark-haired daughter.

She wished she could tell her that it wasn't true, and there was no reason to worry. She wished she could tell her that she would be fine; promise her that things would be as they always had been, and that she would be there for her forever. Yet, even if she did, her words could be empty promises, and Kimmy would know it. Promises, no matter how well-intentioned, were hardly comforting if they were easily broken by circumstance. Instead, Hannah offered what comfort she could and left the rest to Greg. It was a difficult thing to accept, but Greg knew his wife well and loved her deeply. If Hannah could choose anyone to be with Kimberly while she dealt with this news, it would be him.

When they finally hung up the phone, Chris put his arm snuggly around Hannah's shoulders and drew her back against the couch with him. "We need a break," he told her, letting out a deep sigh. They both sat quietly for several minutes, letting their conversation with Kimberly settle. Hannah wiped at tears that continued to flow, thinking of how Kim must be feeling.

"I guess we should have seen that coming."

"What do you mean?" Chris asked.

"All our family has ever known of cancer is death," Hannah told him, looking up into pale green eyes that she loved. "And Kimmy remembers."

Kelsi and Kimberly had been best friends. Kim was the middle sister – two years younger than Kaitlynn and two years older than Kelsi. Kaitlynn was the revered older sister who was always right and always in charge. When they played school, Kaitlynn was the teacher, and Kimberly and Kelsi were the students. When they played house, Kaitlynn was the mommy, and Kimberly and Kelsi were the children. When they did their hair and nails, Kaitlynn was the beautician, and the younger girls were the customers. While they were all good friends, Kimberly and Kelsi were inseparable. And then they were separated for good.

Hannah worried the most about Kimberly after Kelsi passed away. The seven-year-old was too young to understand anything but the fact that her best friend was no longer in the bed next to hers, but instead, in the cemetery north of town.

Now, Hannah could understand perfectly why Kimberly started crying at the mention of cancer and was unable to stop. When Kim heard the word cancer, she subconsciously thought of loss. If Hannah was honest with herself, she felt the same way. A cancer diagnosis was devastating. Dr. Thorlo said he wasn't giving her a death sentence, but no one in their family had ever had cancer and lived.

"This is different, Love," Chris told her as if he could read her thoughts. She looked away, ashamed of the fear she knew he could see. He grasped her chin gently and turned her back toward him. "This is different. That was leukemia."

"It was cancer," she told him.

"Onions and carrots are both vegetables, but they're not the same thing, are they?" he asked gently, winking at her.

She appreciated his attempt to lighten the mood and smiled. "You're right, but neither are as good as chocolate cake."

He cupped his hand against her face. "You are going to be just fine. This will not end the way that ended."

"Maybe not, but I can understand Kimberly having a hard time with it," she told him.

"Maybe not?" he questioned. "Change your thinking, Pretty Lady. You are going to get better! But yes, I can understand it, too." He tugged on a piece of her hair, then leaned back against the couch, putting his hands behind his head and resting against them. "It sure would be easier if we could tell them in person."

Hannah nodded in agreement. She had wanted to wait to tell the kids until Christmas, when they could sit down face to face and explain the diagnosis and what was being done to combat it. That would surely be better, she thought, than giving them the news over the phone. There was just something about being able to see someone with your own eyes, touch them, give them a hug. It took some of the fear and worry out of a situation such as the one they found themselves in.

Still, Chris said that was too long to wait. If they waited to tell everyone but Kara until Christmas, there would be hurt feelings and maybe even some anger. The kids would be upset if they kept something like that from them for so long. As much as she didn't want to admit it, Hannah knew he was right. It was too long to wait. In so many ways, the sooner they told them the better. And so, they had decided to make the phone calls that night.

Joe responded differently than any of the girls. He sat and listened quietly to what they had to say, absorbing the information. He asked how Hannah was feeling. He asked fewer questions than Kaitlynn but more than Kimberly or Kara. When he had his basic questions answered, he prayed – prayed for his mother, his father, and healing. He prayed for the family, for comfort and peace, for the doctors, for wisdom and insight. Hannah felt encouraged and strengthened by his prayer, reminded of who God was and how He loved her. When he finished praying, Joe shared with them about healing, all but preaching a sermon on it to his small but captive audience.

Hannah enjoyed every word, every thought, every

verse, every revelation he shared. She stowed them away in her heart to come back to and reflect upon later. She had a feeling that over the next several months, she would think back to their conversation and remember the encouragement he had shared many times.

Joe had chosen a career in professional football. At least for now. But he had been trained as a pastor, and she still thought he would make a phenomenal one. She couldn't wait to sit in his congregation one day and listen to him preach from the Word, Sunday after Sunday.

Suddenly, like a splash of cold water to her face, she wondered if she would still be around by the time he began his preaching career. The thought was appalling and depressing. She felt sadness well up within her.

"You're going to be healed, Mom," Joe told her, and Chris looked over and squeezed her hand, smiling warmly into her eyes. Joe believed she would be healed. Chris believed it. God was able. Hope was breathed to life in her heart, and it began to overshadow the fear and uncertainty. She was glad they had talked to Joe last.

Lying in bed that night, Chris moved to lay behind her. He wrapped his arms around her protectively, drawing her back against his chest. "How do you feel like tonight went?" he asked.

"I just want to hold them," Hannah admitted.

He chuckled. "They would hardly fit on your lap anymore."

"How does time go so fast, Chris?" she whispered into the darkness, her throat aching again. It didn't seem like it had been that long ago that they were newlyweds with babies. She could remember Kaitlynn's pudgy thighs, big, curious eyes and toothless grin as if it were yesterday. It just didn't feel like it could have been thirty-three years ago.

She remembered putting her babies in cute little sleepers and rocking them to sleep. At the time, she studied their sweet faces, trying to commit every detail to memory, attempting to remember every sweet moment, every gusty sigh and precious giggle. Now, looking back, she was struck again with the realization that those babies that she could still imagine the weight of in her arms, had babies of their own. The thought made her throat ache and her eyes sting.

Where did the years go? If only she could hold them again.

Back then, she and Chris were young and ambitious. They had no idea what life held for them, but they were madly in love and full of adventure. Whatever life had in store, they were confident they would emerge victorious and together!

In those days, thoughts of how she was going to manage to get up with the baby another night and then be a nice mommy all day consumed her mind, along with wondering how to pay the mortgage, and when her in-laws would be able to stay with the kids so she could have a date night with her husband. Back then, their health was something they took for granted. Being healthy was all they had ever known. It never occurred to them that things could be different.

"I don't know, Love, but it sure does, doesn't it?" Chris answered, his voice warm and full of understanding.

"I just wish there was a way to stop it from going any further, or go back and relive it again. We have had a wonderful life together, Chris Colby."

She felt him stiffen. "It's not over, Hannah," he reminded.

She thought about his response, understanding why he had a slight edge to his voice. She grasped after the ability to make him understand. "Parts of it are," she finally said. "I remember how it felt to hold our babies, and I know that I will never hold them again...like you said, they're too big." She let out something between a sob and a laugh. "I remember covering their little freckled faces with kisses and being able to make anything better with an ice cream cone. I remember being young, going skiing and snowshoeing up in the Rockies with you. Now, I wouldn't dare for fear of breaking something."

Chris chuckled again, understanding that she was talking much less about her cancer or their future and much more about their past, and pressed a kiss against her neck. "I remember our wedding day," he offered. "I have yet to see anyone as beautiful as you were when you walked down that aisle toward me. We will never get that day back, but you know what?"

"What?" she asked, smiling and snuggling back against him, where she fit perfectly.

"I've relived that moment a thousand times since, and every time it gets sweeter and sweeter," he paused. "In the moment, there were so many things going on. I was terrified of your dad, my tux was too tight, the church felt warm, I was ticked that Aaron Wood had dared to come to our wedding...as if he was going to steal you away before you could go off and marry me." Hannah laughed at his reference to her old boyfriend, if he could even be called that. She had gone on only a few dates with Aaron before Chris ever asked her out.

"But looking back, in every memory, all I remember is how you looked in your white dress, with your veil down over your face. I remember how your eyes shone, and how I could feel your love crossing the distance between us. I remember thinking that you were the most beautiful woman in the world, and I was the luckiest man in all of history," he continued, then kissed her shoulder. "We'll never get that day back, but I get to enjoy the memory of it forever."

She smiled. "That's true. I guess in the moment, there were poopy diapers, long nights and colicky babies, weren't there?"

Chris chuckled again. "But in your memories, there are only sweet little babies that you rock to sleep and hold close against you. There are only peaceful, sleeping faces, big grins, little laughs and precious coos. The years seemed to go too fast, it's true, Love, but we will enjoy those memories for the rest of our lives."

Satisfied with how he brought perspective to her longing, Hannah fell asleep in her husband's arms. That night she slept peacefully, knowing she was safe and warm, loved and cherished.

The next two weeks were a blur of tests, traveling, doctor's appointments and treatment options. Hannah was on information overload. Her head was spinning with cancer-related jargon, decisions to make, and test results.

A CA 125 blood test was performed and the levels came back high – a good inclination that the cancer had spread outside the uterus. The blood test was followed by CT scans and an MRI to check to see how far the cancer had spread.

As Hannah laid on tables, confined by machines, when needles were poked into her arms, and as she waited while doctors studied images and processed their findings, fear was breathing down her neck, waiting to rush in should she let it. Still, peace filled her. Lying in the confining tube waiting for her MRI, she silently repeated the beloved words of Psalms 23. She had a feeling she said them out of order and had thoroughly rearranged the chapter by the time she was done, but nevertheless, her nerves calmed and peace settled like a blanket.

He led her beside quiet waters. He refreshed her soul. He caused her to lie down in green pastures. Through His love and tender care, He comforted her. Lying on the table, trained specialists studying her insides, she felt like breaking out in song. Cancer or no cancer, she was the beloved of the Most High, and He was with her even in that moment, even in that machine. Her heart responded with love.

When the tests had all been run and the results read, Chris and Hannah sat calmly as the doctor shared the news. What they found wasn't good.

Dr. Hedgins, the oncologist Dr. Thorlo had referred them to, said they would have to hit the cancer hard and fast. Chemo and radiation were recommended, along with a radical hysterectomy. They scheduled the hysterectomy before they left the doctor's office.

Once they were in the truck and on their way home, Hannah fell quiet as she leaned back against the seat. Even though her spirit was well, her flesh felt exhausted. She was full of dread as she thought about the coming days, knowing the events that were already in motion would only serve to exhaust her more.

"At least Dr. Thorlo can perform the surgery so we can stay in Glendale," Chris offered, reaching for her hand.

She nodded. "That's a relief. I would much rather be in the hospital there in town than in the city," she agreed. "You think it's the right decision to have him perform the surgery, right?"

Chris nodded. "He may not have the glitz and glamour of Dr. Hedgins or her colleagues, but he is a good doctor. We know and trust him. And I think the most important thing is that he cares about you. We've watched each other's kids grow up. He delivered all five of our babies. We play golf together. He has a vested interest in the result of your surgery. That's something we wouldn't get in a big hospital."

"That's what I think, too."

"How are you feeling?" Chris paused. "About everything we found out, I mean. ...About the test results."

Hannah sighed. "It's not nice to know that the cancer has spread outside my reproductive system. It certainly isn't what I wanted to hear. I thought a forty-five percent survival rate was bad enough...I definitely don't like thirty percent any better."

Chris pulled his hand over his face. "I don't blame you. I had a hard time with that one." Hannah squeezed his hand. "But here's the thing, Hannah – in a thirty percent survival rate, thirty percent of women have to survive. Thirty percent have to undergo treatment and come out the other side to go on to lead a perfectly normal, healthy life. Thirty percent! Who's to say you're not going to be in that thirty percent?"

"That's very true."

"Don't let today get you down," Chris told her, keeping a firm hold on her hand. "We have to know exactly what we are dealing with, so we know best how to treat it. It's good that we know how far it has spread. And this is what Dr. Thorlo predicted. It's no worse than he thought. Those are all good things...things that we needed to find out."

"I appreciate your optimism," Hannah told her husband, sending him a warm smile.

"There's no sense in being pessimistic," he answered with a grin. She knew he was right. "You are going to be among that thirty percent. You know why?"

"Why?"

"Because you are one of the strongest women I've ever met, because you have the love and support of your entire family, because people across the country are praying for you, and mostly because God is able. He is a God of healing." Chris sounded so sure. His certainty infused her with strength and the peace she had felt earlier returned.

"We should call the kids and let them know what we found out," Hannah suggested. "I'm sure they've been wondering all day."

They spent the rest of their five hour drive home on the phone with their kids, then with their parents, filling them in on the tests that had been run and the results. They told them about the treatment plan – surgery first followed by chemo – and explained it to them. Kaitlynn asked questions, Kimberly cried, Joe prayed. He believed so wholeheartedly that Hannah would be healed, and his words comforted and encouraged them both, breathing hope into a rather hopeless day.

Kara and Justin were waiting for them at their house when they got home, with lasagna just out of the oven. The cancer and its treatment were discussed for the first half hour during dinner, and then the conversation moved on to other things. Chris and Hannah found themselves laughing and conversing, finding blessed relief in being distracted from the reality that had hung like storm clouds over their life for the past two weeks.

Dinner was followed by a game of Monopoly, and Chris strategized and schemed until Hannah and Justin were both bankrupt. Kara held on the longest, but when she landed on his hotel-clad Boardwalk, the game was over, and Chris cleaned it up in jubilant victory.

"Daddy, I've never met anyone who loves to win at Monopoly as much as you," Kara told him, laughing, as she stood up from the table to refill her water glass. He grinned as he left the room to put the box away in the game closet.

"We should get going," Justin said, watching Kara drink her water.

She covered a yawn with the back of her hand as she glanced at the clock. "Wow. I had no idea it was after eleven."

"Neither did I," Hannah agreed, following her daughter's lead, unable to suppress a yawn of her own.

"Yeah, and you guys have had a long day," Justin said, putting his hand gently on Hannah's shoulder. "A long couple of days, actually."

She hugged her son-in-law, who felt more like a son. "We loved having you guys here tonight. Thank you for coming. It's been far too long since someone has challenged your dad in Monopoly." She winked at Kara.

Kara laughed. "Maybe one of these days, I'll actually beat him again."

"I heard that," Chris said, coming back into the kitchen. "Are you guys scheming against me in my absence?"

"Oh, if only it were that easy," Kara told him, giving him a hug goodbye. "We've been scheming for years."

He hugged her back, then Kara moved on to hug Hannah. She hung on a moment longer than usual, and Hannah did likewise. When they parted, Hannah patted Kara's cheek. "Come over for dinner and a game again soon, Honey. Next time, I'll cook."

"That reminds me, the lasagna was great!" Chris told their daughter.

"It was Mama's recipe," Kara answered with a shrug.

"Well, it tasted just like hers," Chris said.

Kara beamed, and Hannah's heart warmed. Her daughter was proud to have done something like her. What more could a mother ask for?

Chris and Hannah walked Justin and Kara to the door and said another round of goodbyes. When the couple had backed up the drive, Chris flicked off the porch light and turned toward Hannah.

"You head on up to bed. I'll lock up, turn off the lights and be up."

Exhausted, she did as she was told. She had enjoyed the nights in a hotel that allowed them to go in for testing subsequent days, but it was nice to be home. She was sure she would sleep better in her own bed.

Lying down, she gave a soft sigh as she settled into the pillow top mattress and rested her head against her fluffy pillow. She loved home.

In a rush, the test results and what they meant came back to her. Over the next few months, she wouldn't be home much. There would be numerous nights in the hospital or in a hotel so she could go in for treatment several days in a row. Chris had reminded her earlier how fortunate they were that they only lived five hours away from her treating hospital. She knew that was true, but five hours was still too far away to maintain a sense of normalcy. It was far enough that Chris would have to take an entire day off work to accompany her to appointments.

"The plans you have for me are good. They are plans to prosper me and not to harm me. They are plans to give me a hope and a future," Hannah whispered, feeling herself sinking toward despair and choosing to fight back. She repeated the words again and again, repeating them until peace began to overtake her heart.

When Chris came to bed a few minutes later, he moved close and wrapped his arm around her, drawing her back against him. When they had first married, they slept like that often; over the years, they had grown to like their space while they slept. They still slept in close proximity in their king-sized bed, both hugging the middle, but were more accustomed now to sleeping far enough apart that they didn't touch, finding that they both slept better that way. Over the past couple of weeks, though, he had begun holding her again during the night. She thought about commenting on it but decided against it.

After all, what would he say? That he was worried he was going to lose her? That he held her again while they slept because she had cancer, and he was afraid? That he wanted to hold her again since being reminded that life was fragile and there were no guarantees?

Her heart ached. She pressed her hand against his and squeezed.

Five

The next morning, Hannah busied herself getting things squared away at home. She was scheduled to go in for her hysterectomy Monday morning, which meant she had the weekend to get everything put in order.

Dr. Thorlo told her to expect to be out of commission for six weeks. That meant no housework, no cooking, no laundry, no women's meetings at church, no running errands, no holding grandchildren, and no helping in the nursery. Dr. Thorlo said the extent of what he wanted her doing was lying on the couch. She wasn't even allowed to climb the stairs to get to her bedroom. To follow orders, she and Chris would be temporarily moving into the spare room – the only bedroom on the main floor of the beautiful home Chris had built for them almost two decades ago.

When the doorbell rang at a quarter till nine, she was shocked to see Kara standing on her porch. "I thought you had to work today," Hannah exclaimed, swinging the door open wide.

Kara's smile was bright. "I rearranged my schedule. I knew you had a lot of things on your plate, and thought I could help!"

"I'm not going to lie, I would love the company, but you didn't need to do that, Honey."

Kara smiled. "I know I didn't. I wanted to." She took off her jacket and hung it on the coat tree. "What's first on the list?"

Hannah smiled gratefully. It wasn't even nine o'clock yet, and truth be told, she already felt tired. The past couple of weeks had been draining, both physically and emotionally. Additionally, the pain in her pelvis was almost constant, like menstrual cramps that never went away. Being alone made the situation seem worse. There was nothing to take her mind off the pain or off the realization that the pain was caused by cancer that was overtaking her body. Having company as she checked things off her to-do list sounded wonderful. "I'm moving things from our bedroom down to the spare room."

"Alright, I needed a stair workout," Kara told her cheerfully. She followed Hannah up the stairs to the master bedroom. Hannah collected clothes, toiletries, her Bible and journal, a few books she had been planning to read, and the photograph of her and Chris on their wedding day that had set on her bedside table since they were married.

Kara made trips up and down the stairs, transporting the items that Hannah set out. When Hannah felt confident that they had the bulk of what she and Chris would need over the next six weeks, she followed Kara downstairs to put things away in the spare room. She hoped to make it feel more homey and less makeshift. To her surprise, Kara had already put everything in its place.

She looked around the spacious spare room, a room she had never slept in, and spent a moment processing the fact that this was going to be her bedroom for the next several weeks. The bed was smaller, a queen instead of the king-sized they were accustomed to, but the walk-in closet was decent sized. There was a dresser for socks and undergarments, and the attached bath was large and beautifully tiled. The walls were gray, as was the fluffy down comforter. The throw pillows were a cheerful yellow, as were the sprigs of flowers that were scattered over the bottom half of the comforter and over the wall paper that covered the wall the headboard sat against. It had been another project that had transpired after watching a home decorating show. She was surprised Chris still let her watch them.

Finishing her appraisal of the room, she noted that the blinds on the windows were in good shape, the nightstands were a good height and the wingchair in the corner was plush and lime green. Noticing it, Hannah shook her head. "Why do I have a green chair in a gray and yellow room?"

Kara laughed, flopping down across the bed and tossing a gray pillow and a yellow pillow onto the chair. "Because it's an antique, and you had to put it somewhere. With a couple of throw pillows, it will be just fine." Kara paused for only a moment. "What's next, Mom?" she asked, distracting her.

"Lunch?" Hannah answered, feeling hopeful. She was hungry.

Kara laughed. "Perfect. Do you want to rest while I make something?"

"All I'm going to be doing for the next six weeks is resting," Hannah told her. "I think I'll help today."

Kara looped her arm through her mother's as they went to the kitchen. "I would like to spend this afternoon cooking, I think," Hannah told her. Kara shot her a curious look. "I want to have a bunch of meals made up and in the freezer so that your dad can just take them out and put them in the oven."

"Oh Mom, I was planning on bringing dinner over for you guys," Kara protested as if Hannah should have known.

"Not every day for six weeks, you aren't." Kara gave her a look that said 'why not?' "I appreciate the offer, Honey, but you have a life of your own. You have a husband. You have a career. You can't be coming over here every night to cook us dinner."

Kara shrugged and shot her mother a charming smile. "Fine. We'll make it every other."

Hannah tugged on a piece of Kara's long blonde hair. She was twenty-five now, a grown woman, yet she was as slender and graceful as she had been in high school. There had been numerous health concerns when Kara was little, but through the years, she had defied the odds. Over time, her doctors had come to admit that she was going to live a normal, healthy life; she was simply going to be petite. And she certainly was.

All three of their girls were small-boned, but Kara was the smallest. Even now, halfway through her twenties, she could easily be mistaken for a high schooler. Hannah took in Kara's exotic green eyes, impish smile and slightly pointed ears. Her pixie look had made her an adorable child; now she had become a beautiful woman, inside and out. "I appreciate you, Honey," Hannah told her warmly, tucking Kara's hair behind her ear before turning away.

While Hannah found recipes and told Kara the meals she was planning to make to put in the freezer, one of which they would take some from to serve as their lunch, she wondered if this was her chance to talk to Kara about having kids. She didn't want to pry, but she was curious as to the reason. If they weren't ready, that was fine. She just didn't want them to be having problems. If they were, she wanted to know. Maybe she would be able to help. If nothing else, she would know how to pray.

"It sure was nice having everyone here a couple of weeks ago, wasn't it?" Hannah started.

"Yeah, it was," Kara answered, digging through the freezer to find packages of frozen chicken breasts.

"Little Ava sure is cute," Hannah continued. "It's nice to have a little granddaughter running around after so many boys."

"She sure is!" Kara agreed, emerging with the frozen chicken. "Every time I see Ava I just want to squeeze her."

Hannah laughed. "And you usually do!"

Kara grinned. "True."

It had not escaped Hannah's attention that Ava seemed to be a permanent fixture on Kara's lap, nor that Kara had sprinkled the little girl with plenty of hugs and kisses. "Hopefully she'll have another little girl to play with sometime soon," Hannah hinted, hoping her meaning wasn't too obvious. She didn't want to come right out and ask Kara.

She wanted to respect her privacy. But she was not above putting a little effort into steering the conversation in a direction that would inspire a baby-related conversation.

Kara looked over, pleasant surprise filling her face. "Do you think Kait will have another? How soon? Do you know something I don't?"

"Kait?" Hannah asked, caught off guard by Kara's question. "Oh, no. I don't know anything...just hopeful I guess. You know me, I love grandbabies."

Kara didn't even seem to hear her last comment. "I wouldn't think she would have any more yet," the young woman said thoughtfully. "As mischievous as her boys are, I think she has her hands full for the time being."

"You're right, they are mischievous," Hannah agreed with a chuckle. Just like that, the conversation turned to the boys only to move from topic to topic, each further away from the baby subject. Ruefully, Hannah came to terms with the fact that the topic wasn't going to simply come up with Kara. If she truly wanted to know, she would have to come right out and ask her daughter why she hadn't had a baby. She wasn't sure if she was ready to be that bold just yet.

The afternoon passed quickly amidst lasagna, chicken pot pie, tator tot casserole, chocolate chip cookies, and three kinds of soup. They made several small disposable pans of each, and, after they had cooled, Hannah stacked them in the freezer. Satisfied with their work, she leaned her hip against the counter and looked at her daughter. "I have thoroughly enjoyed this afternoon. Thank you for coming over. You have made it possible to accomplish five times what I thought I could get done today, and you have made a day of housework enjoyable!"

Kara finished her last bite of cookie and smiled. "I'm glad. But if that was your parting speech, save it. I'm not leaving yet. Look at that sink full of dishes!"

"I'll do the dishes, Honey," Hannah protested. In part, she wanted her daughter to feel free to go home and spend the evening with her husband; but the bigger reason she was sending Kara home was that she felt too exhausted to tackle another project, even if it was just the dishes. It had been a full day, and her energy wasn't lasting like it used to.

"Don't be silly. You're going to go rest while I do the dishes," Kara said nonchalantly, moving past her to start filling the sink with hot water.

"No! I can't do that. I'll dry while you wash."

"Yes, you can," Kara told her with a grin. "I insist."

Hannah felt like she should continue to protest, but didn't have the energy. Additionally, she knew that her sweet, mild-mannered daughter had a stubborn streak a mile wide. Kara had been the easiest of all her children to parent, except for that stubbornness. If Kara made a decision, there was no persuading her. "Are you sure?" she questioned to ease her conscience.

"Absolutely. Go rest." Kara's smile faded into a look of concern. "You need to be taking care of yourself right now, Mom. All these years you've been taking care of all of us. Right now, you're going to have to let us take care of you."

Hannah studied her face. "It's hard," she admitted. "I'm the mom. I'm the one that's supposed to take care of you, not the other way around."

Kara gave her a small smile. "Says who?"

Hannah shrugged. That was just how things were.

Kara shook her head. "Go. You look exhausted. I'm going to get these dishes done, then pull that casserole out of the oven when Daddy gets home. Is it alright if I text Justin and tell him to come on over for dinner when he gets off work?"

"Absolutely," Hannah agreed eagerly.

Kara grinned. "Good. I can't wait to see that man! He works far too many hours for my taste."

Hannah smiled. It felt good to know that her daughter was still in love with her husband after five years of marriage. "He works those hours for you. He wants to provide for you...for your family."

"I know. Sometimes I just miss him."

Hannah thought of her son-in-law who was working so diligently to build his construction business. He was a brilliant builder and was booked several months in advance. Yet his success came with a cost – long hours and a good deal of time away from his wife. "It won't always be like this. It always takes a lot of time to get a business going. Give him five years, and he'll have more employees who will share the workload with him."

"You're right. And I know that. I really do. But that doesn't mean I don't miss him right now."

Hannah patted her daughter's shoulder. "I know."

After Kara directed her to the living room once again, Hannah went. As she stretched out on the couch, she wondered if she had just received a clue to the reason behind Justin and Kara still being childless. Were they waiting until Justin didn't have to work so much? Were they waiting to have children until he could be home more? Good intentions, Hannah thought, but she hoped that wasn't the case.

They couldn't put their lives on hold while he built his business. Days would continue to pass, and then weeks, months and years. Before they knew it, they would both be in their thirties. As someone who had given birth to several children over the span of many years, she could attest to the fact that having small children at twenty-one was very different than having small children at thirty. While it had been just as wonderful, she didn't always have the energy with Kara that she had when Kaitlynn was a baby. She had heard other mothers say the same thing, some who had children much later in life. She hoped they didn't wait too long.

"I know that look," Chris said from above her. She looked up quickly to where he was standing behind the couch watching her, a smirk on his face.

"What look?" she asked, laying her head back on the

throw pillow and diverting her eyes.

He chuckled as he came around and sat on the edge of the couch beside her. He tucked a strand of dark hair behind her ear. "Which one of the kids were you worrying about?"

She thought about denying it. "Kara," she admitted. "I think they may be waiting to have kids until Justin feels like he's built his business. Do you think I should talk to her about it? They shouldn't wait too long. If everyone waited to have kids until they could afford it or until it was convenient, the human race would have died out long ago."

Chris reached down and tweaked her nose with a grin. "I think that our daughter is a grown woman who can make her own decisions with her husband."

Hannah pouted. "Are you saying I shouldn't ask her about it?"

Chris tilted his head, considering her. "I didn't say that. It's your decision. I just thought you asked me to hold you accountable when it came to meddling in our kids' lives. That's all. But do what you think you need to."

It was a gentle warning, accompanied with his charming grin, and Hannah knew he was right. Kara had to make her own decisions. She didn't need her mother getting in the way.

"However, asking about it isn't necessarily meddling, I suppose. It depends on if you're simply curious or hoping to persuade." Another wink. Another charming grin.

"How was work today?" she asked, changing the subject.

"Busy," he answered.

"We knew it would be."

Chris nodded. "With missing work earlier this week and needing to take off most of next, there's a lot to be done."

Hannah felt guilty, but tried not to show it. Chris would just dismiss her guilt, telling her he wouldn't have it any other way. He would say that he wanted to be with her every step of the way. Still, she felt bad taking him away from his work. She knew her diagnosis and subsequent appointments and surgery were going to make his life crazy, both professionally and privately. She thought ahead to what the next several months were bound to be like and cringed. She would consume so much of his time, require so much care. It was a fact that made her skin crawl. For an independent woman, the months ahead promised to be distasteful, even aside from the sickness and treatment itself.

Chris covered her hand with his and applied gentle pressure. "One day at a time, Love. One day at a time."

She looked up at him in time to catch the tender look in his eyes. He had read her mind again, like he had so many times before. "I know," she agreed. "I just hate making life more difficult for you...more difficult for all those around me. Kara is in there washing dishes, while I lay out here on the couch."

"She isn't minding at all. She sounded as happy as a lark when she told me she had sent you in here to rest. She was talking to Jessi. She has one of those devices on – the hands free kind. I thought she had gone mad and was talking to herself when I first walked into the kitchen." Chris chuckled, drawing a smile from his wife.

She couldn't hold back. "You didn't overhear anything about babies, did you?"

Chris looked as if he was trying to recall the conversation. "I heard her say she was expecting in May, but other than that...no."

"What?" Hannah exclaimed, sitting upright, her eyes round for just a moment, before she hit his leg and lay back down. "You're rotten."

He leaned down and brushed a kiss across her lips. "Love, she'll talk to you about having a baby when she's ready. Don't rush her."

Even after Chris left the room to wash up before dinner, Hannah thought about his words. She knew he was right. He usually was. Kara would talk to her when she was ready. She had to be okay with leaving it at that.

Ten minutes later, Chris came back into the room and told her it was time for dinner. They walked to the dining room together, where Kara and Justin were already seated at the table. Dinner was laid out, and their glasses were full of sweet tea. Hannah felt guilty as she took her seat, knowing she had done nothing to help put food on the table. She had never been one to simply show up for a meal, and it felt strange and wrong to do so now.

Once Chris prayed, she thanked Kara, not only for dinner and doing the dishes, but for helping her throughout the day. The conversation moved on, and she was enveloped into laughter and merry conversation amongst her family members, the shadows of guilt chased away by the light of their joy.

Saturday and Sunday were full of miscellaneous tasks that kept Hannah busy from the time she woke up until the time she went to sleep, except for church and Sunday dinner with Chris' parents at the local pizza joint. By Sunday night, Chris was insisting that she stop running around and rest.

"I am going to have six weeks to rest," she answered, continuing to fold laundry.

"You need to rest now. You cannot go into surgery completely exhausted," he told her, his expression firm.

"I have to get this done." She folded one of his white t-shirts and smoothed it with her hand.

"I am just as capable of folding clothes as you are," he told her, exasperated. "I can cook, clean, do laundry and make phone calls too, you know."

Hannah looked up, surprised by the hurt she heard in Chris' voice. "I know you can."

"Do you? Because you're acting like you're the only one in this house who knows how to do anything, and that I simply go to work, come home, and loaf on the couch while you do everything else," he shot back at her.

Hannah felt taken aback by his accusation. "That's not true. You are so helpful around the house. I just want to finish a few things before tomorrow."

"Hannah, leave the laundry and go to bed!" he ordered. "Let me do something for once!"

In a burst of emotion, she threw the shirt she was folding at him. "Fine! Fold it yourself if you must!" she cried. "Don't you understand? You're going to be doing everything for six weeks! Everything! I won't be able to walk up the stairs or push around a vacuum or do any laundry! I won't even be able to get off the couch by myself! I have been running this household for thirty-four years and by tomorrow, I'll be as helpless as a baby, so don't you take my last night of being productive away from me!"

Chris stepped close to her and grabbed her wrist as she reached for a pair of his jeans. With his other arm, he swept the rest of the laundry off the bed and onto the floor. "You are not folding one more pair of pants. Go to bed!"

"I'll go to bed when I finish," she told him, her eyes snapping, shrugging off his hand to free her wrist.

"Hannah, *go to bed!*" Chris roared.

Hannah shrank back. She had only heard her husband yell like that a few times before, and it had never been at her. He looked away for several moments and she stayed still. When he looked back and reached up to take hold of her chin, his hands were shaking. He looked deep into her eyes and ran his thumb over her jaw. "One load of laundry is not worth our next forty years. Please. Go to bed and get some rest. I'll finish this later."

She saw the agony in his eyes, and the fight drained out of her. "Alright. You win."

He gave her a small smile. "Thank you." He pressed a kiss against her forehead and released her. "I'm going to go make sure the doors are locked and the lights are off."

She nodded, stepping away. After changing into her nightgown, she crawled into bed. Once in bed, she laid and thought about what had just transpired. Chris had never yelled at her before. Not in thirty-four years of marriage. And now, on the eve of her surgery, as they began the fight against the cancer that was wreaking havoc on her insides, he did.

When he came to bed a few minutes later, she turned over to face him, even though the darkness shrouded his expression. "It's a routine surgery," she said quietly.

"There's nothing routine about it," he answered quickly. "What does that even mean, a 'routine surgery?' A surgery is a surgery – there's always danger involved."

She had guessed right. He was worried about her. She reached over and laid her hand against his cheek. "I'm going to be okay." She wanted to tack on that the danger wasn't in the surgery as much as it was in the disease that caused the surgery to be necessary. That was what she was worried about, but didn't think it would be helpful to say it.

He pressed his hand over hers and was quiet for several long moments. "I'm sorry I yelled at you." His voice was gruff.

She pulled his arm under her shoulders and laid her head on his chest, wrapping her arm around his stomach. "I know, Love."

Quiet settled over their room, and he ran his fingers through her hair. His gentle caress made her shiver.

"Are you sad? About having a hysterectomy?" he asked into the darkness.

"What do you mean? Sad about having surgery?"

"No. Are you sad about...well, not being complete anymore?"

His question surprised her. She took a moment to think through her answer and examine her feelings. "No. I think I have already dealt with that...I already lost that part of me. When Dr. Thorlo said I had endometrial cancer, I knew that I had lost my reproductive system." She paused. "Does it make you sad?"

"A little," he admitted. "You were so good at giving life to our children."

"True," she agreed, feeling a tinge of sadness herself. Would he love her less when she wasn't a complete woman? "But do you want to have another baby?"

He chuckled. "Hardly. Having the grandkids here, as great as it is, is a good reminder of why I'm thankful to be done having babies. I'm enjoying being a grandpa at this stage of my life." He sighed. "I know it's not like we were going to have any more kids. It's not a big deal. Not really. It just serves as a reminder, I guess."

"A reminder that I have cancer?" Hannah asked, understanding.

Chris didn't speak, only nodded. Hannah understood. Sometimes, it made it much worse to speak it out loud.

"Sometimes, I feel angry with Dr. Thorlo...angry that he didn't find it sooner," she admitted.

"I've had bouts of that myself."

"I feel like he should have been checking me. He should have been asking the right questions. He should have told me of the warning signs," Hannah continued. "But I know it's not anyone's fault. Not even his."

The quiet stretched again. "I believe that God is a God of healing," Chris said.

"You have for many years," Hannah agreed. Her husband loved to pray for people who were sick. He had seen the LORD heal many people over his lifetime, even people with cancer. "I believe that, too."

"How do you think it will change you, being a cancer survivor?" Chris asked.

She had thought of that before. She knew that the LORD was good and that He was a strategic God. She knew that He had a good purpose in letting her deal with cancer. "I think it will help me appreciate life more...you...our children and grandchildren."

"I agree. I didn't realize how much I was taking you,

our marriage, and our life together for granted."

"Me too," Hannah paused before she continued. "I also think it will give both of us a new compassion for those who are dealing with health issues. Other than when I was sick after having Kara, and losing Kelsi, we have lived very healthy lives. We haven't dealt with any major health issues. We haven't faced sickness or death."

"It's funny how you just take good health for granted if you've never known what it is not to have it," Chris agreed. "I don't know that I've ever even given any thought to our health. I just assumed it would be as it always has been, other than joints that seem to be a little creakier and eyesight that seems to be a little worse each time we go to the eye doctor."

"I guess I did, too," Hannah answered. "I never really thought about it."

"I think we will from now on. And I think we'll feel more compassion for others, like you said."

Hannah wrapped the fabric of his shirt around her finger as she thought. "I want to try to keep life as normal as we can during the treatment process. I want it to be as normal as possible for the kids and for us. I want to play games, watch movies, go on shopping trips, go to meetings at the church, get together with friends and have the kids here for Christmas. I want to go out for dinner, and go ice skating and on walks."

"That may not be an option for awhile, Love. You may not feel up for all of that."

"We may need to alter things a little, it's true," she agreed. "But I want to do what I feel like doing. Don't make me lie on the couch and rest, when I feel like being outside. Don't make me take a nap, when I want to be out with the family. I don't want you to treat me like a baby, not you or anyone else. I'm a fifty-four-year-old woman who happens to be in treatment and recovering from cancer; not a baby to be ordered around who doesn't know anything about what is needed."

"Yes, ma'am." She could tell he was amused by her, yet amusement wasn't what she sought.

"Promise me you won't."

He hesitated. "I'll try not to."

That was good enough for her. "Thank you," she said, reaching up to give him a kiss.

"You're welcome," he answered, his tone changing. He kissed her again, then the kiss deepened. She felt familiar butterflies in her stomach, and she snuggled in closer to him.

Six

Chris and Hannah arrived at the hospital early the next morning. After filling out paperwork, they were escorted into a room where a young nurse started an IV in Hannah's arm. Chris held her hand while they waited, neither of them saying anything. Chris received a text message letting them know that Kimberly had arrived at the hospital with Hannah's mother, Kostya. Hannah was thankful they had both come. It felt good to know they were there. It also was good to know that Chris wouldn't be waiting alone.

"Do you want them to come back?" Chris asked, keeping his eyes on Hannah's face. "They'll be coming to take you to surgery soon."

"Yes, I want to see them," Hannah answered. She was touched that Kimberly had gone to the trouble of finding places for her boys to go every day until Greg got off work so that she could come be with her for the week. She was even more touched that Kimberly had coordinated her flight with Hannah's mother's so that they could rent a car and drive to the hospital together. As old as she was, it would feel good to have her mom there.

Kara would have been at the hospital, too, if Hannah hadn't insisted she go to work, knowing Mondays were her busy days. Kara had agreed, only on the terms that Chris would keep her posted on everything that happened and that she would come as soon as she was off work.

Chris stood. "I'll be right back, then," he promised, squeezing her hand. She nodded, and he left the room.

Alone for the first time that morning, she began to think through the next several hours. She would get to spend a few minutes with Kimberly and her mom, then the nurses would come and take her to surgery. She would be put under anesthesia and Dr. Thorlo would perform a radical hysterectomy. She would come out of surgery missing parts of herself, but hopefully with fewer cancer cells, too. She would be sent home to rest and recoup, and when the doctor thought she was strong enough, she would begin her first round of chemo and radiation.

Today was the first step in beating cancer.

She knew Joe was believing that Dr. Thorlo would find that there was no cancer when he went in to remove her reproductive system, and the surgery would be called off. It would be a healing miracle. She knew Chris was hoping for that, but if the surgery had to be done, was believing for the doctor not to find a trace of cancer in her body after the hysterectomy; also a healing miracle, but not quite as extreme. She was hoping for either. She believed the LORD was able.

Still, there was the possibility that He would not remove the cancer, and chemotherapy and radiation would follow. She had to be okay with that option as well, knowing that there was purpose in everything, no matter how hidden. Sometimes the LORD chose to heal through a radical miracle, other times he brought healing through conventional medicine and the wisdom of trained professionals; either way, healing was a miracle, and she wasn't choosey.

Still, her nerves felt on edge. Even though she had assured Chris the night before and again that morning that she would be fine, she felt afraid. She had never had surgery. She wasn't a fan of pain. She didn't know exactly what to expect and that scared her. All she could do was hope that she could handle the pain well and recover quickly. After that, she would think about chemo and radiation. She couldn't yet. It was too much.

"Father, You are good," she said, laying her head back on her pillow and closing her eyes. "You know my limitations. You are strong when I am weak. You have answers when all I have are questions. You know the outcome of this surgery. Father, if it is Your will to heal me, then do so. If not, give me the strength to get through the days ahead. I know that Your plans are good. I trust You."

Hannah thought through the words she had just uttered. They were true. She trusted Him without any doubt or hesitancy. She knew the God to whom she prayed, not in entirety, never in entirety, but in character, in relationship, in history. The Father God had built a rich history with her, and she felt confident in who He was.

Looking back, she saw Him in every season of her life. She saw His perfect will at work. She saw His plan that was good, no matter how it felt at the time. He had been faithful to her and she trusted Him. That didn't remove the unease she felt going into surgery or the bouts of fear and sadness at the remembrance of the disease that was spreading through her body, but it gave her a peace that flowed like a river deep inside. It was peace that ran deep and even covered those occasional moments of fear and sadness.

"Please be with Chris and the kids today. Give them peace, too. Remind them of Your goodness. Remind them of Your sovereignty. Take care of them. Wipe away their fears." Her last requests weighed heavier on her heart than anything else. Would Chris and their children be okay? How would today affect them? Would Joe be okay if the cancer was still there, and the surgery had to be performed? What could she do to help? How could she make it easier for them? It was a routine surgery, but she knew it would be hard for all of them, knowing that it wasn't guaranteed to cure her.

"You trust me with your life, now trust me with your husband and children." The whisper blew across her heart and she felt a pinprick of conviction. Trusting the LORD with her own life had always come easier for her than trusting Him with those she loved. She felt like she needed to protect them, teach them, and comfort them. Now, she

smiled, remembering that He was trustworthy, even with her family, and that He was more than able.

Grabbing her phone, she tapped out a quick text to her children that weren't at the hospital. 'Waiting to be taken into surgery. Finding great peace in Jesus. I'll talk to you when I get out. Love you so much!'

She was sending her text when the door to her hospital room opened. Kimberly came through the door first, looking stunningly beautiful in a gray button-up shirt paired with a navy cardigan, brown belt and skinny jeans. Her hair hung in soft wavy curls, and her green eyes seemed gentle when they met Hannah's. "Hey, Mama," she said softly, coming into the room.

Hannah held her hands out to her daughter, trying not to think of how she must look in her hospital gown, an IV stuck in her arm. "Hi, Honey." Kimberly came and enveloped her in a warm hug. Over Kim's shoulder, Hannah saw her mother enter the room.

For a woman of almost eighty-three, Kostya Marik had aged well. She was still a beautiful woman. She was tall and held herself straight and sure, looking every bit the Slavic that she was. Her blonde hair was arranged in a classy style and her blue eyes were kind and warm. Still, her face held concern, and she had more fine lines than when Hannah last saw her.

"Hannah Kostya," the older woman said softly, coming forward toward her daughter, her hands outstretched. Hannah couldn't remember a time that her mother had referred to her by her first name alone. As far as Kostya was concerned, Hannah Kostya was all one name.

Kimberly moved aside, perching on the side of the bed to make way for her grandma.

"Hi, Mom. Thank you for coming today," Hannah answered, embracing the woman, feeling closer to tears than she had all day. Something about having her mother close made her feel safe enough to break down and confess all her fears. Her mother was a pro at putting things back together. Surely she could fix this, too.

Kostya finally eased back, and Hannah had succeeded in keeping her tears at bay. Kostya stood and held her hands, looking down into her face lovingly. "I would not have stayed home. I could not have."

Hannah smiled. "Well, thank you for coming, both of you. It feels wonderful to know you're both here," she said, continuing to hold her mother's hand while reaching for Kim's with her other.

"You are going to be just fine, Hannah Kostya. This surgery isn't very terrible. I had it myself a number of years back, as you know. You just have to be a good patient and rest when the doctor and your husband say to."

Hannah took comfort in the fact that her mom had undergone a hysterectomy as well, though not a radical one, and was standing here before her. She could tell by the relieved look on Chris' face that he found reassurance in that knowledge as well.

"I will do my best," Hannah agreed. She knew resting had been her mother's biggest challenge after having her surgery. She had wanted to be up doing things instead of resting as instructed. As a result, she took much longer to heal than expected. Hannah appreciated that she was now passing on the wisdom she had gained firsthand.

Kostya smiled. "I know you will. Kimmy, Chris and I will be there to make sure you do."

"The boys were so sad they couldn't come with me this time," Kimberly said, rescuing Hannah from having to respond to her mother's gentle warning.

Hannah turned to smile at her daughter. "Were they?"

"Yes. Especially Caiden. He was begging to come along. He said he could hang out with grandpa during the day, and then sit on your lap during the evenings so you didn't get lonely." Kimberly's face lit up as she talked about her youngest.

Hannah laughed. "That was thoughtful of him. He's such a sweet boy. Where is he going to spend the week? Surely Greg can't take him to work with him."

"No! No, he certainly can't. Caiden is at Mary's this week. She'll pick up the other boys after school, too, and keep them until Greg gets off work. Depending on how long traffic takes him, he may just decide to stay at his parents' house with the boys for the week," Kim explained. Hannah made a mental note to send Greg's mom a thank-you note after her surgery. She appreciated her watching the boys so that Kimberly could come be with her.

A quick rap came on the door, and then it opened. Two nurses entered the room. "Are you ready, Hannah?" the youngest one asked.

Hannah looked at her loved ones in the room, her eyes landing on Chris. He smiled and gave a small nod, and she looked back at the nurse. "Yes."

"Good. It's time to go."

Kimberly gave Hannah a quick hug, as did Kostya. They both stepped back as the nurses made their final preparations and wheeled her from the room. Chris walked alongside the hospital bed as the nurses wheeled it down the hall, holding Hannah's hand. When they came to an intersection of hallways, the young nurse looked up at Chris and smiled. "Mr. Colby, the waiting area is right down that hall," she said, pointing. "Dr. Thorlo will come find you there after the surgery is done."

Chris nodded. "Alright." He bent down so he was close to Hannah's face. "You're going to be fine, Love. You are a strong woman, and Dr. Thorlo is a good doctor. I'll be in the waiting room if you need me, and I'll see you soon, okay?"

Hannah nodded, determined to stay calm and be brave. It was just a surgery. People had surgeries every day. Chris kissed her on the lips, then squeezed her hand and stepped back.

The nurses rolled her down the hallway, made a left turn and wheeled her into an operating room where a man in scrubs, whom she didn't recognize, was waiting beside a machine. "Mrs. Colby, I'm going to put this mask over your mouth and nose, and I just want you to breathe deeply, okay?" he said, busy behind her, hooking things up. When she agreed, he slipped a mask over her face and settled it over her mouth and nose, just as he said he would. "Is that comfortable?" She gave another nod.

That was the last thing she remembered.

~~~~~

Every passing moment felt like an eternity to Chris. He sent Kimberly and Kostya down to the cafeteria for breakfast as they hadn't taken the time to stop to eat on their way from the airport. He would rather wait alone than be forced to make pleasant conversation. He sat quietly, praying and thinking.

It wasn't so much that he was afraid that she wouldn't make it through surgery, it was simply the whole concept – the surgery, the treatment, the cancer. He had prayed and prayed that the test results would come back clean after this surgery. He knew the tests that were done earlier showed that the cancer had spread outside of his wife's uterus, but he believed that the LORD could perform a miracle, and that the cancerous cells outside of her reproductive system could disappear. He was hoping and praying that would be the case.

He dropped his hands to his knees and rubbed his palms against his jeans, asking the LORD once again to heal her.

The fact was, he could not imagine life without Hannah. He barely remembered life before her, and he was confident that he never wanted to experience it again. He knew that they were a long way from facing that kind of a reality, and so much could happen between now and then, but with her in surgery, he found himself beseeching God to heal her...and to heal her quickly.

Just the thought of his strong, beautiful, lively wife being riddled with cancer was enough to make him want to strike a deal with God. Anything – he would give anything to see her well again. He would give up any financial wealth he had accumulated. He would forfeit every plan they had for the future. He would even pay with his own health if it would make a difference. If it were possible, he would trade places with her.

She was the heart and soul of their family. She kept their children feeling connected, loved and supported. She was always there for either of their parents. She kept him in line. She had always been a great listener and offered exceptional wisdom. She was his best friend and knew him better than anyone else on earth. She had the biggest heart of anyone he knew, and everything she did, regardless of whether it was right, was spurred out of love. She was faithful and loyal, loving and gentle, honest and full of integrity. He had never once regretted marrying her or even questioned his choice.

She was exactly what he needed, exactly what he wanted. They had built a beautiful life together.

And now, she had cancer.

He cleared his throat and leaned back in his chair. She would beat it. He knew she would. There was no doubt in his mind. The only thing he worried about was getting from where they were now to that point. How hard would it be on her? On her body? On her mind? How hard would it be on him? On their children? On their parents? On their friends? On their community?

Hannah had been a pillar in Glendale for as many years as she had lived there. Within months of him moving his beautiful new bride to his hometown, she became deeply involved in the community. She was one of those rare individuals who saw everyone as a friend and felt real, genuine love for them.

His cell phone went off, and after checking it, he found it was a text message from Joe, asking how things were going. He tapped out a reply, letting his only son know that she was still in surgery.

Settling back in his seat, Chris found himself wishing that Joe was there. He loved his daughters immensely, it wasn't that he had a favorite among his children, but as wonderful as it was to have Kimberly and Kostya there, he wasn't in the mood to chat. He didn't want anyone trying to distract him with upbeat conversation. For once, he wasn't interested in being a shoulder to cry on or drying any tears. He simply wanted to sit and wait for his wife to be out of surgery. He wanted to pray and think. Joe would understand that.

But Joe was at practice, going over films from his game the day before. While professional football had been a wonderful thing for his son and a dream come true for Chris, it didn't offer much flexibility in Joe's schedule. Chris knew that Joe wanted to be there, too, and for now, that was enough. That, and his text.

Chris' thoughts turned to his daughter Kelsi, and he felt sick to his stomach. He had believed that the LORD would heal her too, and yet here they were, getting ready to mark twenty-five years since she had gone home to be with God. He thought of how painful it had been to see his little girl fighting for her life in the oncology ward, thinner almost every day, with her small head shaved bald. His stomach churned. Back then, he had tried making bargains with God. Lots of them. That's why he knew now that bargains didn't work.

With Kelsi, he had been absolutely helpless to do anything to save her, and that was the most difficult part. He was her dad. He was supposed to protect her. He was supposed to fix things. But he couldn't make it better, just as he couldn't make this better. It was a helpless feeling. Now, he prayed fervently that things would be different this time. He just wanted his wife back healthy, happy and whole again. So that was what he prayed for most of all.

Fifteen minutes after he had sent Kimberly and Kostya down for breakfast, they came back into the room, carrying the breakfast they had not taken time to eat in the cafeteria. Spotting him sitting by the window, Kimberly quickly crossed the distance and took a seat next to him, balancing a piece of coffee cake on top of each cup of coffee that she held. She handed one to him. "Any news?" she asked.

Whether or not he wanted to talk, his daughter's thoughtfulness touched him. She cared as much about Hannah as he did, and she too needed to be close. He felt guilty for having hoped the two women would stay in the cafeteria longer. "Not yet. It will likely be an hour or more still."

Kimberly nodded, and then fell quiet as she ate her coffee cake. Chris took a bite of his, doing his best to swallow it. He hadn't been hungry that morning for breakfast, and he wasn't still. With a large swallow of coffee, he was finally able to get his first bite down.

To their credit, Kimberly and Kostya waited quietly, seemingly content to do as he was – think and pray. On a few occasions, they talked amongst themselves, but graciously allowed him to stay out of the conversation. Kimberly wrapped her slender hand around his after finishing her breakfast and left it there until they saw Dr. Thorlo enter the waiting room. Chris lifted his hand to get the doctor's attention, and Dr. Thorlo crossed the room, his face grim. Chris told himself not to panic as Dr. Thorlo drew near.

"Well, it's over," Dr. Thorlo said. "She lost a lot of blood, but other than that, it went well."

Chris let out the breath he had been holding.

"In a few weeks we'll run more tests and see what we're looking at by then. Best case scenario, the cancer will be gone. Worst case, we'll start chemo and radiation. All we can do now is wait to see how the tests come back."

Chris stood up and shook Dr. Thorlo's hand. "Makes

sense, doc. Can I go see her? Is she awake?"

"No, she's not awake yet, and won't be for awhile. But you can go in if you would like to and sit with her." Dr. Thorlo looked to Kimberly and Kostya. "Just one visitor for now, ladies. When Hannah wakes up, you can all go in."

Chris looked back to his daughter and mother-in-law, who had been listening just as intently. Kimberly waved him forward. "You go, Daddy. She'll want you there when she wakes up. We're fine out here." Kostya nodded her agreement.

"I'll come get you once she wakes up," Chris promised. The two women watched him leave as he followed Dr. Thorlo out of the waiting room.

"Kimmy sure has grown up since the last time I saw her," Dr. Thorlo observed.

"She turned thirty-one last month," Chris agreed.

"Man. Have I been practicing medicine that long?"

"Longer," Chris said with a chuckle, feeling relieved now that Hannah was out of surgery, and knowing everything had gone well. "You delivered Kaitlynn, too, and she was thirty-three in July."

"Wow. Time sure goes fast."

"That, it does," Chris agreed.

"Room number three," Dr. Thorlo told him, pointing down a short hall. Glendale was a small town with a small hospital. There were a total of six recovery rooms. Chris was sure that no more than half were full.

He started toward the second door on the left, where Dr. Thorlo had pointed, but then stopped and turned "Thank you, doctor, for performing the operation, and for all of your help over the years. You've really gone above and beyond for us...and many others, I'm sure. You're a good doctor, and we're blessed to have you here in Glendale."

Dr. Thorlo looked embarrassed. "I don't have patients, Chris. I have friends." His simple statement said it all.

Chris nodded. "I believe you're right." He shook Dr. Thorlo's hand again, then turned and went into recovery room number three.

Hannah was lying in the hospital bed, looking exactly as she had when he last saw her. She appeared to be asleep. She looked peaceful and didn't seem to be in pain. Grateful to be with her again, he bent and pressed a kiss against her forehead. He pulled the recliner close to her bed and took a seat. He sent out a quick text message to Kaitlynn, Joe, Kara, his own mom and dad, and a few of Hannah's closest friends, including Jari Cordel and Carla Martens. After letting everyone know she was out of surgery and it had gone well, he put his cell phone down and reached up and took hold of his wife's hand. He wove his fingers between hers, thankful to be holding her hand once more, and felt her pulse under his thumb. It felt strong and steady. For that, he was exceptionally thankful.

~~~~~

Waking up was difficult. Hannah felt like she was pushing her way through a thick, thick fog that was never ending. Finally, she heard a voice and could actually make out the words and the speaker. It was Chris, and he was reading Scripture. She tried to focus on the words he was reading and eventually determined that he was reading the Psalms. With great effort, she opened her eyes. Everything was fuzzy for a moment and then began to come into focus.

She didn't know where she was. The room was sparsely furnished, and she didn't recognize the slat blinds over the window. Chris stood, drawing her attention as he stepped close, a warm smile filling his face. "Hey Pretty Lady," he said, winking at her. His wink inspired a warmth to flood her, along with a knowing that wherever she was, it was okay.

She opened her mouth to speak, and found that her mouth was very dry. She ran her tongue over her lips to try to moisten them, but had no luck. "Water?" she asked, having difficulty forming the word. The nurse that was standing against the wall charting while keeping an eye on Hannah, nodded her permission. Chris responded quickly, grabbing the cup of water that had a lid and a straw. He held it close for her, and after fumbling around to get the straw in her mouth, she took a long drink. She choked on the water and coughed, which brought about a hot, numb pain in her abdomen. After the worst of it had passed, she took another drink of water, being more careful to swallow it correctly.

"There you go," she heard Chris say as he turned to set the water down. The fog came back up and consumed her. She was back asleep before finding out where she was.

When she woke again, after what felt like days, Chris was standing at her side talking over the top of her to someone whose voice she didn't recognize. She forced her eyes open and turned her head, blinking to cause the person's face to come into focus.

Dr. Thorlo.

In a rush, everything came back to her – the hospital, the surgery, the cancer. "Is it over?" she asked, her words sounding thick even to her own ears. Each one was difficult to form, and her voice sounded foreign.

"Yes, Hannah. The surgery is complete. You did great. Your husband said you had a drink a few minutes ago and choked on your water. How are you feeling now? Do you have any pain?"

Hannah tried to pay attention to her body, but simply felt numb. Swiftly, that same fog came back up to envelop her before she could answer. She didn't have any idea how much time passed as she went back and forth between sleep and being awake, before she could stay awake long enough to utter more than one statement. When she finally had a decently long stretch of time when she was alert and could properly form words, Chris told her he would go out and get her mom and Kimberly. She appreciated his gesture, but was content for the time just to be with him.

She tugged on his hand until he came up and perched beside her on the bed, resting back against her pillow. He slipped his arm behind her head and held her close as best he could without moving or hurting her. She rested her head against his shoulder and closed her eyes, content and comfortable.

"The surgery went well?" she asked.

"Yes, Dr. Thorlo said it did."

"Good. So, what now?"

"Plenty of rest," he answered. "In a couple of hours, they want you to start getting up and walking a little, but for now, just rest."

"I can do that," she told him, feeling sleepy again. "How are the kids?"

"They're fine. They were all worried about you, but I let them know that you are out of surgery and that things went well."

She nodded. "Have you had lunch?"

"Why?" he asked, chuckling. "Are you hungry?"

She shook her head. "No. I just see that it's after two. I don't want you forgetting to eat."

Chris dropped his head, then looked over at her and grinned. "I'll get something when I go get Kimberly and your mom."

She smiled. "Good."

"Oh, Hannah," he said with a slight sigh, pressing a kiss against the side of her head. "Always taking care of us."

She smiled sleepily. "Someone has to."

He chuckled. "How are you feeling?"

"I can feel it," she told him.

"I'm sure you can, Love. It will likely keep getting worse over the next several hours as your pain medications wear off."

"They're not giving me anymore?" Hannah asked, alarmed. She didn't handle pain well. She never had. She had gladly opted for an epidural with each of her children. She had no objection to medication. There was no award for the woman who suffered through the most pain.

"They'll give you more," Chris assured her, chuckling again. "It just won't be as strong."

"Oh," Hannah paused. "A pity."

His chuckle turned into a laugh. "You'll be fine, Love." His voice became more serious. "There will be pain, but just remember, it's worth it. All those cancerous cells are out of your body now."

"*All* of them?" Hannah asked, hopeful.

"Well," he hesitated. "Hopefully all of them. But I was meaning all of the cells in the organs Dr. Thorlo took out. At the very worst, there are way fewer now than there were when we came to the hospital this morning."

Hannah nodded, careful that nothing but her head moved. "True."

They sat together for several long moments, neither of them saying anything. She was content to simply sit with her husband, encircled in his arm, on the recovery side of surgery. Finally, she was having a hard time keeping her eyes open again. "I think I'm going to fall asleep again soon," she told him.

"That's okay. Feel free. I'll be here when you wake up. And I'll have Kimberly and your mom with me."

"That would be nice."

"I love you, Sweetheart," he told her, kissing the side of her head again.

"I love you, too," she murmured sleepily.

The rest of the afternoon passed in much of the same fashion. She drifted in and out of sleep and consciousness. Once she woke up and realized she had been moved to a private room. She was no longer in recovery. When she was awake she visited with her mom and daughter. She caught up on what her siblings were up to in Baltimore. She heard story after story about her grandsons. Throughout the afternoon, Chris stayed close to her side, always ready to give her a drink of water or help her carefully reposition.

When the nurses came to help her stand up, she thought she would black out from the pain. It was searing, seeming to slice through her middle. Unsteady, her head foggy from the pain, she stumbled for a moment before they caught her and helped her regain her balance. Every movement hurt, and she had to focus on breathing, tempted not to even draw in a breath in hopes of avoiding the additional pain it would cause.

Sweat broke out on her face as she took slow, measured steps at the nurses' request, only making it two steps from the bed before she felt utterly exhausted. The nurses allowed her to sit down again and helped her do so as gently as they could. Still, it shot wave after wave of pain over her, causing her to shudder. She held her breath until she was settled, choosing to be slightly uncomfortable somewhat off to the side of the bed rather than repositioning to the middle. Every movement hurt. She let her air out in a gusty breath, easing back against the pillows, blinking back the tears.

Chris was watching her face intently. "You okay?" he asked, brushing a piece of her light brown hair behind her ear.

Biting her lip, she nodded bravely. She wanted to tell him that it was the most painful thing she had ever felt in her entire life, but didn't. He already knew. She could tell by the look on his face. To speak it would only make it worse.

He stroked the hair back from her face and used a cool wet cloth that Kimberly handed him to wipe the sweat from Hannah's forehead. "You did good. And you got your first time over with. You've already done it once now; you can do it again."

She wanted to be as optimistic, but shooting pains were still coming from her abdomen, and she felt like crying. If her mom and Kimberly weren't in the room, she might have. The worst part was knowing that all the cancer might not be gone.

The surgery would improve her chances, Dr. Thorlo had said, not cure her. There was no guarantee that it would get rid of the cancer. The thought of going through all of this and still be facing chemotherapy and radiation, made her feel sick.

She was a strong woman. She knew she was. She had given birth to five children. She had seen them through thick and thin. She had survived losing a child. She had weathered the storms of life, and she had not only survived, but grown as a woman. Over the past fifty-four years, she had been transformed into an overcomer. Still, her medical future looked overwhelming and unpleasant to say the least. She wanted to go home and have it all disappear. She wanted to forget all about it, to unwind the last several weeks and find that the diagnosis of cancer wasn't true. Yet the incision in her belly made forgetting about it all seem unlikely.

Feeling on the verge of a complete meltdown, she closed her eyes and leaned her head back, escaping to a place that brought stillness. "Do not fear, for I have redeemed you; I have summoned you by name; you are mine," she quoted internally. "When you pass through the waters, I will be with you; and when you pass through the rivers, they will not sweep over you. When you walk through the fire, you will not be burned; the flames will not set you ablaze. For I am the LORD your God, the Holy One of Israel, your Savior." The words the prophet Isaiah had penned so many years earlier, which she had committed to memory while in her twenties, came back to her and washed over her roiling thoughts, emotions and physical pain, bringing peace and drying her unshed tears.

Opening her eyes again, she found the concerned eyes of the man she loved, peering down at her. He searched her face, and she could tell there was so much he wanted to say. She could see in his expression that he wanted to take away her pain, her uncertainty, her fear, but didn't know how. If he could take it on himself, she knew he would.

Her husband was a good man; one who had loved her thoroughly and well. His evident concern both warmed her heart and made a deep sadness well up within her. She hated seeing him worry. Wanting to comfort him, she reached carefully for his hand and gave it a firm squeeze, trying to convey a message she would have put words to, had they been alone.

A spark of hope lit his eyes, and she knew that he knew that she had found peace within – peace and strength from the only One who gave both.

Unaware of the special moment they were having, Kimberly stepped forward. "So, we came prepared, Mama. We thought something to take your mind off the surgery might be needed, so...." Kimberly pulled out one of Hannah's favorite movies – an old classic that Hannah had watched so many times with her daughters that they could all quote nearly every line.

Hannah smiled, afraid to do any more than that for fear of causing more pain. "What a good idea, Honey! Is there a movie player?"

"We brought one," Kimberly told her, appearing pleased with herself.

Hannah caught hold of Kimberly's hand, brought it to her lips and kissed it, giving her daughter's hand a firm squeeze. It would be wonderful to have a distraction, something to keep her mind occupied. Without a distraction, she was likely to sit and stew over whether the cancer was gone or if there was more, and if it was gone, if it would come back again. "Good thinking."

Hannah released Kimberly's hand, and Kimberly set to work hooking the video player she had brought up to the television. Before she had finished, Kara walked in the door.

"It's looking like a party in here!" Chris exclaimed as

their youngest draped her jacket across the back of an empty chair, tossing her purse down on top of it, then coming quickly to the side of Hannah's bed. She hugged Chris then reached out to carefully hug Hannah.

"How are you doing, Mama?" she asked, her green eyes full of concern.

Hannah propped up a smile. "I'm doing just fine. I'm glad it's over. You girls, your father and mom are all here, the nurses promised to bring me a glass of apple juice with the soft-crushed ice, and your sister brought a movie – what more could I ask for? That sounds like a pretty good night."

Kara squeezed her shoulder. "I'm glad! Your eyes are bright. I'm glad to see that." Kara turned slightly to the others. "As you can probably smell, I brought dinner. None for you, Mama, sorry. I figured they would probably have you on a pretty strict diet if you were even hungry," Kara paused, and Hannah nodded, waving the thought of food away with a careful movement of her hand before Kara continued. "But I thought the rest of you probably wouldn't object."

"No, ma'am," Kimmy answered enthusiastically. "What did you bring?"

Kara gestured to the brown sack she had carried in. "Burritos."

Chris' eyes lit up. "I thought that's what I smelled!"

Hannah chuckled as her husband quickly left her side to go inspect the contents of the bag.

"That was thoughtful of you, Dear," Kostya said, rising from her seat to hug her granddaughter.

Fifteen minutes later, when everyone was settled with their food and drinks, Kimberly started the movie. As Hannah sat and watched the old, beloved classic, she glanced around the hospital room, her heart swelling. Four people that were oh so dear to her heart, had given up their evening to come sit in a hospital room with her. They could be a hundred other places. But here they were, sitting in uncomfortable chairs, watching a small television that was too far away and hung at an awkward angle from the ceiling. All because they loved her. She was a blessed woman.

The reality of her surgery and even the cancer that had so gripped her heart and emotions earlier, came into perspective. She had been diagnosed with cancer, yes, but she had wonderful children who loved her. She had the unyielding love and strength of her husband. She had supportive parents, in-laws and friends. She had the Great Physician as her Healer. She was truly a blessed woman. There were many who would give everything to have what she had.

As unpleasant as some moments in her near future might be, she had a deep knowledge that it was nothing but a temporary trial. She was surrounded by the things in life that really mattered. Everything else, including her health, was truly a minor detail that would simply fall into its proper place. Everything was going to be okay.

Seven

After spending three days in the hospital, Dr. Thorlo let Hannah go home. By the time she made her way up into Chris' pickup truck and they drove home, the last quarter mile of the trip over their rock-covered driveway, she wished she had stayed in the hospital another day before attempting it. Moving hurt. That's all there was to it. When she lay perfectly still, she was comfortable. Unfortunately, according to Dr. Thorlo and the nurses, lying still was not an option; she had to move. If she didn't move now, she would really pay for it later.

Chris helped her climb out of the truck and stayed with her for every slow, excruciating step to the house, his arm around her side, helping as he could. Perspiration beaded on her brow, and she concentrated on keeping her face pleasant.

Kimberly and Kostya had arrived home first and had already prepared a place for her on the couch. As she settled into the deep, plush sofa and rested against the pillows they had set up for her, she let out a deep sigh.

"How's that?" Chris asked, peering down at her, a smile replacing the lines of worry that had etched his face just moments earlier.

"Much better." She glanced around the high vaulted ceilings, the comfortable living room furniture, the stone fireplace and the trendy collection of family photos hanging over the loveseat. "It's good to be home."

Chris glanced around, too. "It does have a certain charm about it, doesn't it? It feels good after that little hospital room."

Hannah agreed. "Are you going into the office now?"

she asked, changing the subject.

He sat down on the edge of the couch. She kept her face smooth, refusing to show how the change in the cushions caused a stab of pain in her middle.

She was trying hard to be brave and protect her family from having to watch her experience pain. It was hard to watch someone you love suffer and be helpless to make it better. She couldn't put Chris through that. She couldn't put the girls or her mother through that. So, when at all possible, she hid her pain and put on a happy face. She did so again now. Chris reached for her hand, and she gave his a firm squeeze.

"I think I might go in for a few hours, if you're sure you're okay," he answered slowly, as if trying to gauge her reaction.

"I'll be fine," she assured him.

Still, he hesitated.

"She'll be fine," Kostya agreed, coming into the room with a blanket. She gave it a flip and let it settle over Hannah. "I know a thing or two about taking care of my daughter, you know. I think I can handle her care for a few hours." The older woman sent her son-in-law an amused smile.

"I know you can," he answered, looking a little sheepish.

Hannah squeezed his hand again. She appreciated how much he cared about her. "I'll be fine. Go to the office and catch up on whatever you've missed this week."

He bobbed his head in concession. "Okay. But I can be home in five minutes if you need me."

"I know you can."

Chris pressed a kiss against her forehead. "Do you need anything before I go?"

Kostya laughed. "If she needs something, I can get it for her, or Kimmy can. Go already."

Chris grinned at his mother-in-law good-naturedly. "Alright then, I'm going." He turned back to Hannah. "I'll see you in a few hours. Call me if you need anything."

Hannah smiled at him. "I will."

Chris left, and Kostya settled in a chair near Hannah's head. "Kim said she was going to make us all lunch," Kostya told her daughter. "Are you hungry?"

She was. Her appetite had been returning over the past couple of days. The day of her surgery, she had stuck to fruit juice. After that, Dr. Thorlo said she could eat whatever she liked, but cautioned her against foods that caused gas. "Yes, I am. Are you?"

"Famished," Kostya admitted, settling more fully into the chair. Hannah studied her for a few moments. Her mother was tall and stately. Even having passed eighty, she held herself gracefully, keeping her posture straight. Her movements were feminine and dainty, having all the airs of a well-trained, genteel lady. Her complexion was like porcelain. Hannah had always thought her beautiful. Growing up, she thought her sister, Oksana, looked just like their mother, and that she looked more like their father. As the years passed, though, she realized that she had her mother's straight nose, high cheekbones, pale skin and her hands. The similarities were there, just not as obvious as Oksana's.

"What was it like coming to America?" Hannah asked suddenly.

Kostya smiled. "You've been asking me that question since you were a little girl."

Hannah smiled, too. "Tell me again."

Kostya was quiet for several seconds. "It feels like it was a very long time ago now. I only remember parts," she admitted.

"How old were you when you came?" Hannah asked, even though she already knew the answer.

"Four. Your Aunt Alena was five. Miesha was two, and Uncle Rorik was just a baby. I remember we came on a ship, and it seemed very big to me. We used to play jacks on the deck. My mother became ill from seasickness. Alena looked after the rest of us, along with another woman who was immigrating and took pity on Mother. She mostly looked after Rorik." Kostya paused, thinking. "I can't remember her name anymore. She didn't have any children of her own, only a husband. It seems to me like she was young. I wish I could remember her name. Not that it matters, I guess, but I wish I could remember it just the same."

"It started with a 'k,'" Hannah offered. She had heard the story several times.

"Katka! That's right. Her name was Katka. Anyway, my parents came having heard stories of America being the land of opportunity. When we arrived, the country was in the middle of the Great Depression. I remember whole shanty towns made out of whatever people could find. I don't remember much from when we landed in New York City and the weeks following, but I do remember the sounds of children crying, men sitting around with empty eyes, and a sense of hopelessness. We lived in a small shanty made of cardboard for a month and I remember being cold. My mother and father whispered together every night trying to figure out what to do. One day, they announced we were going to ride the rails west.

"My father wanted to farm as he had in the old country. He had heard stories of corn cribs overflowing with corn, barns stuffed with hay and grass as tall as the cattle that grazed it. When we went west, though, we didn't find any of the things he had heard about. Those were the dust bowl days. I remember coughing and coughing and coughing. I remember wearing bandanas that mother had wet down and tied around our faces. We had to run into the house and huddle together under a blanket when we saw the dust storms coming."

Kimberly came into the room carrying a silver tray. On it was a bowl of soup and a sandwich for each of them. She passed them out quietly, not wanting to interrupt Kostya's story. Once Hannah and Kostya had their lunch,

Kim settled down on the loveseat with her own. "What happened then?" she asked.

"We were there for a number of years, trying to eke out a living. My father worked long hours. I remember him working until after it was dark and he would come in with his face clean, but his clothes covered in dirt. I remember being hungry a lot, and working in the garden. We didn't produce much, but we toiled out there every day. We could afford to buy flour from the store for our bread. Other than that, we ate what we could grow in our garden and whatever father could hunt or catch," Kostya paused. "It's funny how much things have changed."

"I don't have the time or place for a garden," Kimberly agreed.

"I had a garden out back for a number of years, remember that, Kim? But, I can't imagine only eating what we got from it," Hannah added. During the summer months, it produced plenty, but she had never learned how to can; in the winter, they would have gone hungry.

"I can't imagine that anymore, either, but that's how it was back then. There wasn't any other option."

"How did your family get to Baltimore?" Kimberly asked.

"Well, one fall I remember the rain coming. By then, we barely remembered what it was. Us children ran out and danced around in it and Mother didn't make us come in. She came out and stood in it too, watching us and smiling up at the sky. Alena, Miesha, and I took mud baths and tried to convince Rorik to eat the mud pies we made."

"Did he?" Hannah asked.

"Yes, he took a bite, but only one," Kostya mused. "I remember that day vividly. I remember how the rain smelled as it soaked into the parched ground, and how it felt hitting my face as I stood staring up at the sky." She smiled, a faraway look in her eyes. "It rained and rained and rained. The drought was over. Trees had been replanted, thanks to

Franklin Roosevelt. The dustbowl days had come to an end. Not long after, the war started. I remember sitting beside the radio with my family, hearing about the attack on Pearl Harbor. None of us were fluent in English yet. We had to help each other understand the broadcast. We only got pieces, but we understood enough to know that America was at war.

"Suddenly, the whole economy was jump-started. Factories came to life, people rallied together, crops were being grown both to feed those within our borders and to send to our soldiers overseas. My father decided to sell our small farm and ride the train back east. He had some experience in factory management and quickly landed a job at a factory. He was smart and had a knack for leadership. He continued to get promoted until he was one of the men running the factory. Mother and Alena worked at the factory, too. At first it was to help put food on the table, but after father got promoted, money was not so much of a concern. Then, they worked simply to help the war effort. American men were going to Europe by the thousands. In those days, many women went into the factories to keep things running in the mens' absence."

"Did you work in the factory?" Kimberly asked, drawn into the story. Hannah smiled. She already knew the answer, but was enjoying hearing her mother tell the stories of her childhood again. This was her background, her heritage, her children's heritage. These stories needed to be retold. In fact, she would love to see them recorded.

"No, I never did. I was left at home to watch over the children. Meisha was just a year younger than me, but Mother didn't trust her with the little ones yet. Adeline and Nadia were just babies when we moved to Baltimore, and Vladamir and Vassily were little boys. Mother always thought I was more mature than Meisha, I guess, so Meisha worked at the factory after school, like Alena, and I went home, took care of the little ones and kept the house. It was during that time that we really became fluent in English, with going to school.

"When we first moved to Baltimore, we lived in a small two-bedroom apartment in the Medford district. All of us kids, except for the babies, shared a room. The girls shared the bed, and the boys had to sleep on the floor on bedrolls. The babies slept in Father and Mother's room in dresser drawers. It kept them contained. When Father was promoted to vice-president, we moved uptown to a bigger house. I had never been in a house so large or so grand. I remember Mother grumbling that it was too lavish. She never did like to spend money...it had always been so tight. But Father said that his house had to match his position, especially since he was expected to do a certain amount of entertaining. He couldn't very well entertain Baltimore's elite businessmen in Medford. I enjoyed having more space, but I didn't enjoy having a bigger house to keep. Cleaning the small house in Medford had been a cinch. Cleaning the new house took hours. It was a beautiful home, though, and I remember that we had a swing in the flower garden. I loved to sit there. It always smelled of roses." Kostya smiled as she remembered.

"How did you meet Grandpa?" Kim asked, her bowl and plate empty now and sitting beside her on the loveseat.

Hannah leaned her head back against the pillows, closing her eyes. She could listen to her mother's voice and her stories for hours. When she was growing up, she and her siblings asked their mother for stories daily. She just had a knack for storytelling. Now, laid up on the couch, she couldn't think of anything she would rather be doing than listening to her tell her stories all over again.

"It was after the war ended. I was fifteen. He was a soldier who had come home. While he had been away, we moved in next door to his parents. I thought he was the most handsome man I had ever seen."

"Daddy is a good looking man," Hannah agreed.

"You should have seen him in his uniform," Kostya told them with a chuckle. "He was confident and charismatic, flirty and charming. The very first time I met him, I fell in love. The only problem was, he was twenty-two...or at least I assumed he was as he had fought in the war for four years. I didn't think he would have anything to do with me, or that Father and Mother would let him. And I was right, at least partly.

"After the first time we had dinner at his family's house after he returned from the war, my mother told me that Father said I was not to go over to their house anymore to visit with their daughter, Cornelia. She said that if we wanted to visit, Cornelia could come to our house, by herself. With Mother and Alena home from the factory since all of the men had returned, I had no choice but to obey. But with them home to help with the house and the children, I had extra time on my hands and I thought about him constantly. We had only shared one conversation, but it had been enough."

"They must have known you caught his eye," Hannah interjected, her eyes twinkling with merriment.

"Or, that he had caught mine," Kostya agreed. "I never did know what it was that tipped them off, but they were adamant. I didn't see him again for two months. When we were finally invited over to their house for dinner again, my parents had no choice but to accept. Our families were friends, and it would have been rude to decline their invitation.

"I couldn't have been more excited. I wore my best dress and had my hair in curlers all day so that my curls would be perfect that night. When I came down to join my family to walk over for dinner, my father just shook his head and sighed when he saw me. I had used some of Alena's new lipstick to paint my lips bright red and was wearing my hair in a new style I'd seen in a magazine only the week before," Kostya admitted with a girlish giggle. "I was determined to turn Jimmy's head."

Kimberly laughed. "Grandma!"

"Did it work?" Hannah asked.

"You bet it did. But then again, he said later that he hadn't needed any help. As soon as we walked in, our eyes met, and I knew right then and there that he had noticed me, too. After dinner, all of us kids were allowed to go out to the backyard to play croquet, while the adults had coffee. Jimmy told us he was the one who had asked his mother to invite us over for dinner. He was standing nearest to me, and when I asked why he wanted us to come, he just smiled. The next week, I came out of the three-story school building we attended, to find Jimmy standing outside waiting for me. He had come to walk me home. I told Cornelia to tell my sisters where I was, and then I let him carry my books while we walked. On our way home, he told me that he was really only nineteen. He had lied about his age so he could join the fighting early."

"Daddy lied?" Hannah asked, shocked to hear that about the man she only knew as honest.

Kostya waved away any scrutiny. "A lot of young men lied about their age then. The military needed soldiers and they didn't question it. Your father was anxious to do his patriotic duty. He was a good soldier, and his age didn't matter."

"So, since he was nineteen, did your mom and dad approve?" Kim asked, eager to get back to the story.

"I didn't tell them. To tell them how old he was would be to tell them that he had walked me home from school, which I didn't want to do. If they didn't know, they couldn't tell me not to walk home with him again, and thus, I wouldn't be disobeying. I made Alena and Meisha promise not to tell Mother and Father, and they didn't. The boys weren't a problem as they always walked home separately so they wouldn't be seen with a bunch of girls.

"When school was over the next day, I raced down the

stairs and ran out the big front doors. He was there waiting for me again. That day, as we walked, he reached down and held my hand. He said I was the most beautiful girl he had ever seen. He asked me to go steady with him. I, of course, said yes. The only thing that was left was for him to ask my parents. He did so that evening. He immediately got sent from the house with instructions never to come back."

Kimberly gave a small gasp. "What did you do?"

Kostya chuckled. "I was so upset I started crying, ran from the room, and flung myself across my bed. Mother came in a little later and said that Father was not ready for any of his daughters to start going steady with anyone. He thought we were all too young. I said I didn't care, that I was going to marry Jimmy Marik with or without his approval. I remember that mother smiled at me kindly and pushed my damp hair out of my eyes. She said I had mentioned marriage awfully fast for a girl of fifteen who had just been asked to go steady earlier that day. Still, she didn't laugh at me, and I appreciated that. That night, after I went to bed, something hit my window. After it came three times, I went to my second-story window and peered out. Jimmy was standing below my window in his yard. I waved, and he motioned for me to come down. I swore Alena to silence, put my dress back on and snuck out of the house."

"Mother!" Hannah exclaimed. She had never heard this part of the story. Who would have thought her parents were renegades in their younger years? "I'm certainly glad you didn't hear this when you were a teenager," she told Kimberly, who grinned and hugged the pillow she was holding.

Kostya just smiled and continued her story, seemingly unconcerned by her scandalous behavior or her daughter's apparent shock. "After I quietly made it off the porch, I ran to him. He caught my hand and pulled me into the back part of his family's property, where the trees grew thick and the shadows were longer. When we stopped, I was breathless and smiling. I felt brave and wild and daring, like a heroine in a novel, and his very presence took my breath away. He must have been feeling the same way, because when he turned to me, he caught me to him and kissed me. It was like nothing I had ever experienced before. When his kiss ended, I showed what a shy schoolgirl I really was – I slapped his face and then turned and ran all the way home."

"You didn't like being kissed?" Kimberly asked, laughing.

"Oh, you bet your boots I did. It was the most glorious thing I had ever experienced. But I was young and shy and didn't know what to do with all the emotions he was stirring up inside of me. I wasn't the least bit mad, just over-whelmed. Anyway, I had managed to sneak out without being caught, but wasn't so lucky getting back in. The second stair from the top creaked and before I knew it, I was facing my father. I got the privilege of sleeping on the floor at the foot of their bed that night and the next day, Jimmy was not waiting for me after school. My mother was."

Hannah laughed. Having had teenage girls herself, she enjoyed how her grandparents had dealt with the situation. Kostya laughed, too, her eyes merry. "I may not have stuck around the night before after our kiss, and Jimmy may have been forbidden from walking me home from school, but that didn't keep me from thinking about him or our kiss. Jimmy stayed away for a week. I was worried he had forgotten about me, or didn't think I was worth the fuss, until there was a knock on our front door, and it was Jimmy. My father went to the door, and I could hear him saying no again, that I was too young. Then the door shut with some force. That night, I had to sleep in my parents' room again, just in case. I felt bad that I had lost their trust by sneaking out, but truth be told, it was probably a good thing that they made me sleep in their room, because if I had seen Jimmy standing below my window, beckoning for me to come down, I may have snuck out all over again. It had only been a week since

I had seen him, but it felt like forever. I remember begging my mother to try to change Father's mind, and pitifully asking Cornelia how Jimmy was and if he still thought about me."

Hannah and Kimberly laughed. "You were quite the drama queen, Grandma."

"Oh yes. That I was." Kostya's eyes twinkled. "There was nothing worse than being fifteen and denied the chance to see the one I loved. It was a grave tragedy."

"So, what happened?" Hannah asked, enjoying the story. She had heard bits and pieces of it before, but never so honestly or thoroughly told.

"Jimmy came back the next three consecutive weeks, each time asking if I could go steady with him. I remember actually accusing my father of being unpatriotic."

"Unpatriotic?" Kimberly asked.

"Yes, for not letting me go out with a United States soldier!" All three of them laughed together. "Finally, my father told him to come back when I turned sixteen, which was three months away. He would think about it then, but not before, he said. Jimmy respected his wishes. So, for the next three months, I only saw Jimmy when my family went to his house for dinner or when they were invited over to ours. Occasionally, we saw each other over the hedge of bushes that separated our two properties, and we would wave at each other. We never talked about it, but I think we both knew we were just putting in our time until I turned sixteen.

"On the evening of my sixteenth birthday, Jimmy showed up on our front porch with a bouquet of flowers from his mother's garden. He asked me out on a date. I looked at my father, expecting him to say no, or at least to say he needed to think about it, but he just smiled and waved me out the door. I had put on my favorite dress and a liberal coating of the new tube of lipstick Alena had given me for my birthday after I got home from school, hoping against all hope that Jimmy would come for me, and I would be allowed to go, so I was all ready. That night, Jimmy asked before he kissed me goodnight," Kostya said, her eyes twinkling again.

"Three months later, Jimmy asked me to marry him. He had talked to my father and Father had agreed, as long as we waited until I was seventeen. We were married the day of my seventeenth birthday. It was quite the social event." Kostya smiled fondly. "And the happiest day of my life."

"I daresay, Daddy would agree," Hannah told her.

"Oh yes, he was even happier than I was. You would have thought that man won the lottery."

"I think he did," Kimberly said with a gentle smile.

A smile lifted Kostya's lips, and she pushed herself to her feet. "I talked so long that my soup is cold. I'm going to go warm it up."

"Good idea. It's definitely best warm," Kimberly agreed.

When Kostya left the room, Hannah looked over at her daughter. "I wish we could find a way to record her telling that story – either in writing or a voice recording. It would be nice to have it in her voice, though, wouldn't it? She's such a good storyteller."

Kimberly grinned and held up her cell phone, which had been sitting upside down on her leg. "Done. I missed the beginning of it, but I recorded everything since I came into the room. I thought it would be neat for the grandkids to hear someday."

"You did? Good thinking, Hon! Except maybe the kids should only hear it once they're all grown up and out of the house," Hannah commented. "I can't believe she snuck out!"

Kimberly laughed. "Yeah, I could see that story being referenced as justification a few years down the road. It's good to have it recorded, though. I'll send it out to Kait, Kara and Jessi."

"Good idea. I'm sure they would like to hear it, too."

When Kostya came back into the room, she settled down in her chair and finished her soup. "I hope you know your father would have been here if he could have been, Hannah Kostya," she said, finishing the last of her sandwich. "He wanted to be but wasn't feeling well enough to travel, nor did he think he should expose you."

"I understand, Mom. It's okay. It's fun having this time just us girls," Hannah told her. She knew that what her mother said was true. Jimmy Marik had always been a loving and attentive father. She had no doubt that he would be there, too, if he hadn't just come down with Influenza the week before. Hannah was glad he had stayed home to rest and recoup.

When Kostya was done with her lunch, they brought a lap desk in for Hannah and pulled a couple of chairs out of the dining room. They sat and played rummy until late in the afternoon. When Kostya brought Hannah a glass of water and pain medication, she suggested that Hannah close her eyes and take a nap before dinner. Having had a hard time keeping her eyes open for the past hour, Hannah didn't object.

Left alone in the living room, she could hear Kostya and Kimberly laughing together in the kitchen as they cooked, and wished she could join them. Being so tired and so unable to take part in what her family was doing, was no fun. As many times as she had jokingly wished for it over the years, it wasn't fun to be waited on hand and foot. She wanted to be up doing things. She wanted to be up taking care of her family, not the other way around.

Still, her physical limitations were real and as a wave of exhaustion rolled over her, she succumbed to sleep. Later, she awoke to Kara's cheery greeting from the foyer, announcing that she had arrived. Seconds later, Justin and Kara entered Hannah's line of sight, and Hannah suppressed a yawn as they came forward to hug her. Kara perched on the edge of the couch, asked about how she was feeling and how her day had been. Hannah tried hard to keep her voice even, despite the burning pain in her middle caused by the change in the slant of the cushion, while she answered Kara's questions and asked about her day in return. Justin relayed a funny story from work, and Hannah smiled at him, thankful for the upbeat distraction.

Hearing the commotion, Chris came from the direction of his home office. He greeted Kara, Justin, and then Hannah, as she had been sleeping when he came home. Seconds later, Kostya and Kim came out of the kitchen and announced that dinner would be ready in five minutes. With Kara and Justin heading back to the foyer to get rid of their coats and shoes, Chris bent over Hannah. "Do you need to use the bathroom or anything before dinner, Love?"

Hannah nodded. She did. And had for awhile. She simply hadn't wanted to get up.

"Alright. Why don't I help you?" His face and voice were gentle, as were his hands as he offered her support.

Letting her set the pace, he held his hands firm as she used them to pull herself to a sitting position, then scoot to the side of the couch. Pain exploded within her until dark shadows were fading in and out around the parameters of her vision. She groaned as she stood, feeling lightheaded.

"It's bad this time, huh?" Unable to speak, she nodded. "How long has it been since you were up?" he questioned.

"Since we got home," she admitted through clenched teeth. At first, she had forgotten that Dr. Thorlo had told her to get up every two to three hours to keep the muscles stretched out as they healed. By the time she remembered, it was late afternoon, and she was scared to move, afraid of the ensuing pain.

"Hannah," Chris chided gently. "This wouldn't be so bad if you had kept moving throughout the afternoon."

"That's helpful," she told him, pain making her words have a bite to them. "Thanks for reminding me." He gave her a chagrined look. Once she got to a standing position and stood absolutely still for several long moments, the pain slowly subsided enough that she could attempt shaky steps into the bathroom connected to their makeshift master bedroom. When she finally made it back to the couch and Chris helped her lower herself down onto it, she let out a long sigh and relaxed.

He took her chin in his hand, his touch gentle but firm. "We're doing this again in two hours, do you hear me?" She nodded. Getting up more frequently had to mean less pain in the long run. Surely it would be better than what she had just experienced.

They had dinner in the living room that night. Kim and Kostya had made broccoli and cheese stuffed chicken breasts with sides of baked potatoes and steamed asparagus. They all ate together, talking and laughing. Hannah looked around the room full of joyful people, her mood reflective. If her cancer had caused this room full of people that she loved to all have dinner together on a Thursday evening, then it wasn't all bad. It had brought her family together. Sudden tears pricked her eyes. Was that it? Was a purpose of her sickness to bring people together? Was this just the beginning?

Their family had always been close. However, she couldn't deny that over the past several years, the kids had become busier and busier in all different parts of the country, resulting in less time together. For the last two years, they had only all been together once a year. She realized that families grew busy and didn't see each other as frequently once the kids grew up, moved out, and started families of their own. Still, if her cancer would cause them all to come back together again, she would enjoy every minute of that family time. Surely that was a blessing amidst the ashes.

After dinner, Kara and Kimberly insisted that everyone else remain seated while they took care of the dishes.

Hannah could hear them laughing together in the kitchen, and it warmed her heart. Kara had been twelve when Kimberly had gone off to college. They had played together some when Kara was little, but it had only been a couple of years sprinkled over their childhood that they had been interested in the same kinds of things. Kimberly had always tried hard to act older like Kaitlynn, and by the time Kara was ready to really play, Kait and Kimmy were getting too old for her kind of games. By the time Kara was old enough to really fit in with her sisters as a young woman, Kimberly was married with children, and once again, they found themselves in different seasons of life.

Hannah contemplated the girls' relationship. They loved each other very much. She knew they were close. But she realized that they may never have been super good friends, simply because of a lack of common ground. It was good to hear them talking and laughing now, just the two of them.

While the girls were doing dishes, Chris flipped through television channels until Justin stopped him. It was a show about Alaska and both guys were instantly transfixed. "Is this okay, Love?" Chris remembered to ask over his shoulder, only glancing briefly at Hannah before turning back to the television. She laughed carefully, glancing at Kostya. Kostya smiled back.

"I always have been interested in the forty-ninth state," Kostya said.

"Me too," Hannah agreed, giving her permission. Satisfied, Chris settled back in his chair and propped one ankle up on the opposite knee. When the girls came in a few minutes later, they found all four of them involved in the show and sat down to join them. Kara sat on the loveseat with Justin, leaning back against him and positioning herself to see the television screen. He wrapped his arm around her shoulders and chest, letting it settle there. Hannah watched from her place on the couch, a small smile on her lips.

Justin had loved Kara since they were little more than children. He took good care of her.

Again, Hannah found herself wondering when they would have children. *'When God?'* she asked. *'Please don't let there be a problem. If anything was harmed when she was an infant, please heal it. Let her have children.'* Kara glanced at her, feeling her attention. Hannah smiled before turning back to the television show, continuing to pray.

The evening passed pleasantly between lively conversation and quiet television watching. When the grandfather clock in the corner struck nine, Kara stretched and then stood, Justin following suit. "We'd better be going," Kara said, coming over to sit beside Hannah.

"The morning comes early, doesn't it?" Hannah asked, picking up Kara's hand and holding it in her own.

"It does. It never seems to care how busy the day before was or how late I was up. That alarm clock goes off at the same time, regardless," Kara said, her voice as cheerful as always.

Hannah patted her hand. "Thank you for coming tonight."

"You're welcome. It's good to see you home again," Kara told her, her expression serious for just a moment. She leaned in and gave Hannah a hug, then pressed a kiss against her cheek. "Get some rest, Mama. I'll stop by tomorrow."

"I will. You have a good day at work."

Kara stood to say her other goodbyes, and Hannah returned a careful hug from Justin. After seeing Justin and Kara out to the front door, Chris came back into the living room, stopping beside Hannah's couch. "Are you ready to turn in for the night? I think I am."

Fighting to keep her eyes open, Hannah smiled up at her handsome husband, grateful to be known so well. He was giving her a choice, even though he knew what she was going to say. "I think I'm ready for bed, too." His smile was full and rich, and she savored it like she would a piece of chocolate cake. She committed it to memory, tucking it away with so many other memories.

He was charmingly handsome, and as the years had stolen his youth, they had given him something equally as attractive – wisdom. She looked at the laugh lines around his mouth and eyes, the streaks of gray at his temples, the history that she saw in his eyes. Even after thirty-four years of marriage, her heart skipped a beat. After letting herself enjoy his smile for another moment, she turned her head back toward the others.

"I think I'm going to turn in. Are you guys going to stay up awhile longer?"

Kimberly turned to Kostya. "I'm not tired yet. Are you?"

Kostya sent her a mischievous smile. "I'll take you on in Scrabble."

Kim laughed. "Done. You're going down, Grandma." Hannah enjoyed their easy banter. "I guess we are," Kimberly answered. "But I think it's good for you to go to bed. After what your body just went through, you need rest."

"Agreed. Get some sleep while you can. In six weeks, you'll be up and at it again," Kostya told her. "But for now, you need to rest and recover."

Although playing Scrabble sounded like fun, Hannah knew they were right. "Well, goodnight then. You guys have fun."

Kimberly and Kostya echoed their goodnights and watched as Chris helped Hannah from the couch. Their exit from the room was painfully slow. Once they made it into their room, Chris helped Hannah get ready for bed, then pulled back the covers so she could lie down. Being careful not to cause additional pain, he pulled the sheets and blankets up over her and reached down to smooth back her hair. "I'll be back in a minute," he promised, and seconds later, she heard him brushing his teeth and readying himself for bed. Finally, he plugged his cell phone into the charger as he crawled into bed beside her.

Inching his way closer to her, he took her hand and held it in his own, letting it rest against his heart. The comfortable silence stretched for several moments. "Does it hurt you when I move?" he finally asked, his voice sleepy.

"No, I can barely feel it," she answered. "I'm glad we chose this mattress."

"That's right. We debated on that quite awhile, didn't we?" he asked, amused. "I hope this will serve as a reminder that I'm always right."

Hannah laughed heartily, regretting it the moment she did. Overcome with pain, she stilled until the worst of it had passed. Helpless to ease her suffering, Chris laid still and simply stroked the back of her hand comfortingly, as if she were one of the kids.

When she let out the breath she had caught, he kissed the back of her hand and then laid it back on his chest, his fingers still woven between hers. "You doing okay?"

She took her time answering, giving herself a moment to process his question and her emotions. "I hurt, but I think that's expected. Mentally...I just wish this was all for something."

"What do you mean?" he questioned, incredulously. "This is for your life...for our future...for our children. What more is there?"

Hannah cringed at the hurt and confusion she heard in Chris' voice. She hadn't meant it like that. "You're right," she paused, searching for a way to put into words the dread she felt. "It's just that I'm in all this pain and have undergone a major surgery, and for what? I still have cancer."

"You don't know that," he told her. "You could be cancer-free. They have to run more tests before they can say either way."

She recognized his hope and was reluctant to crush it. "That's true." She wanted to remind him that they already knew the cancer had spread outside her reproductive system, and had been warned that a hysterectomy would not remove all traces of it. Still, the hope she heard in his words was like a lifeline, and in the darkness, when she let herself think about the cancer that was waging war on her body, she desperately needed something to cling to.

"Besides, at the very least, there are significantly fewer cancerous cells than there were in the beginning," he added.

Significantly less, she repeated back to herself. That was something. "You're right."

The silence stretched. Finally, Chris broke it. "Your answers are so patronizing. I feel like you're not convinced any more than when the conversation started. You sound so pessimistic...so resigned."

Hannah gripped his hand more firmly. "I am not giving up, Chris Colby. Not in any way, shape, or form."

"I'm glad to hear that," he told her. "You were worrying me for a minute."

"I'm sorry. I'm not resigned to having cancer. I promise you I'm not. I'm just ready to be well again. I'm ready to have the cancer gone and have all of this behind us."

"You and me both, Love. You and me both." He kissed the back of her hand again. "It will happen. And soon. A year from now, we'll be looking back on this time, thankful it's over and enjoying life together, healthy as can be."

Lying still in the darkness, the peaceful quiet of their home settling around them, Hannah clung to her husband's strong hand, hoping and praying he was right.

Eight

"What do you mean it's still spreading?" Chris asked, repositioning in his seat, clearing his throat. They were sitting in Dr. Hedgins office. The test results were back. "We...we did the hysterectomy."

Dr. Hedgins dipped her head. "I know you did. And we had hoped that would stop the spread of the cancerous cells, or at least slow them, but it hasn't." She shifted her attention off of Chris. "You have a very aggressive form of cancer, Hannah," she paused. "I'm sorry. Really, I am. I know you hoped that the surgery would make it go away. We were all hoping for that. Unfortunately, it just didn't happen."

Hannah nodded slowly, feeling numb. She had tried to prepare herself for the very words Dr. Hedgins was speaking, hoping that she would find herself overwhelmingly surprised and grateful for the news that would actually come, but now, actually hearing it was even more difficult than she had expected. The surgery, the pain, the weeks of recovery – it was all for nothing. The cancer was still spreading aggressively.

Chris was rubbing his forehead, and the look of disappointment in his eyes made Hannah's heart sink. She knew he wasn't disappointed in her, knew he didn't blame her, yet she knew she was the reason for it. She turned back toward Dr. Hedgins. "What do we do now?"

"We begin chemotherapy and radiation," the doctor answered simply.

Hannah knew that was the next step, and yet the words were difficult to hear. They carried so much uncertainty and fear. They carried so many memories. "When?"

"As soon as possible. I can get you scheduled for to-morrow, if you're agreeable."

Hannah wanted to shout at her that she wasn't agree-able. Not at all. She didn't want to undergo chemo and ra-diation. She didn't want to have any treatments. She didn't want to have cancer! Inside, she was shaking. She felt like screaming. She felt like slapping Dr. Hedgins and telling her to take it all back. The ferocity of her emotions startled her, and she cleared her throat. "How often will the chemo be administered?"

"Daily. Through an IV. You'll have to stay in the hos-pital."

"Daily?" Chris questioned, sounding deflated and in despair. Hannah couldn't bring herself to look at him, couldn't risk the high likelihood of a complete meltdown if she did.

"Are there any other options?" she questioned.

Dr. Hedgins looked at her sympathetically, folded her hands on her desk, and leaned forward in her chair. "Hannah, Chris, I know this is all very sudden and very sur-real to you both. I would not recommend anything that I didn't feel was absolutely necessary. You need to start treat-ment, Hannah, and you need to start it as soon as possible. Do you understand?"

Hannah understood. She understood what Dr. Hedgins wasn't saying. "Am I dying, doctor?" she asked for the sec-ond time in the past month and a half, her throat aching, the words hard to form. Beside her, a groan escaped from Chris. She felt his agony with every fiber of her being. Tears stung her eyes, knowing how much pain he was in, hearing the news they were hearing. She reached around for his hand, not taking her eyes off the doctor, and found it by instinct. She clung to it, and his grip was so firm that she knew he wasn't letting go. Not now, not ever.

Dr. Hedgins' face filled with compassion. "There is still hope, Hannah. That being said, you have a very aggressive form of cancer, and there is no time to think about other treatment options or to get things situated at home. You need to be ready to check in tomorrow, and we need to begin treatment."

Hannah's head was spinning. Dr. Hedgins had not answered her question. In that fact alone, she knew the answer. Fear rose up around her like an angry ocean; uncertainty, anger, sorrow, and disbelief breaking over her like waves churned up by a storm. There was nothing she could do but grab hold of the one lifeline that had been thrown to her. "Okay. I'll be ready for my first treatment tomorrow."

Dr. Hedgins smiled. "Good." She gave them further instructions about where to be and when. She told them more about what to expect, and gave them pamphlets about chemotherapy – the treatments and the side effects. Then, she bid them good afternoon and showed them to the door, promising to see them the next day.

Once out of her office, Chris and Hannah walked quietly down the halls of the hospital to an elevator that took them to the ground floor. Without a word, they walked out of the hospital, across the street, and through the parking garage to Chris' truck. When the doors shut around them, they both just sat for several moments.

"I can't believe this is happening," Chris finally admitted.

Hannah's shoulders lifted in a shrug. "I didn't think the cancer would be completely gone. Dr. Thorlo warned us of that, but this? I didn't expect this," she agreed.

Hearing the wobble in her voice, the fear in every word, the protective instincts within Chris rose up. He turned to his wife and took her hands firmly in his. "You are not going to die of cancer, Love. I will not let you! We are going to follow the doctor's advice and treat this cancer as aggressively as it is attacking. You are a fighter, Hannah Kostya Colby – you have been since the day I met you and you still are today. You are strong enough to beat this. We are going to pray to the LORD for healing and take every necessary measure to fight this. We are not defeated. Look at me, Love." She raised watery eyes to meet his and felt overcome by the love she saw there. "We are not defeated! We serve a powerful God!"

His passionate words inspired courage and confidence in her that she was far from feeling on her own. She reached up and pulled his face down to hers, kissing him soundly. "I love you, Chris Colby."

He ran his thumb over her cheek. "Not as much as I love you."

She couldn't help herself. "Will you always love me? No matter what happens?" Her voice was shaky, her need for reassurance great. She felt needy, sick and afraid.

Chris let out a deep breath, having to look away or be overcome with emotion. After composing himself, he glanced back at her and stared straight into her blue eyes, his hands on either side of her face. "Hannah, I will love you until the end of time. Nothing," he paused, "*nothing* will change that. Do you understand?"

She nodded. She did. She knew the words he spoke were true. She knew they were true before he spoke them, and yet she had needed to hear them again. When she thought of what the days, weeks and months ahead would be like, she needed to hear him profess his love for her one more time. She needed to be reassured that in the darkest days, he would be there. She needed to know that she held a place in his heart that was transcendent.

'Father!' she cried out silently, over and over. Her husband was flesh and blood, wonderful, yet human. As much as she needed reassurance of his love, she knew she needed something more. She knew her heart was crying out for reassurance from God – the Great Physician, who knew her inside and out, whose love truly could extend to the end of time. Would He be there with her during the darkest days? She needed to hear Him say that He would.

'Father, please come and heal me! Cleanse my body. Cleanse my blood. Restore it to the way You created it to be. And please, sweet Holy Spirit, be with us now, because I don't know how we're going to get through the next twenty-four hours without You.'

Ever unified, Chris began to pray out loud, still holding her hands. He prayed for strength, for comfort, for stamina. He prayed for wisdom for the doctors and wisdom for them. He prayed for healing. He prayed for a miracle. He prayed for restoration of Hannah's body and he prayed for peace. When he finally said 'amen,' Hannah wanted to weep. Instead, she looked up through a small trickle of tears and smiled. He reached out and caught her tears on his thumbs as he held her face, gazing deeply into her eyes.

"Tomorrow, we are going to come back to this hospital, walk in that door and give the best fight against cancer those doctors have ever seen, but tonight," he paused and wiped another tear. "Tonight we're not going to talk or think about cancer anymore. We're going on a date. What do you want to do, Love? We'll do anything you want."

Hannah wanted to think of something creative and exciting. Heaven knows she had spent years daydreaming about dates in the city where Chris agreed to do everything and anything she wished. But as the clock on the dash edged toward five o'clock, all she could think of was how tired she felt.

The long walk through the hospital had worn her out. Her surgery was not far enough behind her that her strength and energy had fully returned. She was walking better, but slowly and not far. Going to a museum sounded fun, or perhaps walking around the historic downtown, but she was realistic enough to know she would never make it. Going to a play would be something out of the ordinary, but she didn't feel capable of even walking through a big parking lot or climbing stairs. "Do you know what I want to do?" she asked suddenly, a smile filling her face.

"What?" he asked, ready to give her whatever she wanted.

"I want to go back to the hotel, order in pizza, and watch a movie on TV while you give me the longest back-rub of my life...at least an hour's worth."

Chris tipped his head back and laughed. The comforting sound chased the sorrow away and seemed to break up the dark cloud that had settled over them. "Oh, Love, you don't waste an opportunity do you?" She had been asking for backrubs since before they were married. He always obliged, but they were short-lived, as his arm tired quickly. She, on the other hand, never tired of receiving them.

"You said anything," she reminded, her eyes laughing.

He rubbed his thumb over her cheek again, still smiling. "Yes, I did." His expression grew serious for a moment. "Are you sure that's it? Just pizza and a backrub?" He had expected something more elaborate.

"It's what I want," she told him.

"Then, that's what we'll do."

He backed out of his parking place and turned his pickup toward the hotel where they had reservations. He noted mentally that he would have to see if he would be allowed to stay in Hannah's room with her, or if he needed to make reservations at a hotel closer to the hospital. There was one just a block away from the hospital campus, but they had always avoided it, wanting to stay some distance away from the large complex that was quickly becoming unpleasant. However, if Hannah would be staying in the hospital, distance was the last thing he wanted.

"We need to call and tell the kids," Hannah said, despair creeping back into her voice.

"Hey! I said no thinking or talking about any of that stuff," he reprimanded, not confessing to the fact that he had been thinking about it as well. "What kind of pizza do you want?"

She named her toppings, and again he chuckled. "You

really are getting your goody out of this chance to have whatever you want, aren't you?" His gentle tease was met with a charming smile. "This is the one time you'll see me eating a mushroom. Why anyone would want fungus on their pizza is beyond me."

"You can pick yours off and give them to me," she offered. He chuckled.

On the way to the hotel, he pulled the truck into a busy parking lot, making a pit stop at a restaurant that was known for their decadent cheesecake. Hannah stood at the glass display case for over half an hour, 'ooing' and 'ahhing' over the different flavors and choices. For once in his life, he didn't rush her. Forty-five minutes later, they emerged with a slice of white chocolate blueberry cheesecake and a slice of chocolate turtle cheesecake.

Once they arrived at the hotel, he left her in the truck to rest while he checked in and got their room keys. After parking, he carried their bags and the cheesecake while motioning for Hannah to go ahead of him.

He was thankful she had chosen staying in for their date. He could see how exhausted she was by the careful way she walked, the slight slump of her shoulders and the look of pure concentration on her face. He had forgotten how taxing walking was for her still, and chided himself for not having insisted she let him push her through the hospital in a wheelchair. Her dignity would be a whole lot easier to mend than her body; he would rather deal with her stinging pride than the pain he knew she was in.

He breathed a sigh of relief as he unlocked the door to their hotel room and held it open for her to go in. She immediately sat carefully on the side of the bed, then laid down, drawing in a slight gasp of pain, then letting out a long sigh of relief as she stretched out. He had been right. She was physically exhausted.

He left her to rest while he got their luggage situated and called out for pizza, giving the hotel name and address, along with their room number. Flipping on the television, he flipped through channels until he found a movie Hannah wanted to watch. Once he did, he set the remote aside and nudged her arm. "What do you say about me starting on that backrub? If it's going to be the longest of your life, I'd better get started."

Rolling over carefully, she shot an impish smile over her shoulder. "There's not much of a record to beat."

He poked her in the ribs as he chuckled. "Hey! I can't help that my arm cramps up."

With her head turned away so she could watch the movie, he felt her grin more than he saw it. He ran his fingers lightly over her back, drawing imaginary straight lines, then crisscrossing and going freestyle. When a sharp knock on the door came, he was relieved to have a break. His forearm was already cramping. After paying the pizza delivery guy, he carried the hot pizza back into the room, his mouth watering. Despite the mushrooms Hannah had ordered, their dinner smelled good.

She reclined against his chest as they ate their pizza and watched the movie. Hungrier than they had thought, they put away the entire large pizza. Taking a sip of her soda, Hannah glanced up at him, her face full of guilt. "I can't believe I ate four slices," she admitted.

He looked at the extra room in her clothes, and wanted to remind her that she had lost weight over the past few months. It wouldn't hurt her to put those pounds back on. Additionally, it may be the last good meal she had without feeling ill in weeks. But, he reminded her of neither; he didn't want the light to go out of her eyes again the way it had earlier. Instead, he grinned and said, "Don't feel bad. It was thin crust. Thin crust just doesn't fill you up like the others."

"Still. The calories in the toppings are just as high. I'm ashamed of myself."

"Don't go becoming a calorie cruncher on me. There's no need. You're one hot mama." His words drew a laugh from her, and he smiled. Mission accomplished.

When they finished their meal, he helped her reposition carefully, then stood, collecting the napkins and plastic glasses they had been using. He threw them away, then returned to the bed with plastic forks and their slices of cheesecake. He watched in amusement as Hannah savored her first bite, taking one bite to his three. "This is pure heaven," she told him, slicing into her cake to break off her next bite. He couldn't argue. He couldn't remember the last time he had eaten cheesecake so creamy and good.

"It's like a luxury vacation for my taste buds," he agreed, drawing another chuckle from his wife. He relished her laughter.

He finished his cheesecake first and set the plastic container aside. He made a pot of coffee while Hannah finished. After disposing of the discarded dinnerware, Chris carried two cups of coffee back to the bed and settled down beside his wife. She took two sips of hers, which he knew was all she would drink, then put a pillow across his legs and laid carefully on it. Knowing another cramp in his arm was in his immediate future, he set his mouth in a grim line and got to work, carefully running his fingertips back and forth across her back. As he did, he found himself wishing he had taken the time to do more of it over the years, despite the ache that was already developing in his forearm. With her face turned toward the television and her attention off him, he allowed himself to think of the illness they were facing, the treatment that would start in the morning, and what it meant for them.

His interest in the movie gone, he began to pray. He prayed for healing, prayed for his wife, prayed for his children and for himself. He prayed for endurance to get through the coming weeks, to have the strength that Hannah would need from him, the wisdom to know how to help her and the grace of God to handle whatever came next. He had no doubt that God would heal Hannah, but he knew it could be a rocky and emotional road until that moment came.

His thoughts shifting, he began to think about calling the kids in the morning to share the news. He didn't know how to tell them, or even where to start.

Despite the fact that they were all adults and were being realistic about things, he knew they were hoping for a good report that the cancer was gone or at least greatly diminished, as much as he had been. He knew the hope he would hear in their voices when each of them answered the phone in the morning. To tell them that the cancer was still growing aggressively, and the doctor thought it necessary to start chemotherapy as early as the morning, would be a hard blow. His chest ached just thinking about it.

Below him, Hannah laughed, startling him from his melancholy thoughts. Glancing at the movie, he realized he had missed a funny part. He forced out a chuckle to ward off her suspicions. He knew his wife. If he didn't laugh at things he normally did, she would notice. Then the questions would begin. Was he into the movie? Was something else on his mind? What was he thinking about? Was he thinking about the cancer? And the chemotherapy? Was he nervous? There would be a whole string of questions designed to draw out of him what she already knew, leading into a conversation that he wasn't ready to have.

He knew she would eventually turn those big blue eyes up to him and ask him the two questions he most feared – was he okay? And was he scared? He feared honesty would be the final straw that broke the camel's back. If not for both of them, at least for himself. And so, he laughed at the movie in appropriate places while tracing lines and circles over his wife's back, all the while crying out to God for a miracle.

~~~~~

Later that night, quiet tears ran down the sides of Hannah's face, running below her ears, across her neck and wetting her hotel pillow. It had been a good evening. A quiet, restful one. Their dinner had been a treat, the movie funny and distracting, the mood light. Her backrub had filled her love tank, and the hot shower she took after the movie had served to completely relax her body. Slipping into a night-gown she hadn't put on in years, she had surprised and de-lighted her husband. She had convinced him that she would be okay, and that it wouldn't hurt.

She had lied.

With not many weeks having passed since her surgery, it had been painful. Yet, not painful enough to keep her from withholding something that she wasn't sure she would be able to give again anytime in the near future. And Chris' pleasure had made up for the discomfort she felt. Yet, it was in that moment when she saw something that now caused her tears.

For one moment, just one moment as Chris' actions had moved from loving to possessive, she saw the despair and desperation in his eyes as he had frantically tried to hang on to something that was ending. For the half hour prior, he had felt confident and in control. Things felt nor-mal, and they had both forgotten about what was waiting for them in the morning. During that time, as he held her, he had felt capable of *holding* her – of holding on to her, of holding things together. As it all came to an end, he realized that he was no more capable of holding on to her than he was of making the deep pleasure of their encounter last for-ever. It was then that she saw the fear in his eyes – fear that she was slipping away from him just as the moment was.

In another moment, his eyes had shuttered, and all she had seen in them was love and adoration. But hours after Chris had fallen asleep beside her, it was that brief look of fear, despair and desperation that kept her awake.

Her fingers spanning across her stomach, her finger-nails bit into her flesh as her frustration rose. She wanted the cancer gone! She wanted to fight it, to resist it, to will herself better. And yet how could she fight something she couldn't see? How could she resist something that stealthily stole more and more of her healthy cells, slowly making its way through her body until every bit of her would be corrupted and crippled by the angry cancer? How could she will herself to be better when the cancer continued to spread, no matter how optimistically she had been thinking, or how many times she had told herself it would be gone? How could she fight something that was in her own flesh and blood? She felt helpless and overwhelmed.

She also felt guilty. Guilty that she had been weak enough to get cancer, guilty that she hadn't discovered it sooner, and guilty that she wasn't doing a better job of fighting it now. Surely she should be able to have some control over it. Surely she should be able to beat it. And yet, here she was. It was still spreading. It was still aggressive. And she was starting chemotherapy in the morning.

Taking a thick strand of hair between her thumb and forefinger, she rubbed the silky tress between her fingers feeling the weight and thickness of it. She knew that chemotherapy oftentimes caused people to lose their hair. Not always, but usually. She hoped she would be one of those who didn't. She didn't consider herself a vain or prideful woman, but she didn't want to lose her hair.

Needing a distraction from the sorrow she felt welling up inside of her, she slipped quietly out of bed. Careful not to wake her sleeping husband, she stepped into her jeans and pulled on a sweatshirt. Grabbing her cell phone and making sure she had a room key in her pocket, she slipped out of the room into the hotel corridor, quietly pulling the door shut behind her. She slid down the door until she was sitting against it, and dialed a familiar number.

"What's wrong?" Carla Cordel's voice was filled with alarm. Hannah could tell her friend had been sleeping. Her words were a little fuzzy. And understandably so, as it was nearing one o'clock in the morning on the East Coast. Carla probably thought something had happened to Joe, Jessi, or one of the kids.

Carla was Joe's mother-in-law, Jessi's mother. Hannah and Carla were related through marriage now, but friends on their own accord. It was a friendship that started during Carla and Jessi's year in Glendale, when Joe and Jessi had been high school sweethearts, and it had grown and deepened since.

"I start chemo tomorrow. The cancer is still spreading." Speaking the words out loud caused Hannah's voice to catch, and she fought against tears. Why was it that speaking something made it so much more real – and so much scarier?

"Oh Honey." Carla's quick response full of concern and compassion broke the dam, and Hannah cried. Hannah could hear rustling on the other end of the line, and knew that Carla was getting out of bed and going somewhere she could talk. Hannah wanted to apologize for calling so late, wanted to thank her for getting up to talk her through her midnight battle, but knew there was no need. With as deep of a friendship as they had, no explanation or apology was necessary.

"We went to the oncologist today to get my test results," Hannah told her, tears streaming down her face. "It's not good, Carla. The cancer has increased since the tests they ran before my surgery, not decreased."

"It hasn't decreased at all?" Carla questioned in dismay.

"No. I asked if there were options other than chemo, but she said we don't have time to consider other options. She said the cancer is very aggressive, and that we have to start treatment as soon as possible...meaning tomorrow." Hannah paused and wiped her eyes with the back of her hand. "Carla, I asked her if I was dying, and she didn't answer me other than to say that there's still hope. There's still hope. I'm dying of cancer, Carla, and the hope...the chance is that I won't. Do you understand? It's not that I have cancer, but they're treating it, and there's a chance I could die. I'm dying with a chance I could live." Hannah's words were ragged and choppy between sobs, and her throat and incision ached.

"Hannah," Carla answered, and Hannah could tell she was crying now, too. That was all. Just her name. Somehow, it was oddly comforting. Carla knew her too well to offer some shallow cliché. She would remind her of truth and of hope later, but for now she simply let Hannah talk.

"We didn't tell the kids yet. I thought we should, but Chris wanted a night for just the two of us first."

"They're going to take it hard, but they'll be okay. They'll want to come up and be with you while you have chemo," Carla said, offering what comfort she could.

"Joe will take it the hardest," Hannah told her. "He was so sure I would be healed."

"He is so sure you *will* be healed," Carla reminded. "And he'll be okay. His faith is strong, Hannah. What looks bad in the eyes of the world will be no more than a temporary distraction from what he knows is true."

"What's that?" Hannah asked, needing encouragement.

Carla was quiet for a moment, and when she answered, her voice was gentle. "That there is healing in the wings of Jesus."

An hour later, after processing the news they had received earlier that day with her closest friend, Hannah made her way back into bed. Lying down beside Chris, she settled into the soft mattress and fluffy pillow, more at peace after having a chance to talk it all out. As the quiet of the room settled over her and sleepiness began to wash over her in waves, she thought of the verse from Malachi that Carla had been referencing. "The Sun of Righteousness will arise with healing in His wings," she whispered into the stillness of the hotel room.

She went to sleep imagining that great, beautiful,

white feathered wings like those of an angel's that she had seen in a storybook once, were being folded over her as she slept. She imagined the darkness of the room was the darkness of being sheltered beneath those wings where it was warm and still. There, she was sheltered from every bad thing, and she found respite from fear. There, under the wings, she knew she was close to Jesus, and with that knowledge came an understanding that everything was going to be okay.

Come what may, she was tucked in close to her Savior and His wings were covering her, not only in her imagination, but in the realm of eternity, which felt nearer and more real to her than it ever had in her entire life.

Nine

"Good morning, Beautiful. How did you sleep?" Hannah blinked sleepily a few times and then yawned.

"Were you watching me sleep again?" she questioned with a groan. It had always been a habit of his that unnerved her. What if she made weird faces in her sleep? Or, heaven forbid, what if she drooled? And he saw? Chris shrugged with a sleepy, lopsided grin. She grimaced, then decided if he still loved her after watching her sleep for thirty-four years, he probably wasn't going to stop now.

The bed felt wonderfully comfortable. She was still hovering between sleep and being awake. She felt still, quiet and happy inside. "Really good, actually. That was the most pleasant night of sleep I have had in a long time," she answered, snuggling down in the bed, relishing the feel of it.

Chris' grin was quick. "Good. I'm glad it was so *pleasant.*"

She smiled. "It was," she told him, protesting his gentle tease. "It was...peaceful."

Chris kissed her cheek, then rolled over onto his back, putting his hands under his head. "Who were you talking to last night?" Chris asked closing his eyes, his lips lifting in a still-sleepy smile.

"Carla."

"I figured. Did you tell her about yesterday?"

"Yes."

"Did it help?" he asked, sounding like he genuinely hoped it had.

"It did. It helped to talk it out with someone I wasn't afraid of hurting by being honest," she answered slowly.

Chris was quiet for a moment. "I understand."

She checked his face to see if he was hurt, but found that he truly did understand. Oh, did she love that man. She loved that he understood what she meant, even when it wasn't what she said.

It hadn't always been like that. There were definitely times in the beginning when she felt like there was nearly constant miscommunication. Then again around thirteen years into their marriage, they went through a rough patch where they were always thinking the other person meant something they didn't. It was then that they learned that entering different seasons of life meant they had to relearn how to communicate and be a couple in the midst of their new circumstances. They had been more prepared for the communication lapse that followed after Kara went off to college. Becoming empty nesters was a huge adjustment for them, both individually as well as in the context of being a couple. It took awhile for their communication and emotions to adjust to the change. In each of those seasons, though, she had been consciously thankful for her husband's patience, eagerness to work through things to arrive at a good place again, and willingness to forgive. He was a good man.

It was quiet for a few moments. "How are they doing?"

"They're good," Hannah told him, thankful to have a good report once again. About three years back, Carla and her second husband, Tim, had gone through a rocky season. Carla had teetered dangerously on the edge of an affair, while their marriage hung by a thread. Deciding that she wanted to stay with Tim was the first step in the right direction. The following year and a half was tricky as a wounded relationship was never healed in a day. It had been about a year since the first time Carla told Hannah that things felt good between them again. After months of counseling with the family pastor at their church, in addition to both of them being purposeful about having a healthy and enjoyable marriage, Carla could honestly say she was in love with her husband, and they felt healthy and happy. In the months since, Hannah enjoyed hearing her friend's voice brighten whenever Tim came up in conversation.

"Is she still liking her new job?"

"She loves it," Hannah answered. Carla couldn't be happier with the change she had made in her career. She was at a smaller firm, making less money, but felt like she was making a difference in the world and loved the people she worked with. Another perk was that it was closer to home, giving her more time with Tim.

"When do they leave for Africa?" Chris asked, keeping one hand under his head and scratching his jaw with the other.

"June," Hannah told him. "They're going back to the same village they've gone to for the past two years to teach about sanitation and clean water. From there, they'll go out into the surrounding villages to the west, where they haven't been yet."

"Clean water," Chris mused. "The people think they're just bringing them clean water when in reality, they're bringing them Living Water."

Hannah mulled over what he said. Living Water. She was thankful she had drunk from that cup. Though one day she may die, she would live.

It was quiet for several minutes as both of their thoughts wandered. "We need to call the kids," Chris finally said. "Do you want to do it before or after breakfast?"

Hannah turned her head to look at the clock. "After."

"Good idea. I'm starving!" Chris was out of bed and pulling on his clothes, before she made a move to sit up.

She laughed. "So I see."

They went down to the lobby to eat breakfast, and took their time, lingering over the meal. Chris looked at the omelet she had barely touched, and nudged the plate she had pushed away, back toward her. "You need to eat more," he told her.

"I'm full," she lied.

"You've taken three bites." Those three bites had taken her the better part of an hour.

She considered his face, then her shoulders slumped. "I don't have an appetite."

His face filled with compassion. "Nerves?" She nodded. "Over telling the kids or starting treatment?"

She shrugged one shoulder. "Both."

His head bobbed. "Me too."

She couldn't resist a teasing smile as she glanced pointedly at his empty plate. "Yes, I can see that it really took a toll on your appetite."

"Trust me. It's happening internally," he told her with a grin. He tapped on the side of her plate. "Eat some more, Love, even if you're not hungry."

She scooted the plate closer to herself dutifully, and put a bite of the now-cold omelet in her mouth.

"That a'girl," he told her. When she had taken four more bites, successfully getting down over half of the omelet, he relented.

After she finished her orange juice, and he drank the last of his coffee, they went back up to their room. In the privacy it offered, they sat on the bed together, Chris' cell phone between them. "Who first?" Chris asked, forcing his voice to sound cheerful.

Hannah knew the news they had for their kids would be hard for them to hear. As a mother, she loathed doing or saying anything that would bring her children pain – especially over the phone. If she could be there with them to give them a hug and hold their hand as they processed the bad news, it would be different. As it was, they were hundreds of miles away, and she had to be at the hospital in two hours. Considering she still needed to take a shower, and there were four calls to make, there was not time for anything other than a quick phone call to each to share the news and lay out the little they knew about the plan for the future. It felt harsh and hurried, but there were no other options. "We might as well go in order."

Chris agreed and found Kaitlynn's number in his contacts list. They sat together, both looking grim as her phone rang, then as her greeting came across the miles to them from Texas.

Sharing the news was just as hard as Hannah imagined it would be. Sharing it not once, but four times, felt like torture.

Their kids responded much as they had the first time. Kaitlynn had questions – more questions than they had answers for. Kimberly cried. For a moment, disappointment weighted Joe's tone, but then he prayed and encouraged them that the LORD was able to heal. Kara had simply said she was on her way. That was the final straw. Hannah had simply sat with tears coursing down her cheeks as Chris told their daughter that everything was okay, that she didn't need to come up, that she should stay and continue on with her work. Not one to be easily dissuaded, Kara simply responded that she would be there by evening.

When they finished calling their kids, they called both of their parents to give them the update. Both phone calls were similar. Their mothers cried, their dads were grim. Then, as the news sunk in and they realized that, like it or not, it was how things were, they offered encouragement and reminded them that thousands and thousands of people undergo chemotherapy and come out the other side cancer-free. What they said was true, and Hannah felt encouraged.

When the dreaded phone calls were over, Hannah went in to take a shower and get cleaned up. She took her time, wondering when it would be that she would take a shower outside the hospital again. When she was ready, she found Chris sitting at the small table by the window, his Bible laid open in front of him, his head back, his eyes closed. Comforted by the sight of him praying, she moved to zip the suitcase shut rather than disturbing him. When he was finished, he stood to join her. Sending her a calm smile, he kissed her cheek and reached around her to set the suitcase on the ground. They made their way down the hall to the elevator, down to the ground floor and out to the truck. Chris opened Hannah's door for her before loading the suitcase and getting in himself.

On the way to the hospital, he held her hand firmly in his. She watched out the window as they passed restaurants and shopping malls, car lots and office buildings. They passed single family homes and apartment complexes, movie theatres and a football stadium. Everything appeared so normal. It felt like any other day in any other city. Except, it wasn't. Not for her and Chris. This was the city where she was receiving treatment for her cancer. This was the day she started chemotherapy. Real life – the life she had always known and been accustomed to – had never felt more distant.

At the hospital, Chris parked in the main parking garage rather than in the two hour parking like before. The permanency of their stay struck Hannah, and she fought against panic and fear as Chris came around to open the door for her. He held her hand as they walked toward the main entrance. Thoughts laid siege to her mind, bringing up an endless litany of what ifs. As she stepped through the automatic door at the front entrance, she had the brief, fleeting fear that she would never walk back out of the hospital. Dismissing it as ridiculous and dramatic, she took a deep breath and matched her steps to Chris'.

"You doing okay?" he asked, looking down at her as they rode the elevator to the fifth floor.

She smiled and nodded, stuffing down everything that begged to differ. There was no room for emotions, fear or drama. This was simply how things were.

She had cancer. She needed chemotherapy. She was starting treatment today. No matter how much she didn't want it to be, that was the reality. She had to accept that. She had to take things in stride.

"Are you?" she asked, studying his face. As hard as this moment was for her, she couldn't imagine what it was like for him. She was thankful that it was her starting chemo, and not him. As selfish as it might be, she would much rather go through it herself than to watch him go through it. As much as she disliked pain and discomfort, she found it even more unbearable to watch someone she loved experience either.

"The LORD is my strength and my song," he told her with a smile, and she wrapped his words around her heart like a blanket. Leave it to her husband to so appropriately remind her that when she was weak, God was strong.

She grabbed Chris' hand and felt life, strength and confidence come through it into her own hand, up her arm and into her heart. She stepped out of the elevator onto the oncology floor feeling braver than she had all morning; her steps sure, her heart and mind wonderfully quiet.

Getting to the desk, they checked in and sat in the waiting area while Hannah filled out paperwork. They were shown to a room with two hospital beds and two chairs. Both beds were empty. The nurse chatted with them as she got them settled, giving them brochures about what to expect and telling them about the television and the buttons on Hannah's bed.

Hannah didn't miss how the nurse mentioned that there was a lot of information to go over and absorb, as most patients were given chemotherapy educational materials a few weeks before their first treatment. She was further convinced of the severity of the situation when the nurse off -handedly told them that most patients came in for a treatment, then went home, coming back only when it was time for another treatment.

Hannah's mouth pressed into a firm line when the sweet young nurse left the room, never knowing how she had served to increase their anxiety or demonstrate the advanced stages of the cancer. Chris patted her hand. "Better to stay in the hospital and get treatments several times in one week than to go home in between. The sooner you get your treatments, the sooner we can go back home for good, and the sooner you'll get better."

"That's true," Hannah agreed. She would rather get it over with than to have it drag on.

They flipped through the educational materials together, looking up only when a lady in scrubs knocked quickly, then came in. "I'm here to take your blood," she said cheerfully.

"Lucky for you, she's an easy stick," Chris said, sending the woman a good-natured wink. Hannah watched, amused.

In their early years of marriage, she was suspicious and overly-aware of the way Chris winked at other women. After all, it was that same wink that first made her take notice of the dashingly handsome and jovial Colby boy during her college years. After confessing her unease with it and hearing how surprised Chris was that she thought anything of it, she realized it was simply a disarming tactic that he used interchangeably with, and most often at the same time as, a smile. Chris' dad was a winker, as was his granddad. After realizing that, Hannah didn't think twice about his winks. He was as loyal as the day was long, and he loved her. Of that, she was certain.

"Well, that is some of the best news I've had all day," the nurse replied with a smile. She tied a tourniquet tightly around Hannah's upper arm, felt for a vein, prepared her butterfly needle, and slid it smoothly into Hannah's skin. Almost instantly, dark blood started filling the test tubes the nurse had prepared.

"First try. Very nicely done," Hannah told her, smiling.

The nurse laughed. "Well, this isn't my first rodeo."

"So, what's this blood going to be used for?" Chris asked, watching the nurse fill four tubes with blood before sliding the needle out of Hannah's arm and pressing a cotton ball against the small puncture wound.

"The doctor has ordered a CBC. It's routine. The doctor will use the results to make sure your wife's white blood count is high enough for her body to be able to handle the treatment."

Chris nodded, satisfied with the answer. Collecting her tubes of blood and bidding them goodbye, the nurse left. "Now what?" Hannah asked, looking around the small room, then smoothing the covers back on the bed.

Chris shrugged. "We wait."

"For what?" Hannah asked, wanting specifics. She felt nervous and afraid, and she needed to know the schedule of events.

Chris smiled, his expression sympathetic, as he gave a slight shrug. "For whoever walks in that door next."

The wait turned out to be long. Knowing they both needed a distraction or else they would go mad from the uncertainty of the illness and the treatment, Chris picked up the television remote and turned on the electronic device that hung on the wall.

"All that's on this time of day is soap operas and talk shows," Hannah protested.

"And fishing," Chris answered with a grin. He flipped through the channels until he found a fishing show.

"Just what I was hoping for," she told him sarcastically. He grinned and handed her the book she had brought.

"You said yesterday that you were just getting to the good part. Go ahead and finish it," he said, his words spoken with confidence. It was apparent that he had planned the compromise – she could read if he could watch a fishing show.

It worked for her. She accepted her book with a smile and carefully sat on the edge of the hospital bed, moving back until she could rest against the raised backrest, which was hidden under several pillows. She found her bookmark and began to read, the peaceful tones of hushed men's voices, and a rushing mountain stream filling the room.

Half an hour later, both Hannah and Chris looked up, surprised, when Dr. Hedgins entered the room. She offered them an encouraging smile and a greeting. After the pleasantry had concluded, she let them know that Hannah's blood test came back good, and she had enough white blood cells to be able to withstand the treatment. She told them what to expect the rest of the day. She said that a drug cocktail specifically for Hannah's treatment was being mixed as they spoke. Once it was ready, they would give it to her via an IV, which a nurse would be coming in to start momentarily.

"How often will I have these treatments?" Hannah questioned.

"You'll have four this week, along with daily radiation treatments. How your body tolerates the treatments will determine what the treatment schedule looks like for next week. In three weeks, we'll run more tests and see how your body is responding."

"Three weeks?" Hannah echoed. "Will I be home in time for Christmas?" In just under four weeks, all the kids were coming.

Dr. Hedgins gave her a sympathetic smile. "I'm not making any promises, but yes, hopefully. As long as your body is handling the treatments okay, you should hopefully be able to go home for a couple of days at least."

Hannah took a deep breath. A couple of days would be better than nothing. At least she would get to see all of the kids. "Will I lose my hair?"

"Everyone responds to treatment differently. Most people do lose their hair while going through chemotherapy, yes. However, some don't. If you do, it will likely start sometime next week or the week after." Dr. Hedgins' face was serious, but kind. Her pager went off, and she checked the number. Looking up, she glanced at Chris and Hannah. "Do you have any other questions?"

Hannah wanted to tell her yes, that she had nothing but questions, hundreds of them, but she couldn't seem to formulate even one. She finally shook her head.

Dr. Hedgins nodded. "Good. I'll be back to check on you before I go home tonight. Sit back, try to relax, and enjoy your afternoon to the best of your ability."

Hannah forced a brave smile and folded her hands on her lap. Chris reached up and took her hand in his. "We have a whole afternoon together, we serve a kind God, and our daughter will be here by this evening. We definitely will enjoy this afternoon."

Hannah took a deep breath. He was right. She was alive. She had so many things to be thankful for. She had a whole afternoon with her husband. She had a daughter that loved her enough to drop everything she was doing and drive hundreds of miles, just to be with her. She had loving family and friends. And she was sheltered under the wings of the Most High.

She closed her eyes and repented of any hopeless, bitter words, or thoughts she'd had over the past twenty-four hours. She was thankful to be alive. When she opened them again, Chris was rummaging through a full backpack he had carried in. She had wondered about it at the time, but had been too preoccupied to ask. Now, she didn't hesitate. "What's that?"

He looked up and grinned. "I thought we might need a little fun."

His grin made her countenance brighten. "What did you bring?"

With great flare, he whipped out a deck of cards. "I bet I can beat you in a game of Go Fish!"

She laughed. "Go Fish is for kids."

"Good thing that's all we are, then – two old kids!"

Another grin. "To prove it, I brought...Go Fish crackers!" He pulled out the cheesy snack their grandkids loved, and Samuel had mistakenly identified when he was young. The name had stuck.

Hannah laughed and accepted the box of crackers, pouring a small pile out onto a napkin Chris had put on the rolling bedside table. She laughed again when Chris pulled a juice box out next, sticking the small plastic straw through the top of the box and handing it to her. Chris sat on the end of the bed, shuffling the cards after he took a juice box for himself out of the bag. Once he got the cards dealt out, he held up his juice box. "A toast to remembering how young we are," he declared with a grin.

With a juice box in her hand, cheese crackers on a napkin, and Go Fish spread out on the table between them, she felt young. She laughed as she bumped her juice box against his. "To being young," she agreed.

Fifteen minutes later, Chris was deep in thought, trying to decide what to ask for, when a nurse rapped on the door, then peeked her head in. "I've come to start your IV," she told Hannah, waiting for them to beckon her in. Chris did so, folding his hand of cards and laying it on the table as he stood.

"Come on in," he told the nurse. "She's ready."

While the nurse started the IV, Chris' phone rang, and he stepped out in the hall to take the call. Hannah chatted with the nurse while she worked, then waited quietly for Chris to return. When he did, his smile was bright.

"That was Pastor Ted. He called to see how you are doing. They sent an email out on the prayer chain today, letting everyone know that you're starting chemo and asking them to pray."

Hannah smiled. "I think I can feel their prayers."

He looked at her, surprised, as he took his seat and picked up his cards.

"Yeah? How so?"

"I feel peaceful," she told him simply, sipping her juice box. "The nerves from earlier have passed, and I just feel calm. We're simply doing what needs to be done."

"Well, that's very true, and I'm glad to hear that." He fanned his cards out. "Did you look at my cards?" he asked suspiciously, studying her over the top of them.

She laughed and shook her head. "I can beat you without cheating."

"Oh ho ho! You're pretty sure of yourself over there."

"When you're good, you're good," she told him and laughed when he pinched her knee.

"Alright, Cocky, can I have your sevens?" She handed them over. "Boom!" he exclaimed as he slapped down his first set of four. She rolled her eyes at him and motioned to her own three sets. "Oh, you just wait, Little Lady, you just wait. It's still my turn."

~~~~~

Hannah lay in her bed, her hand on her forehead, her eyes closed. Her stomach was churning, and something seemed caught in the back of her throat right over her gag reflex.

Her chemo treatment had ended hours earlier and in its wake, nausea had taken a firm grip on her. Ever at her side, Chris held a plastic bucket for her as she lost the contents of her stomach, not once but four times. Miserable, she wiped her mouth and watched him empty the bucket and rinse it out. When he returned, she turned beseeching eyes up toward him. "Would you mind pulling my hair back out of my face?" He gave her a questioning look. "It hurts to move," she explained quietly, putting effort into keeping her voice even. The heaving had not only exhausted her, it had also made the pain in her lower abdomen sharp. She hoped she hadn't broken anything open.

Understanding filled his face, and he made quick work of pulling her shoulder length brown hair into a low ponytail. Finished, he sat on the bed beside her and washed her face with a warm washcloth, then simply sat and held her hand until she asked for the bucket again.

An hour later, as the nausea subsided, she opened her eyes and studied her husband. He had scooted the recliner as close to her hospital bed as he could, and was sitting on the edge of the seat, his elbows on his knees, his hands clasped, his forehead resting on his hands. He was praying again. No doubt for her. She watched him, taking in every detail of his handsome face.

His nose was straight and sure, his jawline strong, his lips thin. A dusty shadow was visible along his jaw and chin, and she knew that if she kissed him, he would feel scruffy. His thick dark eyebrows drew low over his closed eyes as he prayed, longer lashes than any man had the right to have, spanning over his cheeks. Behind those lids were fathomless, pale green eyes that struck a stunning contrast to his dark chocolate-colored hair. Laugh lines were etched deeply into the tanned skin at the corners of his eyes and around his mouth. Despite his fifty-six years, the fabric of his long-sleeved polo was stretched tight across his chest and shoulders, and he still looked smoking good in a pair of jeans. She was a lucky woman.

Suddenly, her stomach lurched again, interrupting her perusal of her husband. "I need the bucket, Love," she told him even as she reached for it. He sprang into motion, grabbing the bucket and holding it for her as her stomach emptied again. He smoothed her hair back from her face as dry heaves racked her, sending splintering pains through her abdomen. When it finally passed, Hannah sank back against her pillows, utterly exhausted and spent.

She wanted to cry. She felt sick, she hurt, and she knew that she would feel like this at least four days out of every week for the next three weeks. It felt overwhelming and indefinite. Still, she had determined in her heart to be brave and think positively. She had to – for herself and for her husband. So, she kept the tears at bay and propped up a smile for Chris when he came back from washing the bucket out once again.

"Try to drink some water, Love," he told her, holding out a cup with a straw in it. Drinking was the last thing she felt like doing, but she had heard Dr. Hedgins say it was important to stay hydrated, just as he had. She sipped as much water as she could get down, hoping that it wouldn't come back up. Setting the cup aside, he stood beside her and smoothed the hair out of her face. "Are you doing okay?"

She nodded bravely. "It's just part of the process, isn't it? It's all for the sake of getting healthy."

His smile was quick. "Yes, it is. You'll be as healthy as a horse again in no time."

She nodded, wanting to believe him.

"Alright, I think it's time for a distraction," he told her, going back to his backpack. After rummaging around, he came out with a DVD and held it up for her to see. It brought a smile to her face.

"So, you decided to finally watch it with me?" she asked, referencing her favorite musical, which he was holding.

He grinned and turned toward the hanging television. "Well, I gave it a good run. I've held out on this harmonious headache for thirty-four years. All good things must come to an end eventually." He stopped abruptly. "Oh but wait, there's no DVD player."

Despite the nausea rising within her again, Hannah smiled. "Aw. I guess you're going to miss out on it again."

"Never fear! Mr. Preparedness is here!" Chris went on, dramatically turning back to his backpack and pulling out his laptop. She laughed, despite herself.

"If you keep on like this, I'm going to need a little wine to go with all this cheese," she told him. His only answer was a grin. He set to work getting the movie ready to play on his laptop, which he put on her rolling table, and Hannah watched him, thankful for the distraction.

Ten minutes later, music filled the room, and beloved scenes played out on the laptop screen. Hannah couldn't think of anything that could have been more comforting. She squeezed Chris' hand, and smiled right into his eyes when he glanced over at her. "I hope you know how much I love you," she whispered, and he smiled back, a sheen in his eyes.

"I do," he answered. After sharing another smile, they redirected their attention back to the movie.

Another hour passed before a quiet knock drew their attention to the door. Whoever it was didn't walk in as the nurses and doctors did. "I bet its Kara," Chris said, jumping to his feet and crossing the room quickly. When he opened the door, Hannah felt her heart leap at the sight of her youngest standing there, a winter coat draped over her arm and a purple stocking cap still on her head. Despite the years, she didn't look very different than she had as a little girl, and it warmed Hannah's heart. The aching sadness she had grown accustomed to over the past month, returned.

Where had the time gone? It felt like only yesterday that her kids were little enough to cradle in her arms. Surely it had been only a moment ago that Hannah had pulled a purple stocking cap over Kara's blonde pigtails, carefully stuffed her little hands into matching purple mittens, and sent her out the door to play in the snow with her dad and siblings for the very first time. Now, here she was standing at her hospital door, a full-grown woman.

In a small way, it made Hannah want to weep. Oh, to have those days back again! To rock her babies to sleep, cover their faces in kisses, dream with Chris about their future, and know that their next sixty to seventy years stretched out before them like a blank canvas before an artist. In those days, their biggest concerns were how to pay for groceries plus new tires on the car, and whose family to spend the holidays with.

Chris was ushering Kara in, giving her a hug, thanking

her for coming, and asking about the roads. Hannah was thankful their greeting gave her time to compose herself. As weak and sick as she felt, it was not a good time to take a trip down memory lane.

Setting her purse down and tossing her coat over a chair, Kara approached Hannah's bed, her smile bright, her eyes clear. "Hey Mama!" she said, reaching out for Hannah's hand.

Hannah smiled. "Hi, Honey. Thank you for coming. Really. We appreciate it more than you know."

"Mama, there's no way I could have stayed home knowing you were starting chemo. We're a family. We're in this together."

Hannah squeezed her hand, too overcome with emotion to speak. She knew she had the love and support of her family, but to hear her daughter make such a statement made her heart full. "Thank you," she finally managed.

Once she had carefully pushed the IV stand back out of her way, Kara perched lightly on the side of her bed. "How are you feeling?"

"Your dad put on a movie. That helped."

Kara's smile was faint. "I've heard it's best to keep your mind occupied and off the cancer as much as possible."

Hannah nodded. "That seems to be true."

"Well, hopefully I can help with that when Daddy runs out of ideas."

"Kara, do you *know* who you're talking about? I never run out of ideas."

Kara grinned at her dad. "I was just saying hypothetically, Daddy. I could hypothetically help if you hypothetically ran out of ideas."

They joked back and forth for a little while longer and Hannah found herself struggling to keep her eyes open amidst the easy banter going back and forth between them. She fought sleep, but it was a challenge. She knew she was losing the battle when Chris said, "You hungry, Kid? Maybe we should go down to the cafeteria and see what they have."

"Great idea. I'm starving," Kara agreed quickly. Hannah tried to open her eyes wider, but yawned.

"Do you want anything, Love?" Chris asked bending over her. Hannah shook her head.

"I don't think I could keep anything down," she told him honestly.

He nodded. "Alright then. Well, we'll go on down and have some dinner and we'll be back in an hour or so. Why don't you lean your head back and get some rest?"

Hannah agreed, relieved. Chris kept the musical playing, and left with Kara after kissing Hannah's cheek. She watched a few more minutes of the movie before sleep claimed her, and she drifted away on a comfortable wave of peace.

~~~~~

That night, after Chris and Kara came back from dinner and they had made it through Hannah's first evening after a treatment and gone to bed, Hannah's sleep was anything but peaceful.

In her dreams, they were in another hospital, sitting before another doctor, being given another diagnosis. They were talking in hushed tones, less the little girl who was sitting several feet away, coloring, could hear them.

Hannah's heart had stopped the moment she heard the word leukemia.

Later, after the doctor stepped away, Chris had gathered her into his arms, and she wept, her face turned away from Kelsi. Joe was a toddler, and Hannah was pregnant with Kara. They had enough going on medically with the complications Hannah was having with her pregnancy; to think about having a child with leukemia was too much. And yet, all of that paled in comparison to knowing that her sweet daughter was being attacked from within by a destructive force.

It was something Hannah couldn't protect her from. It was something that neither she, nor Chris, nor anyone else, could save Kelsi from. They had sat by helplessly as her small body succumbed to the disease.

In her dreams, she scooped Kelsi up again as she had that day, and held her in her arms, kissing her face and hugging her close. The next months had been a terrible whirlwind, like a bad dream she could never wake up from. She watched helplessly as her daughter lost her beautiful pale hair, became little more than skin and bones, and grew weaker and weaker each day.

Over and over in her dreams, she once again lifted Kelsi's emaciated body easily into her arms and rocked her, trying to keep her tears from dripping onto the little one's face. She covered her face in kisses and went down on her knees beside the hospital bed in speechless desperation.

Losing Kelsi had been the single hardest event in Hannah's life, and she relived it over and over again that night. She had wept over the lifeless body, refusing to let her go, until Chris was forced to unwrap her arms from her child's still form and hold her back while Kelsi was taken from the room. Hannah had cried out for him to let her go, and when he hadn't, she had moaned like one in great physical pain as they took the lifeless girl from her. She reached out after her, shrieking for them to bring her back.

Hannah awakened abruptly, not knowing if she had called out in her dream or out loud. Shakily, with the effects of the dream still making her heart race, she reached up and felt wetness on her face. She wiped away her tears, focusing on taking deep breaths. The nightmares she had after Kelsi died had stopped years ago, and she had not dreamed so vividly of her daughter or her death since. Now, she lay awake in the darkness for a long time, feeling the aching loss as if it had happened just yesterday. She had never fully recovered from Kelsi's premature death. She didn't think she ever would. And her first round of chemo had opened the old wound.

Throughout the rest of the night, every time she slept, she dreamed of Kelsi. Sometimes, she was laughing and healthy, as she had been before the cancer. Other times, she was thin and sullen, riddled with the disease. In every dream, Hannah was weeping, knowing how the story ended, twenty-four years of missing her daughter all coming out in a single night.

She had never been so glad for the sun to peek out over the Eastern horizon, which she could see from the one window in her room. Utterly exhausted and spent, she sought solace in being awake. At least when she was awake, she saw something other than Kelsi's face, heard something other than her sweet voice, and felt something other than the slight weight of the child in her arms.

She never wanted to forget her daughter, not for a moment, but now, in this place, with cancer waging its silent war against her body, she did not want to remember her death.

Ten

Hannah looked around her hospital room, feeling restless. She was waiting for her second chemotherapy treatment. Her blood work had come back and her white blood cell count looked good. Now the drugs were being mixed and when they were done, the treatment would begin.

Chris had gone out to rent a movie for later and return a few work-related phone calls. Kara had stayed, and was now reading in the chair beside Hannah. Reading, as Hannah should be. She had started, but soon found herself laying her book aside. She felt nervous. As much as it should have been about the upcoming treatment, she knew it had more to do with the young woman sitting next to her.

Today she would ask the question she had wanted to ask for months. She had made up her mind. Being in the hospital with an aggressive form of cancer gave one all sorts of time to think. She didn't have time to put things off, nor did she want to have any regrets. No, she was asking Kara the question she had been mulling over for months, and this was her chance. Now, if only she knew how to start.

She looked over to study her sweet daughter. Unable to keep the question in any longer, it came out in a rush, sounding blunt and nosy. "Why aren't you having children, Honey?"

She watched as Kara glanced up in surprise, then slowly shut her book, keeping her finger in it to mark her place. Hannah couldn't decipher the look on her daughter's face and was worried she had hurt or offended her. "I'm not trying to pry, Hon, really I'm not, but I lay here recovering from a hysterectomy, waiting for my next dose of chemo, and I'm so, so grateful that you're here – that I have you, and your brother and sisters. I want this for you, Kara! I don't know what I would do without you guys! You're not getting any younger, and I know that fifty-four seems far away, but trust me, it goes by in a blink of an eye. I know that Justin wants to get his business going—"

"Mom," Kara interrupted.

Hannah held her hand up to stop the protest. "I know that he wants to get his business going," she repeated, "and that's a good thing, I just think there's always going to be something to do first before having kids, and all of a sudden you'll wake up and realize you're forty-two with a great business, but no children to leave it to. I know this probably sounds like I'm making a big deal out of nothing—"

"Mom," Kara interrupted again.

"But I just want to see you happy! I see how you look at your sisters' kids. I see how you held Joshua on your lap last time Joe and Jessi were home, and how you had tea parties with the girls. You love kids, Kara, and so does Justin. I just want to see you guys happy!"

Kara folded the page corner over in her book and stood up. She stepped close to the bed and took Hannah's hand. "Mama, I should have told you this awhile ago," she paused, looking ashamed. Hannah held her breath, guessing what Kara might say. She was sure that Kara was going to say that there was something wrong with her reproductive system, that she had miscarried or that they had begun fertility treatments. "But…I'm pregnant."

Hannah was stunned by Kara's admonition, accompanied by a shaky smile. She gave her head a slight shake, attempting to shake off the shock. "You're pregnant?" Hannah echoed, struggling to comprehend it. Kara nodded, her shaky smile giving way to a bright grin. It took another minute for what Kara had said to truly sink in.

Suddenly, it was like a switch was flipped. Joy exploded within her. Years worth of prayers had been answered! The LORD had worked a miracle, and Kara was able to have children, despite the prognosis the doctors gave her as a baby. After years of praying, worrying, wondering, and praying some more, Kara was going to be a mother!

"Honey, you're pregnant? You're going to have a baby?" she cried, her voice full of joy and jubilation. Finally, her youngest was going to join her siblings in parenthood.

Kara laughed, nodding. "Yes! You're going to have another grandchild!"

Hannah hugged her tight, laughing even as she felt tears running down her cheeks. She had so many questions! "Well, how long have you known? Did you just find out? When are you due? Are you feeling okay? Have you been sick? Have you told Justin?" All of her questions came pouring out, one over another.

Kara's hug lasted a few moments longer than Hannah would have expected, and when she pulled back, Kara didn't meet her eyes. "We've known for a little while."

Hannah didn't understand her demeanor. She would expect her daughter to be jumping with joy, but instead, her eyes were downcast. "Well, how long? When are you due? Aren't you excited? Isn't Justin?"

Kara's eyes flew to Hannah's face. "He's ecstatic! We both are! You should have seen his face the night I told him. I had known all day because I took my test that morning, but he had already left for work. I wanted to tell him in person so I waited until that night. It was perfect because we were already going to Log Cabin anyway, so it made—"

"Wait," Hannah stopped her. "You went to Log Cabin in August." She remembered because the quaint, fancy restaurant was an hour and a half from Glendale and going was no small occasion.

Kara's eyes slid away from hers, and then Hannah knew. Her heart fell. "Honey, why didn't you tell me? If you found out in August...that would make you over four months pregnant!"

"Almost five, actually. I'll be twenty weeks next Tuesday," Kara admitted.

"Kara!" Hannah exclaimed, laughing, but hurt. "Why didn't you tell me?" All fall she had been worrying about her daughter for nothing! Not only were they not having problems conceiving, she was pregnant! All the wondering if she should say something, all the worrying, all the tears, all the desperate prayers were completely unnecessary!

Hannah had always told her own mother immediately when she found out she was pregnant. In fact, when she was pregnant with Joe, she called her mom and told her before she told Chris. Yet Kara had waited four months to share the news, and now only because Hannah had asked. How long would she have waited? Would she have told Hannah once she was in labor? Hannah tried to reign in her hurt, blinking back tears.

"I wanted to! In fact, I was going to! But Justin really wanted to wait until twelve weeks to tell anyone, just until we were out of the first trimester, and we knew that it was a healthy pregnancy. So many first time pregnancies end in miscarriage, and we just didn't want to get everyone's hopes up until we knew for sure," Kara explained.

"Twelve weeks was a long time ago," Hannah pointed out.

"I know. Remember that night I came over to your house? That night that…you found out about…all of this?"

Hannah nodded, her heart sinking as she connected the dots. "You were coming over to tell us you were pregnant, weren't you?" she asked, her heart breaking. Kara must have come over nearly bursting at the seams with her good news, only for them to throw a bucket of cold water on her joy.

Kara shrugged. "I had turned twelve weeks that day. I couldn't wait to tell you. But then…then I found you and Daddy in the truck, and I found out about all of this and," she took a deep breath, "I just couldn't tell you. It didn't feel right. I've been trying to find a time ever since, but there just hasn't been an opportunity when it felt appropriate."

Hannah wanted to weep. She understood why Kara hadn't told her. Now it made perfect sense. She felt selfish and ashamed. She had made such a big deal out of her cancer, that her daughter hadn't felt free to share her happy news. Hannah had been so consumed with her illness that Kara hadn't trusted that she would be able to feel joy over the news of a baby. Despite that sinking realization, she knew about the baby now, and she wanted to give Kara the gift of handling it well. It would be pure selfishness to make the moment any more about herself, which is what would happen if she expressed sorrow at her own selfishness throughout the past fall.

So instead, Hannah reached for both of Kara's hands and squeezed them before pulling her into a tight hug. "I am so, so happy for you, Kara!"

"Really?" Kara asked, sounding touched.

"Absolutely! This is the best news I could have gotten! This is my early Christmas present. It's the one thing I really wanted this year!" Hannah dashed at a few happy tears and squeezed Kara's hand, her eyes on her daughter's bright face that had transformed into a ray of sunshine. She had never told Kara of the doctors' predictions about her inability to have children, and she never would. Kara would never understand the depth of joy that Hannah felt, knowing that Kara was pregnant, but she knew that her daughter could feel it. Tears sprung into Kara's eyes, too.

"Thank you, Mom, for not being upset that I didn't tell you earlier."

Hannah squeezed her hands. "I understand." She did. "And how could I ever be upset when you just gave me the very news I have prayed and prayed for? To say I'm ecstatic is a severe understatement!"

Kara smiled and swiped at a few happy tears. Suddenly, she laughed. "There has been so much I wanted to talk to you about!"

"Like what? Tell me everything!" Hannah said, her eyes lighting up.

"Well, for starters, I had an ultrasound the day before yesterday!"

"You did?" Hannah squealed.

"We're having a girl!" Kara announced, doing a little dance, her face glowing with joy.

"A girl?" Hannah exclaimed, covering the hurt of not being at Kara's ultrasound, with the joy of having another granddaughter. "Kara! Yay!" Hannah pulled her daughter into another hug, laughing. "Finally! Now Ava will have another little girl to play with, and I'll have another grand-daughter! Do you guys have a name picked out yet?"

"I know! We're thrilled! I was hoping for a girl all along," Kara answered. "And no, we don't have a name picked out yet. As easy going as Justin is, he's turned out to be very picky when it comes to names."

Hannah laughed. "Well, picking a name is a big deal. That little girl is going to be called that for the rest of her life."

"True," Kara conceded.

"Do you have any names that you like?" Hannah pried. She loved baby names. She loved hearing couple's thoughts, what they liked, and then what they chose in the end. She loved it even more when the baby in question was her granddaughter.

"I like Isabella, and call her Bella, but Justin isn't a fan. Justin likes Kennedy, which is pretty, but I don't know. I don't feel like it's quite right. We have a few others we've been kicking around, but nothing that both of us can agree on. I feel like we haven't thought of the right name yet. I think when it's the right name, we'll both love it."

Hannah instantly loved the name Kennedy, but kept her thoughts to herself. "Yes, when it's the right name, you'll know."

"That's what I think, too."

"So, when is your due date?"

"April twenty-third," Kara answered, still beaming.

"That's so soon! This is going to feel like the shortest pregnancy ever...at least for me. I can't believe you aren't showing yet!"

"Oh I am," Kara assured her. "You can hide a lot under a sweater."

"What are you hiding under a sweater?" Chris asked, coming into the room. "You been smuggling things in, Kara?"

"Just a baby!" Hannah answered, and Kara laughed. Chris looked confused. "Kara's pregnant!" Hannah explained.

Hannah watched as her husband's face went from surprised to thrilled. He never tired of his grandchildren. He congratulated and hugged Kara, then asked all the same questions Kara had just answered for Hannah. When the nurse came in to give Hannah her treatment through her IV, his questions continued, but their voices grew quieter.

Hannah's mind didn't stay on the treatment she was receiving through the tubing in her arm or the illness that inspired it, for even a moment. A smile filled her face, and her attention was on the happy answers Kara was giving Chris. He patted their daughter on the back, grinning, and tousled her hair. "We've been wondering when you were going to have news to share," he told her. As Kara responded, her voice bright and excited, Chris glanced at Hannah, meeting and holding her eyes.

His look communicated his message oh so well; she could almost hear him saying, 'I told you there was nothing to worry about.' She smiled at him, happy that he had been right. His eyes gentled, and she could feel his love and joy as if he had wrapped his arms around her. They both loved their daughter, and now they shared great joy at her news.

For years, they had prayed together for her. Now, they would celebrate together.

Hannah's mind wandered as Chris and Kara continued talking about the baby. This must be one of the greatest joys of being married for three and a half decades, she thought, and being parents to the same children. Both of them loved Kara with a depth you could only feel for your own child. Seeing her so happy, knowing she was having a child of her own, knowing that one of her biggest dreams was being fulfilled right before their very eyes, was something that brought a joy that only the two of them could feel and understand.

There were days when the kids were young when Hannah had dropped into bed, completely exhausted, feeling utterly spent, discouraged and disillusioned. In those moments, she wondered about their sanity in having five children in eight years. And yet, moments like these made every one of those days worth it.

She was going to be a grandma. Again.

The ten grandchildren they already had didn't make this one any less special. Perhaps, instead, they made it more so – they already knew the joy a grandbaby brought.

Throughout the rest of the day, even when she was so sick that she kept the bucket constantly at her side, the joy from that moment carried her through. It was a reminder that God was great. He was sovereign. Even the knowledge brought by modern medicine did not have the power to deem what was possible or impossible.

Kara was pregnant after being told conceiving would be impossible for her. If that wasn't impossible for God, what was? She knew the answer. Nothing. Nothing was impossible for Him.

Like the sun rising after a very dark night, faith rose within Hannah.

She served a great God. She had full confidence that He not only existed, but that He was in control. Additionally, He was not some distant deity that had no time for the constant tragedy of human frailty. Instead, He was intimately aware of her existence, her needs, her emotions and her desires. She knew He was, because He was the Good Shepherd. She belonged to Him, and she knew that she could not be snatched from His hand.

Her heart hummed to life in a way it hadn't in weeks. Fear fell away as her heart took up a cry that she had chosen for years. "Let it be unto me as You will," her heart shouted, feeling a familiar peace as she remembered that her life was not her own, nor was her diagnosis of cancer the absolute authority.

As she told Chris about the return of faith she had experienced, he smoothed the hair back from her face, and smiled. He was stretched out beside her on her hospital bed, lying on his side, his elbow next to her pillow, his head resting on his fist. "I've been thinking about the same things all afternoon," he told her. "This cancer did not surprise God."

"Nor did it ruin His plan," she agreed.

"When the Author of Life planned our story, Love, He knew this would be part of it."

Hannah thought about that, drawing comfort from it, even as questions rose. "So, do you think He gave me cancer?"

Chris was quiet for a long time. "No, I don't."

"How does that work? He could have prevented all of this. He could have taken it away before the first test was run. Or, He could have kept the cancer from forming in the first place. But, He didn't. Why?"

Hannah's questions weren't accusatory. She wasn't demanding answers as much as she was seeking understanding. Chris understood her heart, and wished he had great wisdom to share. Instead, he was a simple business man who had loved the LORD greatly for many years, but had never read the Bible in its original language, spent a day at seminary or taken a theology class beyond those offered during Sunday school.

"I think that we live in a fallen world that has been corrupted by sin," he answered slowly. Heaven knows he had wrestled with the very same questions for the past few months.

"Is my cancer a result of a sin I committed?" Hannah asked. She had wondered it so many times. She had struggled with feelings of guilt, even shame that she had cancer, as if it must be her fault.

"No," Chris answered quickly. As wonderful as his wife was, as much as he loved her and wanted to comfort her, his answer was based more on his theology than her need. "Our God is merciful. I think sometimes sin brings consequences, but you have lived a good life, Hannah. You are a righteous woman. It's not a sickness borne from a promiscuous lifestyle, not taking care of your body, harboring bitterness or the poison of unforgiveness. You have done your best to live according to His laws. To think that your cancer stems from one time that you must have stumbled and sinned during your past fifty-four years, would be a grave misrepresentation of the mercy and heart of God. I think we simply live in a world that embraces sin, and because of that, sometimes bad things happen."

Hannah agreed. She had come to the same conclusion in her mind, but in her heart, she was still trying to resign herself. "It just doesn't seem fair," she admitted.

"Because good things should happen to good people, and bad things should happen to bad people?" Chris asked, tracing the side of her face with his finger. She felt embarrassed by her immature thinking, but nodded. Letting out a deep sigh, he turned over onto his back and stared up at the ceiling. "Sometimes, I think the same thing."

"Just sometimes? What do you think the rest of the time?" Hannah asked.

"I think that we cannot begin to perceive the meaning and workings of justice. I think we fail to think in the terms of eternity."

"I don't understand," she told him honestly.

"How different does justice look if you think of it in terms of a hundred years, versus three thousand? Or, if you think of it out of the context of conceivable time? In our limited understanding we see justice as good things happen to good people in the eighty to one hundred years that they're on this earth. But, in the span of eternity, maybe it's more about victory rather than comfort, with the great reward coming later," Chris paused, and reached down for Hannah's hand. "I think believing that our lives will be easy and comfortable is an illusion that is far more comforting than it is real."

"Is it bad to like the comforting?" Hannah asked half-heartedly, drawing a chuckle from Chris.

"I think that's pretty human," he answered.

She was quiet, digesting all he had said.

"However," he continued, "I think expecting to emerge victorious in every situation, and in every trial, is an accurate reality."

"What do you think victory looks like for me? For us? In this situation?" she questioned, thoughtfully.

"I'm going to believe that it's complete and total healing. I know that whatever happens, though, through Christ, victory is imminent – the outcome has already been decided."

"On the cross," Hannah agreed.

"Yes, on the cross," Chris echoed.

"For God so loved the world that He gave His one and only Son, that whoever believes in Him shall not perish but have everlasting life," Hannah quoted softly. The verse from John had always been one of her favorites. "In Jesus I will live forever – we both will. That's victory, Chris, isn't it? That's justice."

Chris took in the glowing smile on Hannah's face, the light in her eyes. She was absolutely right – both healing and redemption from death had been decided on the cross. One way or another, Chris was certain his wife would experience the victory of Jesus. He prayed that it would be physical healing, and that she would experience it in the land of the living.

Eleven

"Is the baby moving?" Hannah asked, watching the delighted expression on her daughter's face. It was Kara's last day to be with her in the hospital. She needed to go back to work, and she needed to go home to spend time with her husband. Hannah was grateful the young man had been willing to share his sweet wife with them for as long as he had. She couldn't ask for more than the week Kara had already given them.

They had spent the morning playing cards. Now, Hannah was getting another treatment by IV, and all three of them were reading. She had paused when she noticed movement other than the occasional page flipping, out of the corner of her eye. A faint smile had lifted the corners of Kara's lips, and her hand flew to her stomach. The young woman stilled, then her smile grew broader.

"I think so," she told Hannah, her smile big. "I'm not completely sure that's what I'm feeling, but I think it is. I've felt this a few times in the last week or so. It's definitely not anything I can feel from the outside yet, but I think it must be the beginning."

"Does it feel like small flutters? Like you have butterflies inside?" Hannah questioned, enjoying the look of pure wonder on her daughter's pixie face.

"More like a goldfish going 'tink, tink, tink' on the glass of a fishbowl," Kara answered with a laugh.

"That sounds about right," Chris chimed in from his chair.

"How would you know?" Kara questioned.

Chris shot her a look over the top of his reading glasses. "I've been around the block a few times," he told her. "I may never have been pregnant myself, but I've been through five pregnancies with your mom, and more than that with your sisters. As a man, you hear things." His answer drew laughter from Kara and Hannah, and he shook his head and started reading again.

"I wish I could feel her," Hannah said wistfully. Feeling Kara's baby move would provide a welcome distraction from the way her body was feeling.

Nausea was her constant companion now, along with a dry mouth and a bitter taste that nothing seemed to chase away. Foods tasted different than they ever had – more bitter than she remembered – and her appetite continued to decline. She was pleased if she could force down a few bites at every meal and actually keep it down. Chris had become a food Nazi, making sure she ate and always encouraging her to take at least one more bite than she thought she could. Her strength had waned over the past week, and getting out of bed and walking as far as the bathroom and back was exhausting.

Still, her spirits were high, much in part to the faith that had seeped in and sustained her, along with the presence of her husband and daughter, and the hope of a new baby.

"So do I," Kara told her. "Soon. Hopefully by Christmas."

"Christmas," Hannah echoed. The holiday had never seemed so far away, and yet she knew that when it did arrive, she wouldn't be ready. From the hospital, she couldn't do all of the Christmasy things she normally did to get ready for the holiday, and even once she went home, she doubted she would have the energy. The thought made her sad, but at least they would all be together.

"I've been meaning to talk to you guys about Christmas," Chris said, setting his book down. He looked between his wife and his daughter, who were both watching him curiously. "I think we should cancel our plans." He saw the protests before they even started and held up his hands. "Or, at least alter them drastically."

"Everyone's flying in," Hannah told him, immediately defensive. "The tickets have already been purchased."

"I've thought of that, but Hannah there's no way you're going to feel well enough to get the house ready or make big meals for everyone, and that's if you even get to go home," he protested. "Maybe everyone could come here," he suggested after a pause.

"All the plane tickets would have to be changed. And it wouldn't feel like Christmas if we weren't home. No, it's the one time of year that everyone is actually home at the same time. I want to actually be at home for that."

Chris stood quickly to his feet and walked to the side of Hannah's bed, taking her hand, his battle between frustration and sympathy obvious. "I know you want it to be like it always has been, Love, but I'm just not sure it's a good idea this year." He didn't point out the guarantee that she wouldn't have the energy to carry out the Christmas traditions. The commotion of so many people would wear her out within mere minutes, and it wouldn't feel the same to her whether they were home or not, if there were no wrapped gifts under the tree, and she wasn't in the kitchen making cookies with her kids and grandkids. "It's just one year," he told her. "We can have a normal Christmas next year."

"I want a normal Christmas *this* year," Hannah answered, too afraid to speak her greatest fear. In her mind the troubling question bounced around. *What if she wasn't around for next Christmas?*

"You guys, you guys, you guys," Kara said, shaking her head as she stood and came to the side of the bed, too. "I've already talked to the girls, and we have it all worked out."

"What do you mean?" Chris asked skeptically. He wouldn't risk putting any additional stress on Hannah, not for any holiday – her body was already under enough distress as it was.

"Kimmy is coming with the boys a week early. Jessi and the kids will get to Glendale just a few days after Kim. Kait is busy at work, getting their Christmas issue out the door, or else she would come early, too. The three of us will get the house decorated and make all the Christmas goodies. Everything will be ready by the time you guys get home."

"What about all the commotion?" Chris asked bluntly. "You know we love them, but having all the kids around..." He let his sentence dangle.

"Chris!" Hannah chided. She never wanted to give the impression that they didn't love having their grandkids around. Not even now, when she herself had wondered how she would deal physically with the extra energy in the house.

"Again, I've already talked to the girls. Grandpa and Grandma and Justin and I will stay at your house. The others will stay at our house and just come over to visit. That way, there will be at least some moments of quiet throughout the day. Mom, you can be out with everyone when you can be, but there will be no shame in needing to go spend some time in your room, alright? We'll be around so that you know we're close, but we don't want to tire you out in any way."

"That many people will never fit in your house!" Hannah protested.

"Nonsense. We have three bedrooms," Kara answered.

"Three bedrooms for sixteen people?" Hannah questioned. "Where will all the kids sleep?"

"On the floor," Kara answered simply.

"They can't sleep on the floor! It's Christmas! They should stay at our house where we have beds for everyone."

"They'll be fine on the floor," Chris said firmly. "They're kids. Their young bones don't creak like ours do."

Hannah looked between her husband and daughter, seeing that neither of them would be of any help. She made a face. Christmas wouldn't be Christmas without having everyone home, in *her* home. It wouldn't be Christmas without a handful of sleeping bags laid out in front of the Christmas tree on Christmas Eve, a line of people waiting for the bathroom, little ones up bright and early peeking at stockings, and big pans of cinnamon knots coming out of the oven Christmas morning. No, she would just have to dig deep to find extra energy within. She wanted a real Christmas.

Chris saw the protest in her face before she even began. "We do Christmas like Kara and the girls have planned, or we don't do Christmas at all," he told her. "It's not worth it."

"It's not worth what? What isn't being together as a family worth?" Hannah questioned, stubbornly. Getting all of her kids and grandkids under the same roof was rare enough. She wasn't going to waste this opportunity.

"This has nothing to do with us being a family," Chris told her, his tone firm and final, upset that she dared to disagree. He was frustrated that she wasn't letting him take care of her, frustrated that she wasn't taking care of herself. She needed to accept her own limitations and stay within them to allow her the chance to get better. At her age, he thought she would know that.

"I'm going to go grab a snack," Kara said, slipping quietly from the room.

Neither of her parents noticed.

"We're going to be a family whether we all get together for Christmas or not, and certainly whether or not we all stay under one roof! Thank goodness family ties aren't dissolved that easily!"

"You know what I mean," Hannah muttered, the disagreement already beginning to sap her strength.

"Your children love you," Chris told her. "They have devised a plan that allows them to spend Christmas with you while letting you get the rest you need. If you're exhausted, your body isn't going to be as capable of fighting this cancer, and they know that. You need to accept that, and let them take care of you." Frustrated, he wanted to add that she needed to let *him* take care of her. If she wasn't going to use caution herself, then she needed to start listening to him. But he left that part off. Better to make it about the kids, then to turn a battle into a war.

He watched the fight leave her face and knew that he had won. Oddly, knowing that brought up a sorrow that made his chest and throat ache. She had given up so easily. He could see the exhaustion that even this small battle of wills had caused. His wife, whom had always been so frustratingly feisty, which drove him crazy but also strongly attracted him to her from the beginning, had given in after no more than a mere discussion.

"I at least want everyone there Christmas Eve, and I want to sit in the living room with them while presents are opened, and while you read the Christmas story," she capitulated.

"Done," he agreed, his voice hoarse. For the first time ever, he wished she had fought him longer. He wished her eyes were still fiery. He wished he saw stubbornness in her face, rather than exhaustion. He wished he could share some of his strength with her. If only he could get her to eat more, he lamented. Perhaps then, she would have more energy.

"And I want to get everyone Christmas presents."

"We'll give cash or gift cards," he told her.

"No, I want to give real presents," she protested, leaning her head back against her pillow.

"You can't go shopping for hours, and you know there's no way I would get the right things."

His last statement brought a small smile to her face. "We'll shop together online," she offered.

He could live with that. "Alright, then we should get started. We'll do some of our shopping tonight after Kara leaves." Hannah nodded.

With the Christmas dispute settled, Chris moved back to his chair. Impulsively, he turned and picked up Hannah's hand, pressing his lips to the back of it. She smiled and squeezed his hand. When Kara came back in with her cup of fresh fruit, Chris and Hannah were both reading peacefully again.

~~~~~

Hannah yawned as she woke up, covering her mouth with the back of her hand. Sitting up, she swung her legs over the side of her hospital bed, going slowly, sitting there for several moments before standing. After two weeks of chemotherapy, she had learned to stand up slowly to give herself time to adjust before trying to walk. She was definitely still mobile, but she grew tired and lightheaded easily.

Her mouth pressing into a thin line, she remembered that she was scheduled for another treatment later in the day after having the day before off. Another day of sickness was what was on her schedule for the day.

In the bathroom, she brushed her teeth carefully with a soft-bristle toothbrush, now used to her teeth and gums being extra sensitive. Once that task was complete, she straightened and washed her face, then pulled her hair out of the ponytail she had gathered it into the night before.

Her stomach plummeted as she looked down and saw the large clump of brown hair in her hand. Glancing quickly to the mirror, she leaned close and inspected her head. Her heart sank as she noticed little patches of baldness. She looked down at the brown hair she held in her palm again, and tears started to form.

She was losing her hair. The doctor said this might happen, probably would, in fact, but she had held out hope that it wouldn't. Being sick, away from home, having cancer, that was all wearing enough, but to lose her hair....

She thought of her husband asleep on the hospital bed beside hers, and dreaded having to tell him...or worse yet, having him notice.

They were in their fifties. He wanted a wife who was vibrant and beautiful, active and full of life; not a wife who was weak and sick and, to top it all off, bald.

She considered sitting down on the bathroom floor and crying. She almost did, in fact. But like a cool breeze on a hot summer day, familiar words floated through her consciousness. *'Don't be concerned about the outward beauty of fancy hairstyles, expensive jewelry, or beautiful clothes. You should clothe yourself instead with the beauty that comes from within, the unfading beauty of a gentle and quiet spirit, which is so precious to God.'* The verse from 1 Peter was one she had made each of her girls memorize in their teen years. It was a verse that spoke truth to her now.

With the words still lingering in her mind, she knew that whether or not she had hair, didn't have anything to do with her worth or her ability to carry out her purpose in life. It had no influence on her ability to love or be loved, to experience joy or bring joy to another. Her beauty came from within. It came from a lifetime of cultivating patience, gentleness, peace, love, joy, kindness, goodness, faithfulness and self-control. That beauty could never fade, fall out or be taken away. And that was why her husband loved her, not because of the thickness of her hair.

Smiling sadly, she remembered telling Kelsi something similar the first time the sick little girl had looked in the mirror after they had shaved her head. It had not been vanity, but fear that made Kelsi cry that day. She no longer recognized the person in the mirror. It had been a hard day. Hannah had felt deep grief, but buried it within to keep her spirits up for her daughter. They had spent most of the day cuddling on Kelsi's bed and coloring pictures of princesses together.

But Hannah was a grown woman, not a little girl. There was no need to fear her reflection or her body's physical reaction to the chemotherapy she was undergoing. It was all part of the process.

Taking a deep, steadying breath, she dropped the clump of hair into the waste basket beside the sink. She brushed her hair carefully, collected the hair that came out in the bristles, and disposed of that, as well. She pulled her hair back into a loose ponytail, knowing that she would be thankful she had done so when the nausea hit her later. Then, she applied her makeup and made her way back out to the bed, thankful to sit down again by the time she got there.

As she sat on her bed and rested back against the pillows, she glanced at Chris, seeing that he was awake. He yawned and then smiled at her. "Good morning, Beautiful," he told her, and the fact that he had said it thousands of times before, didn't make it any less special. She tucked his sleepy smile and his endearing greeting away in her heart.

"Good morning," she answered, smiling warmly. "How did you sleep?"

"I don't remember, so I guess that means good." He sat up, swinging his legs over the edge of his bed. They had become used to the noises associated with being in the hospital, and had learned to sleep through them. While it wasn't as restful as being at home, it wasn't as bad as it first was. "You look nice this morning," he told her, stepping in for a kiss.

She smiled at him sadly. "I'm losing my hair, Chris."

She could see she had surprised him with her quiet statement. His expression changed to one of sorrow and compassion, and he sat down carefully on the side of her bed. "Are you okay with that?" he asked.

She couldn't help a small laugh. "Well, if I had a choice, I would keep it, but considering no one asked me...." She let her sentence dangle. She took another deep breath and smiled at him. "I'm okay."

"Really?" he pressed.

She smiled again and nodded. "Really. As long as you can love a bald woman."

He leaned forward and hugged her, his hold gentle and

long. "I love you no matter how you look," he promised, his voice full of emotion.

"I know you do," she told him. And, she did. His love had been steady and unwavering. She wrapped her arms around his strong back, and they just sat there for several moments.

"I was hoping you wouldn't lose it," he finally said, sitting back. "Not for my sake, but for yours."

She understood what he meant. "So was I. I mean, I knew it was probably going to happen, but...I guess you always hope you'll be the exception." She looked up at him. "Is that wrong? Is that vanity?"

He chuckled. "I don't think so." He picked up her hand and held it loosely in his. "We can get you a wig if you would like. Or you can embrace your new look. Whichever you prefer."

She thought about her options. She thought about going home for Christmas and having all their children and grandchildren there. She thought about how the little ones would respond. "I would like a wig," she decided.

"But when it's just you and me, don't wear it," Chris told her.

She looked at him, surprised by his request. "Why?"

"Because I don't just love the girl that you were when we got married or the wife that I had three months ago. I love the woman you are right now." His voice was thick with emotion, and she felt tears sting her eyes. She squeezed his hand and pressed her lips to his palm, unsure how to accurately express how much she appreciated his reassurance.

They were both quiet for several moments. Finally, Hannah broke the silence. "I was thinking about Kelsi this morning...about the day we shaved her head."

Chris nodded. "I just had a moment of that, too."

"What do you remember?"

"How big it made her eyes look. I remember I sat in that wooden rocker we had tucked into the corner, and we sat and snuggled. She just stared up at me for the longest time while we rocked. I remember looking into her big eyes and feeling so much love." Chris was smiling.

Hannah watched him for several moments before speaking. "Sometimes, the memories still make me sad," she admitted.

"Me too," he told her, still smiling but letting out a deep sigh. "She was one special little girl." Hannah nodded her head. "You know, I'm not sure what it will be like when I get to heaven. I don't know if I'll fall down and worship before the throne of God, if I'll come face to face with Jesus, if there will be time to reconnect with those who have gone before me, but I have to think that hugging her will be one of the very first things I do," he continued.

Hannah smiled. "Me too."

Chris reached down and wiped a lone tear from her cheek. "We may have missed out on time with her here on earth, but we will spend eternity with her, Love. And I think when we are face to face with her again, if we asked her, she would never regret being taken so early. I think she is rejoicing that she only had to spend five years out of the physical presence of God."

Hannah was quiet, letting that settle, wrapping her mind around what Chris said. She liked the picture he painted. The sadness within her began to wane.

He stood. "I'm going to clean up, and then do you want to go to breakfast?"

She nodded, relaxing back against her pillows. She would rest while he got ready, so she would have the energy to make the trip down to the cafeteria. After he had taken a shower, they walked together, Chris matching his steps to hers, down the hall to the elevator, then through the maze of hospital halls until they reached the cafeteria. Going through the cafeteria, Hannah looked for something that looked appetizing. Her appetite had almost disappeared completely over the past couple of weeks, and it was a challenge to make herself eat.

Chris certainly didn't have the same problem. She looked at his tray as he rejoined her and laughed. He had cereal, an omelet, a plate of sausage, and a bowl of fresh fruit. He grinned at her. "So, what are you going to have?"

She looked over the breakfast choices again. "The raisin toast looks good," she answered. Chris grabbed a plate of the bread in question and a couple pats of butter.

"What kind of protein do you want?"

"What's in your omelet?"

"Broccoli, cheese, green peppers, ham and tomatoes."

"I might have a few bites of that," she answered. He nodded.

"Do. I got it hoping you would. Do you want anything else? Bacon?"

He knew her weak spot. Even when she had no appetite, there was always room for bacon. Reading her mind, he put a plate of bacon on his tray with a grin. Carrying their food, he paid, then went to find a table in the bright and spacious dining room. The large room was nearly full. Doctors and nurses occupied about a third of the tables, while patients and their loved ones filled the rest. Some were dressed in street clothes, others in hospital gowns; some looked like they had just stepped out of a magazine, others as if they were on the brink of death. As she followed Chris to a table, she wondered which category she fit into.

Finding a seat, Hannah sank down wearily. The walk had almost been too much for her. She spread butter on her bread and ate it slowly, forcing herself to finish it when she could have been happy with half. Chris slid half of his omelet onto her plate, and she dutifully took up her fork and ate about half of it. Satisfied, he ate the rest, while she munched on her bacon. Finally, she drank the apple juice he sat in front of her.

Chris nodded at her. "Good job."

She felt sick to her stomach and full to the brim, but

she was glad she had eaten as much as she had. For the first week, she had succumbed to how her body felt, only eating when she felt hungry. It resulted in weakness and fatigue, which kept her confined to her room. In the past week, she learned that she had to eat whether she felt like it or not. Since then, her strength had slowly been returning, and she had begun to accompany Chris to the cafeteria for breakfast, even if she was exhausted by the time they got there.

She enjoyed the chance to get out of her hospital room, and the cafeteria was warm and bright, letting in all the winter sunshine without any of the drafts or cold. The large room had ceilings that were several stories tall, and over a hundred tables were situated around the area, some on different levels. Planters full of dark leafy plants acted as privacy screens, separating many of the booths, and there was a large enclosed bird cage on the far end of the cafeteria where a number of brightly colored birds chirped and played. It was a comfortable place filled with the hum of simultaneous conversations and laughter.

Hannah enjoyed the opportunity to be out around people. But what she enjoyed most of all was after breakfast when Chris would slide their Bibles out of the backpack he carried. Sitting across from each other, they would have their individual quiet time with the LORD. It was in those times that Hannah found the strength for the coming day and the peace that sustained her.

After they spent time with the LORD individually, they came together, shared a scripture or experience, and prayed. They prayed for their children, their grandchildren, missionaries overseas that they supported, governmental leaders, societal leaders, their church back in Glendale, and the doctors, nurses and other patients they came in contact with. Then Hannah prayed for Chris, and Chris prayed for Hannah.

After they prayed, they would go back through the hallways, up the elevator, down the hall and back to Hannah's room where they would wait for the nurse to come in and take Hannah's blood, always checking her white blood counts before giving her another treatment.

Today was no different. After breakfast, they spent time in the Word and prayed together. When they were done, they returned to Hannah's room, where they waited for her next round of chemo. When Chris got a phone call while the nurse was in the room talking to Hannah about how she was feeling and setting the mixture of medicines up to enter Hannah's bloodstream through her IV, he stepped out. He didn't return for over an hour, and Hannah grew curious as to where he was.

When he finally returned, his face was alight with joy. Seeing him so happy, his face full of hope, made Hannah's heart jump expectantly. "What happened?" she asked, never considering that it was bad news. Her husband was an open book. If it were bad news, she would have known the instant he walked in the door.

"It's Michele!" he told her, shutting the door behind him, then crossing the room quickly, coming to stand beside her.

Hannah couldn't hide her surprise. She expected him to have talked to one of the kids, or one of his associates at his office, or perhaps he had run into Dr. Hedgins, and they had good news back from a test. She hadn't expected the good news to have come from the woman in the room next door.

Michele was in much of the same situation she was. She had been diagnosed with breast cancer early that summer. After going through a mastectomy, she and her husband learned it had not been enough; the cancer had already spread. Told that she, too, had a very aggressive form of cancer, she had been undergoing chemotherapy in the hospital for the past three weeks, two of which Chris and Hannah had known her. This was her third round.

"What's going on with Michele?" Hannah asked.

"She's going home!"

"Before her next round of chemo?" Hannah asked.

"No, there is no more chemo," Chris told her, grabbing her hand, his eyes full of light. "They just got some tests back. The cancer isn't just in remission, Hannah – they can't even find a trace of it!"

"What do you mean?" she asked, her voice shaky. Could it be…?

"She's been healed!"

"Healed?" Hannah asked, weakly. It was something they prayed for constantly, yet thinking about the reality of everything being over, getting to go home without having to worry about the next round of chemo and radiation, what the cancer was doing, or how long you had to live, felt inconceivable.

"Yes, healed," Chris told her, his voice firm and full of hope. "Her results came back, and they can't find any cancer. None at all. Her tests came back perfectly clean, Hannah, and they're going home!"

Her heart catching up with her mind, Hannah's face blossomed into a bright smile. "Are you serious? Chris! That is amazing! Praise the LORD! And just in time for Christmas! What a blessing!"

"They thanked me for praying for them, Hannah, they told me to thank you, too. They said they know God healed her."

Hannah swiped at tears that were leaking out of the corners of her eyes. "Thank God," she murmured. Hannah felt real joy in her heart – joy and gratitude. She thanked God for answering their prayers. She thanked Him for His healing. She thanked Him for His love for Michele that had prompted Him to move in mercy. She thanked Him for the reminder that He was able to heal even cancer. Miracles were not just for the days of old, they were happening here, all around them, in this day and age.

Michele was one of the main patients they prayed for

every morning at breakfast. They had been praying for her every evening, as well. She had a family – children who needed her. Michele and her husband were both believers, and they had been a big encouragement to Chris and Hannah, and vice versa.

"As much as I'll miss her, I'm so glad for her," Hannah said.

It had been a great joy to have Michele and Rick in the room next door. With so many days of having nothing to do, Hannah had enjoyed visiting with them. Additionally, Hannah and Michele walked the halls of the oncology ward together every day. Although their walks weren't long, the fellowship was good, and it gave them a way to keep their bodies somewhat conditioned.

"Same here. They said they would stop by before they leave to say goodbye. I think they're friends we'll keep for a long time."

Hannah couldn't disagree. A friendship formed in such an uncertain and difficult time, was one that she was confident would last. She was glad they would stop in before leaving.

"Do you know what this means, Hannah?" Chris asked, sitting lightly on the side of her bed.

"What?" she questioned, expectantly.

"God is in the business of healing cancer. Here. Now. In this hospital." He squeezed her hand, the hope in his face evident. She felt her own heart skip a beat. He was right. If God could heal Michele, He could heal her, too. "I have needed this!" Chris continued. "I feel like we pray and pray and pray...*everyone's* praying – our kids, our church, our kids' churches, our family, our family's churches, our friends...people we don't even know are praying! I believe that the LORD is going to heal you, hands down, no question, but man is it good to see someone healed! It restores hope...it builds faith."

She couldn't agree more. She believed she was going

to be healed. Chemotherapy and radiation might be the tool the LORD used to heal her, but she was sure she would be cancer-free and go on to live many more years. Still, it was comforting to see Michele healed.

In the hospital, where everything was about treatments, test results and cancer, healing could feel millions of miles away. It felt impossible in the middle of such an evidence-based institution. Hearing that Michele was not only in remission, but cancer-free was a much-needed reminder that with Christ, all things were possible. Chris was right, it definitely built faith.

Both Chris and Hannah were cheerful and full of hope as the IV continued to drain the potent mixture of drugs into her bloodstream. They chatted about Christmas, about who they still needed to order gifts for, and about their last phone call with Joe.

Hannah was excited to see him at Christmas. She and Chris had been to Minnesota in early August when preseason was just starting, but they had not seen their son, daughter-in-law, or their three grandchildren since. Four months felt entirely too long.

Hannah glanced to the small Christmas tree Kara had set up on the table under the television and felt her excitement grow. It wouldn't be long until she was back home, surrounded by all of the people she loved.

An hour later, there was a light knock on the door. Hannah was in the middle of her treatment, and felt queasy. Yet, seeing Michele walk in with her street clothes on, and Rick pulling their packed bags, made the shadow of her physical reality pass.

Michele hurried to the side of her bed, sharing the news again that Chris had already shared. Michele's face was shining, almost glowing, and joy was pouring out of her every word. Hannah held Michele's hands tightly and told her how glad she was that she was better and going home. They praised the LORD together, tears collecting in both of their eyes.

Before they left, Michele and Rick stood around Hannah's bed, and they all prayed. They prayed for more good reports when Michele's doctor ran follow-up tests in the next several weeks and months, and for her strength and health to return quickly. They prayed for Rick's work as a builder, that a flood of business would come in now that he could return home and start working again. Then, they prayed for Hannah, that she too would get good test results and not a trace of cancer would be found. They prayed for a miracle, in total faith that it could and would be performed – after all, they had just seen it happen.

After Rick and Michele left, while Chris sat on the edge of Hannah's bed and stroked her hand tenderly, holding the bucket nearby, even as she pinched her nose tightly to stop the flow of blood that was coming from it, he said, "Rick and Michele should be out of the city by now and on their way home."

Hannah felt too sick to even respond, but gave a subtle nod, barely moving to refrain from aggravating her churning stomach or her nosebleed.

He smiled down into her blue eyes. "That's going to be you soon, Love. That's going to be us."

Twelve

By the time they left the hospital for Christmas, all of Hannah's hair was gone. In fact, she had taken a razor and shaved her head when it became too scraggly. Struggling with accepting reality and not wanting to go home and see all of her family and friends without hair, she pulled her wig on and fluffed the shoulder-length brown hair, blinking back tears.

Having grown accustomed to being bald was one thing in the hospital, where most patients in the oncology ward looked the same way. Going home to Glendale was altogether different. She dreaded facing her children and seeing the look in their eyes when they saw the toll the illness had taken on her body. She knew it would be then that the full reality of her condition would hit her. Most of all, she dreaded facing her grandchildren. What if they didn't recognize her? What if they were afraid of her? What if the little ones didn't allow her to hold and rock them?

Sensing her mood, Chris gave her a warm smile from across the room. "You look beautiful," he assured her.

Tired and feeling ill, she sat on the edge of her bed and looked at him. Her emotions were roiling and her head ached. "Why do you love me?" she asked, swiping at a tear that escaped and was rolling down her cheek.

Chris grinned, but didn't laugh at her. He walked over to the bed where she sat and put his hands on her shoulders. She sat looking up at him dismally. "Because you are Mrs. Colby," he told her lightly.

"So is your mother."

He laughed. "And I love her, too."

"Chris, I'm not joking around." She lifted her shoulders, then dropped them. "Why? Why do you love me? Why have you stayed here with me? You've given up three weeks of your life just to be holed up in this little hospital room. Before that, you were basically home for four weeks. You haven't worked, you haven't been with friends, you haven't even been to church! And why? Because I'm so fun to be around? I'm sick the majority of the time! Because I'm so beautiful? I'm bald! Because I take care of you? I can barely stand up and walk across the room!"

Chris frowned. "Where is this coming from? I love you."

"And what do you get out of that love? The chance to empty my puke bucket ten times a day or worry about things like if I ate enough dinner, if my nose will start bleeding in the middle of the night, or if my mouth is dry? Is it because you always saw yourself married to a bald bombshell?" Hannah couldn't keep the bitterness out of her voice.

"Stop!" he commanded. She did. She saw the pain in his face, and she crumpled. Her harsh words had done more than just paint a painstakingly accurate picture of his life for the past couple of months. They had deeply hurt the man she loved more than anyone else in the world. "Hey," he said softly, sitting down next to her. He put his arms around her as her head dropped forward, and she began to cry. "Hey," he said again, rubbing her back and pressing a kiss against the side of her head.

"Do you want to know why?" he asked. She nodded, still crying, unable to summon the strength or courage to look at him. "Because I fell in love with you in college, and I fall more in love with you each day. You are strong, brave, caring and full of compassion. I've never met anyone who has as big of a heart as you. And your smile...it still melts my heart." He set his chin on her bony shoulder, his arms still wrapped around her. "You make me laugh when I want to cry, and when you love, you really love. You're loyal and faithful, and you make me feel more loved, like really loved, than anyone ever has."

His words were like cool balm to her heart. She turned into him, wrapping her arms around his solid waist, and pressing her face into his shoulder. "Is that all?" she asked, making him chuckle.

"No. It's also because, just a few short years ago, I promised to love you in sickness and in health, in the good times and the bad, and you promised the same to me. You've held up your end of the bargain, and I figure, if I've found a woman who could manage to do that with someone like me, well, then I better hold up my end of it, too."

She tipped her head back and smiled up at him. In a moment of tenderness, he gently wiped the leftover tears from her face. "It's time to go home, Love. Your last treatment is over. It's time to go home to our own house, sleep in our own bed, and be surrounded by our family."

She nodded. It certainly was. She was tired of this place, tired of the treatments, tired of feeling sick. She was ready to go home to the quiet privacy of their own home. She was ready to hold her grandchildren on her lap, talk with her daughters, laugh with her son, and dream about the future with her husband.

As she held Chris' hand as they prepared to leave the room, their suitcase in tow, she had a sweet feeling that she would not be coming back for more treatment. That season was behind them. It had come to a close. She looked around the hospital room one last time, then watched carefully as they walked down the hall, past the nurse's station and out of the oncology ward. It had been a good hospital; the nurses were kind, the care excellent. Still, she felt ready to move on. It was time.

She couldn't explain it, but she just knew that she wouldn't have even one more treatment. She thanked God, as certain as if she had received the news from the doctor.

On the long drive home, her heart soared. They were

done with chemo and radiation. Now, her strength would return. Her hair would grow back. The nausea would end. Her appetite would return. Her mouth wouldn't be so dry. The nosebleeds would disappear, along with the bitter taste in her mouth. She would put on enough weight that her clothes fit again.

It was over. The night had gone and the morning had come.

It was dark when they pulled into town. Hannah watched fondly as they passed the 'Welcome to Glendale' sign. They had only been gone three and a half weeks, but it felt like a lifetime.

She watched out her window as they passed all the familiar businesses and restaurants. They passed the high school her children had attended. They passed the park, where they had gone on walks as a family. They passed the drive-in diner, where she had led someone to the LORD for the very first time. They passed the bowling alley, where she and Chris had been on a bowling league for seven consecutive years when they were first married. They passed the hospital, where every one of their children had been born. They passed the church, where they had spent countless hours over the past thirty-four years, enjoying their church family and worshipping God.

A deep, rich, satisfying sense of homecoming washed over her, and she gave an inward sigh. Everything was going to be okay. They were home.

"I think it would just be wrong to go home without stopping at Sweet Dips for a cone," Chris told her, pulling into the parking lot of the small ice cream shop. "What do you say? Are you up for it?"

She smiled. "Can I have mint chocolate chip?"

"A double dip or a triple?" he asked as he parked.

She laughed. "I'll stick with a single."

"Good thinking. Kara did say they were waiting dinner for us." Chris had talked to Kara just an hour before, letting her know that they were about to get off the interstate. The update let their family know when to expect them.

"If they're waiting dinner, why are we stopping for ice cream?" Hannah asked, amused. "It's already seven o'clock! I'm sure the kids are starving."

"Because," he told her, sliding out his door while sending her a wink, "we're *home*."

She understood completely. "It feels good, doesn't it?"

He turned his head, looking at the familiar town around them, his breath visible in the late December air. Christmas decorations from the 1980s hung from street lights, lining the streets. A 'Merry Christmas' banner was tied high above Main Street; high enough that even the semi trucks on their way to the grain elevator wouldn't touch it. Hannah looked, too, a smile touching her lips. Unlike Chris, she wasn't born in Glendale, but she loved it just the same. She loved the people who lived here. She loved the memories she had at nearly every street corner.

"No matter what people say about the allure of the city, I know I would sure never want to live anywhere else," he told her.

"Me neither," she agreed, amused by the irony. When he had first brought her home to meet his parents, she vowed she would never live in such a small town. It was a far cry from her home in Baltimore. Yet, she was willing to follow Chris Colby anywhere, even if it was to sleepy little Glendale. Starved for the real world – malls, crowds, rush hour traffic, and enough grocery stores to choose from, she had initially felt disconnected in tiny little Glendale. But little by little, the town had grown on her, making its way into her heart, until now, she couldn't imagine living anywhere else.

"I'll be back out with the ice cream in a jiffy," Chris said, closing the truck door. She watched through the window as he approached the counter, walking right up to order rather than having to wait in line.

For the first time, Hannah let herself really think about the fact that it was almost Christmas. Kimberly and her boys, Justin and Kara, Jessica and the kids, and Hannah's mom and dad were already in town and waiting for them. Joe, her only son, would arrive in two days, as would Jake, Kaitlynn and their kids. Excitement rose within her until she wanted to drag Chris out of Sweet Dips and drive them home herself.

She had missed her family so much. She could barely wait to get to them now. Reminding herself that they had all week together, she forced herself to stay calm.

When she saw Chris turn and come out to the truck with her single-dip mint chocolate chip ice cream in one hand and a triple-dip cone of chocolate chip cookie dough in the other, she laughed.

"What about dinner?" she asked as he handed her the dish of ice cream. She appreciated his thoughtfulness. She hadn't even thought about the fact that an ice cream cone could be torturous on her sore mouth, but he had. He grinned as he climbed into his seat and took his first bite of ice cream.

"Oh, don't you worry. I'll be hungry. We haven't eaten a home-cooked meal in almost a month. That's a long time."

"That is a long time," she agreed.

"You know what sounds fantastic tonight?"

"What?" she asked, amused by his excited tone. She took a bite of her ice cream and watched his animated face, the lines at the corners of her eyes crinkling as she smiled.

"Your homemade lasagna! You haven't made that in forever!"

"That does sound good," she agreed. At least it did in theory. In reality, she had become shy of anything with tomato sauce. Being as sick as she had been, she had learned that tomato sauce stained. Still, those days were behind her now, and she made a mental note to make Chris lasagna as soon as she felt well enough to cook. It would be the first meal she made.

When Chris had finished the first of his three scoops of ice cream, he put the truck in drive and continued home. For the first time in a long time, Hannah finished something. She was taking her last bite of ice cream as he turned onto their gravel driveway.

Suddenly nervous, she flipped down her visor. "Does my wig look okay?" she asked, self-conscience of her sickly appearance.

"Not that anybody will care, but yes. It looks fine."

Her mind flitting away from her appearance, she craned her head to see around the bend, wanting just to see even the vehicles of their family parked in the driveway. What she saw took her breath away.

The eaves of the house were expertly strung with colored lights, transforming their beautiful home into a stunning likeness of a gingerbread house. Lighted deer were set out in the front yard, and white lights were strung down either side of the sidewalk leading to the front porch, which had big red bows tied on each of its pillars. Light shone through all the windows on the main floor, and electric candles burned in each of the upstairs windows.

Home.

The front door opened, and people streamed out. Everyone was standing out on the driveway, waiting for them, by the time the truck pulled up to the garage.

"I think they're anxious to see you," Chris told Hannah, looking over at her with a big smile as he pushed the garage door opener.

"Us, Love. They're anxious to see us," she corrected. Justin came around and was standing at her door, so Chris hit the unlock button. Justin opened Hannah's door to help her out.

"Hey! Glad you guys made it!" Justin said.

"Me, too. Hi, Justin," Hannah said, beaming at her son

-in-law. Taking her hand, he helped her down, then gave her a firm hug. "Welcome home, Mom," he told her, his deep voice cheerful. Kara came around the back of the truck, squealing. "Hey Mama! It's so good to have you home!" she said, running the last few feet and throwing her arms around Hannah.

"Look at you!" Hannah exclaimed, laughing. "I can see your baby! How did she grow so much in just two weeks?"

Kara laughed. "I told you I could hide a lot under a sweater!" The formfitting shirt with a cardigan, skinny jeans, and boots showed a lot more than her bulky sweaters had when she was at the hospital, and Hannah couldn't get over it. She put her hand on the gentle bulge of Kara's stomach, wonder filling her. Babies were truly a gift straight from the Father, a little miracle only forty weeks in the making.

Like a tidal wave coming at her legs, the grandkids ran at her for hugs. Justin put his arm firmly around Hannah's waist, offering support, and Kara held her hands out, even as she smiled. "Remember what we talked about!" she quickly instructed the eager group. The kids backed up and approached Hannah one at a time, giving her careful hugs, their little faces alight with joy.

Hannah couldn't keep the tears from her eyes, as she embraced Kelsi and Kamryn, then little Joshua. It had been far too long since she had seen them. For a moment, she regretted again that her treatment had forced them to cancel the trip they had planned to go out to see them for Thanksgiving; but with so many bright smiles, chubby little arms, and sweet childish greetings, she couldn't spend time on regrets.

She hugged Clinton and Caiden, then received hearty hugs from Carson and Samuel. Having all the children embrace her as they did was like a drop of healing in her heart – they hadn't been afraid of her or wary of her sickly appearance. Once she had greeted all the grandchildren, they ran off to tackle their grandpa. Hannah embraced Kimberly and then Jessica, each for a long time.

"It is so good to see you," Jessi said, her crystal blue eyes shining. "So good."

"Oh, it's good to see *you*," Hannah said, laughing, wiping at more tears. "We have missed you all so much."

"We have both wanted to come so badly," Jessi told her. "It's been just about killing Joe that he couldn't come be with you. If it weren't for his football schedule, he would have been here…if it weren't for the kids, I would have been," Jessi finished with a small laugh. "Somehow I didn't think those three in a hospital room all day sounded like a good idea."

"No, that may not have worked well," Hannah agreed with a laugh.

"Joe can't wait to get here," Jessica continued, looping her arm through Hannah's as they started toward the front door. Kimberly and Kara attempted to round up the kids as they went into the garage to greet Chris.

"Neither can I," Hannah agreed. "But, I'm so glad that you and the children got to come early. And Joshua! What have you been feeding him? He's huge!"

Jessi laughed, and the musical sound of it filled Hannah with joy. She had missed her only daughter-in-law, who had become like one of her own daughters long ago. "He sure has. He wants to play ball like his Daddy, so he's been cleaning up his plate at every meal. That was the trick, Joe said, to growing big and strong, and Josh has taken it to heart."

"I can tell!"

Going through the front door of her house, Hannah felt a flood of relief. Home was warm and cozy, with Christmas music coming from the living room, and heavenly aromas wafting out of the kitchen. Hearing the commotion, Kostya and Jim came out of the kitchen. For a brief moment, Hannah saw the look of shock and sorrow on her parents' faces, causing her a moment of stinging insecurity. But then it was gone, and bright smiles replaced their shock.

Kostya pulled Hannah into her arms first, kissing her cheek, telling her how glad she was to see her, and how worried she had been. When she finally relinquished her hold, Jim embraced his daughter, kissing the side of her head and holding her for a beat longer than he ever had. By the time the greeting was over, everyone else had made their way into the house. Hannah caught Chris' eye over the top of Kimberly's dark head, and she smiled at him. He winked at her, even as he was drug into the living room by Carson and Samuel to look at the new remote control cars their mother had let them unwrap early.

Hearing about their early Christmas presents, Hannah looked knowingly at her second eldest. "Did you have some busy boys?"

"Oh, they were driving me crazy!" Kim admitted, laughing as she swung Joe's Joshua up to her hip. "I had to do something to entertain them, or I would have ended up knocking their heads together!"

Hannah went to the dinner table laughing with her daughter.

She forced herself to eat as much of the turkey and noodles as she could, and then let Chris insist that she rest on the couch while the girls cleaned up dinner. She felt thoroughly exhausted from the trip home and the evening with her family, no matter how wonderful it had been.

Weary through and through, she allowed Chris to help her settle on the couch, and she patted the sliver of cushions in front of her, inviting Kamryn to climb up with her. The eight-year-old didn't need any more encouragement. She climbed up on the couch and lay down in front of her, resting her head on Hannah's chest, chattering gaily about school and her friends. Hannah ran her fingers through Kamryn's silky blonde hair and closed her eyes, not remembering a time when she had felt happier. She fell asleep to the sweet lulling of her granddaughter's voice.

Thirteen

Hannah *enjoyed* Christmas. She enjoyed it more than she remembered enjoying a Christmas in a very long time, if ever. Each day, each hour, each conversation, each moment with her family felt special...somehow sweeter than it ever had before. She felt overwhelmingly thankful for each day she had at home with them and thankful for the family that surrounded her.

She ate the frosted cut-out cookies her daughters and granddaughters made. She watched the boys' constant renditions of epic superhero battles. She stole private moments with Chris when he walked with her up to their room so she could rest. She finally felt the tiny movement of her unborn grandchild after spending collective hours with her hand on Kara's stomach. She played cards with her parents and visited with her son-in-laws. She listened to Christmas music and drank hot chocolate with marshmallows. She snuggled with Ava and Joshua on the couch, holding them close for as long as they would allow.

Her Christmas week was filled with things she didn't often take the time to do. Without having to worry about cooking or cleaning for the large group, she had time to enjoy her family members. The result was a heart-full of beautiful memories she would treasure for the rest of her life.

Sadness started creeping in on the evening of Christmas Day, as she knew the blessed week would soon be over. Greg and Kimberly had to fly home in the morning, and Jake and Kaitlynn and Joe and Jessi would go the day after. Justin and Kara would be moving back into their own house, and her mom and dad would start the long drive home.

The presents had all been opened, the Christmas story had been read, and the kids had gone through their stockings. They had eaten the big Christmas dinner the girls had prepared, and the sun had gone down, sending even the bravest of the sledders back inside. Hannah could hear commotion going on in the kitchen, and knew the leftovers were being pulled out of the refrigerator. She would go in and join them for dinner soon, but for now she rested on the couch and looked out the large bay window to where the back light chased the darkness away from the snow covered patio.

She smiled, thinking again about how thankful she was that it had snowed, and they were able to enjoy a white Christmas.

"Mind if I join you?" Hannah looked up to see the quick grin of her only son. "I can't feel my toes and thought the fireplace might feel nice," he said.

She laughed. "Please do!"

When Joe approached her couch, she moved her feet, and he sat down on the end of it, pulling her feet and the blanket she had covered up with, onto his lap. He handed her one of the two plates he held, and she saw that on it was a thick wedge of the multi-layered chocolate cake the girls had enjoyed making that afternoon. "I thought I would snag us each a piece before it's gone," he told her, his eyes laughing.

"What about dinner? We can't have dessert before our dinner," she scolded.

"Mom," he paused, giving her a look that said she was being ridiculous. "It's chocolate cake! And if we wait until after dinner, it will likely be gone."

Hannah laughed. "Good point. I guess we can bend the rules, just this once."

Joe grinned and took his first bite. She did likewise and savored the rich chocolate flavor. "Which one of the girls made this?"

"It's Jessi's recipe, but I think they all chipped in. Good, isn't it?" he answered with another grin.

"Amazing!" she agreed. They both sat in comfortable silence while they ate their cake. Hannah started feeling full halfway through her slice, but it was so good, she kept going. Any other Christmas she would have felt guilty for eating the generous piece that her son had brought her; this year, she just made sure to enjoy every bite.

"How are you feeling tonight?" Joe asked, breaking the comfortable silence that had settled.

"Pretty good," she answered.

"Really?"

She smiled at his question and patted his arm. "Yes, really. The nausea is getting better the farther out from chemo I get, and you all have been doing such a good job of making me rest that, overall, I feel pretty good," she paused. "How are you doing?"

He glanced at her, then set his empty plate on the armrest of the couch and put his head back against the headrest. "It feels good to be home. It's been hard to be away."

"We understood," she told him, detecting a hint of guilt in his voice. "You are a grown man with a career and family of your own. Besides, it hasn't been very eventful or very pleasant. I wish your father didn't even have to go through what he has for the past few weeks. I certainly didn't want anyone else there."

"Do you think you'll have more treatments?" he asked, curious.

"No," she answered simply. It was one thing she had become more and more convinced of since being home. She was done with the chemo and radiation – not that she would refuse it if Dr. Hedgins suggested more, but she simply knew that she wouldn't.

Joe grinned. "I agree. You're going to be okay, Mom."

"Yes, I am," she answered quietly. She wondered if she should tell Joe about the knowing that had been growing within her over the past week, but decided against it. It was premature. She kept it to herself and changed the subject. "I have been so thankful for your support during this," she told him.

He sent her a sad look. "I wish I could have done more."

She shook her head, seeking to disperse the guilt she saw etched in his face. "Your phone calls and text messages were exactly what I needed. When I was sad and discouraged, all I needed was to talk to you. You have been such an encouragement...over the past few months, that's what I've needed more than anything else."

Joe grinned and squeezed her hand. "I'm glad, Mom. The LORD is going to heal you. He is faithful and good. And He is more than able. We can't lose hope or lose faith."

She met his eyes, a quietness filling her. "You're right. He is faithful and good, Joe. That's something we can never forget." She paused, the serious moment passing. "Can you feel your toes yet?" she asked, watching as he lifted his legs and wiggled his toes, then grinned at her.

She studied his face, a face she had loved for twenty-seven years. His dimpled grin was the same. He had grown stunningly handsome over the years, but his charm and his grin had never changed. Neither had the pale green color of his eyes that was so like his father's, or the dark brown sheen of his hair. Her eyes moved over his broad shoulders and well-muscled arms. He was the spitting image of Chris at his age. The thought made the corners of her mouth lift.

"Just about," he answered. "I was just going out to sled with the girls and Josh, but when Kim's boys challenged Greg and I to a snowball fight, well, then it was on."

"Who won?" Hannah asked, amused and enjoying the one-on-one time she was having with Joe. He had proven to be a popular guy over the last few days. When one of his three kids wasn't hanging off him, he was talking football with one of his brothers-in-law, joking with one of his sisters, or taking a look at a project in the garage with his dad. It was Hannah's first chance to be alone with him, and she wasn't eager to have the moment pass.

"Oh, we pummeled them," he told her with a smug grin.

"Joe," she half-scolded, laughing. "They're little boys!"

"They asked for it," he said in defense, his tanned face stretched in another grin. "Believe me, they asked for it."

She laughed, then her smile turned mischievous. "Was that before or after you were kissing Jessica?" She laughed at the look on his face. "That's right, you've been caught, Son. I saw you smooching out there in the snow."

Recovering, he chuckled. "Well, I guess there's no use denying it. I love my wife, and she looks beautiful in the snow."

Hannah smiled at him. She had thought the same thing when she saw Jessi outside. The girl's dark hair hung in loose curls that were dusted with snow. Her fitted wool coat made her look as slender as when she was in high school, and her matching scarf and mittens were stylish, especially paired with her boots. A full smile had filled her pretty face and her blue eyes were alight with merriment. "That she does."

Joe grinned.

A peal of laughter came from the kitchen, and Joe and Hannah both glanced that way. "Do you need to go have dinner with your family?" she asked gently, hating to see the moment end, but not wanting to keep him.

"No, ma'am. I told Jessi I was going to hang out in here with you for awhile. I figured after those slices of cake, we wouldn't be hungry anyway."

Hannah's heart warmed, knowing that he had come looking for her and was as eager to get one-on-one time as she was. "Well, I'm glad you did."

He smiled at her then, his warm, tender smile that always melted her heart, just as it did now. "Me too, Mom."

"Josh is getting big," she mentioned casually.

Joe bobbed his head. "He'll be three this spring."

"Crazy how fast it goes, isn't it?"

"It sure is. It feels like he was just born."

"Think you guys will have any more? If you're thinking about it, the sooner the better – that way Josh and the baby can have each other to play with like the girls do."

Joe's grin came quickly, and he shot her a sideways look. "Well, we weren't going to tell anyone yet, but since you asked...."

Hannah stared at him for a moment in shock, then gave a little squeal. "Jessi's pregnant again?"

"Not exactly," he answered. He turned to face her more fully. "We've started the process to adopt."

Hannah caught her breath. "Are you serious? Joe! When? How? Are you doing an international or domestic adoption? When will you get a child?"

He laughed and held up his hands. "One question at a time, Mom." His grin faded and his expression turned serious. "Remember when I took Jess to the homeless shelter when we were in high school?" Hannah nodded. She certainly did. "Remember those two little girls I told you about – Morgan and Montana?" Another nod – her granddaughters were named after those girls. "Well, that night Jessi and I decided that we wanted to do foster care someday. We've had it in the back of our minds for awhile now, but feel like this is the right time. We started classes in November, and finish up in February. We don't know how long it will be before they have a child for us, but once we're certified we'll just wait until we get the call."

Hannah's heart was full. Though they had never adopted, it had been heavy on her heart for many years. She was so glad to hear now that her son and daughter-in-law were going to. "I'm so happy for you, Honey! That's wonderful news!"

"Yeah, we're pretty excited about it," he answered, grinning.

"Do you know what you want? A boy or a girl? What age?" Hannah questioned.

"Well, we don't want a child that's older than our own, so anyone under three. We know there is a big need for families who will take older children, so maybe we'll adopt again in ten years or so, but for now we feel like we need to have a child who is younger than Josh in consideration of him and the girls."

Hannah nodded. "I think that's wise."

"We would be happy with either gender, though I'm sure Josh would appreciate a brother," Joe finished with a wink.

Hannah agreed joyfully. "Probably so! I'm sure the girls are thrilled!"

"We haven't told them. We don't want the word to get out quite yet and," he shot her another sideways grin, "you know telling them is like telling the world."

Hannah laughed. It was true. With all of her granddaughters' admirable qualities, keeping a secret wasn't one of them. "Well, I'm sure they'll be happy when you do."

"Oh, I'm sure," he agreed.

"You should tell them soon," she finished. "They'll need time to adjust to the idea of having another brother or sister."

He nodded in agreement. "We will. We're going to tell them after Christmas."

Hannah looked at him and spent a few moments contemplating the man her son had become. He was a wonderful husband and an amazing father. She had enjoyed watching him with Jessi and their kids over the past few days. He had truly turned into a good man. Now, he was opening his home and his family to the fatherless. She could not be prouder.

Reaching out, she grasped both of his hands, waiting

until he met her eyes. "Joseph Colby, I am so proud of you." Her words were deliberate, and a grateful smile filled his face.

"Thanks, Mom." They both let the moment linger, and then moved on when it ended.

"We watched your games every week, even when we were in the hospital," she told him. "You're having a great season."

He bobbed his head modestly. "I played every one of those games for you."

She smiled at him and patted his arm, feeling loved and cared about. Their conversation continued, and all too soon, other people were flooding into the room. Joshua wanted to be held, and Joe lifted him easily up onto his lap. Chris brought Hannah a plate of food, and she sat up to eat it. The living room filled with people, laughter, and conversation. Hannah felt a pang of remorse that her conversation with Joe was over, but like so many other moments over the week, she tucked the memory of it away inside to remember and treasure later.

Over the next few days, when everyone had to leave, Hannah found herself hugging them a little longer than normal. It wasn't that she was afraid of what came next as much as she was more aware of how much she loved each and every one of them, and how thankful she was for the time they had spent together. When the last group left, she returned to the couch at Chris' urging and promptly fell asleep, sleeping late into the evening. She was guilty of sugar coating things just a little when people had asked – the truth was, she was exhausted.

Despite the fact that she was done with treatment, her body was still depleted and recovering, and the fatigue felt overwhelming. She was thankful for the chance to sleep, but equally as thankful when Chris woke her up that evening.

"Good morning, Sleepy Head," he told her with a smile.

She rubbed her eyes, smiling up at him. Seeing that he came bearing plates of food, she pushed herself to a sitting position. "Pizza?" she asked in surprise.

"I thought it might be a nice break from turkey."

"I agree."

Chris found a movie on television, and they ate their pizza while they watched it. When Hannah finished the slice of pizza Chris had put on her plate, he offered her another, but she declined. She was well aware of how her clothes hung on her, making her look like a shell of the woman she had been, but she was full. Determined to get more calories in her, Chris returned from the kitchen with bowls of ice cream an hour later. Never able to say no to ice cream, Hannah ate it and enjoyed every bite.

After Christmas, Chris and Hannah enjoyed a whole week at home together. Hannah enjoyed the sunshine that streamed through the large windows, the quietness of the comfortable rooms, the peace that had settled, and the chance to simply be at home with her husband.

They spent New Year's Eve at home, just the two of them, as Justin and Kara went to Justin's family to bring in the new year. Justin invited them, as did his mother, but Chris declined, saying they were just going to lay low and enjoy a restful evening at home. Everyone understood. Chris and Hannah spent the night eating boxed macaroni and cheese and playing board games in front of the fire.

With January underway, Justin and Kara came over for dinner the night before Chris and Hannah were scheduled to go back to the hospital for more testing.

After dinner, Chris and Justin disappeared to the garage to work on one of Chris' projects, and Hannah and Kara sat in the living room and talked. They talked about how Kara was feeling, the baby, ideas for the nursery, baby names, how a baby would fit into their schedule, and made preliminary plans for the baby shower. They decided on a Saturday in March. Hannah thought it would be best to wait as long as possible, so she could regain her strength before the joyous event. Sitting on the couch together, she felt the baby move again.

They discussed how Hannah was feeling, and if she was nervous about having testing done. They talked about the marathon that Kaitlynn and a few of her friends would be running in May to raise support for cancer awareness. Hannah told Kara how pleased she was to hear of Kaitlynn thinking of such a positive way she could support Hannah in her healing process, even from Texas. She told her how much it meant to her to hear Joe say he was playing every game for her. She expressed again how thankful she was that Kara came to the hospital and for all the times she and Justin had come over during the past several months. She shared how encouraged and supported she felt by her family.

She wanted Kara and the entire family to know how blessed she felt and how thankful she was for their support.

When Justin suggested it was time to leave that night, Hannah wasn't ready to let them go. She enjoyed her daughter so much. They could have talked all night. But, it was late, and Justin was right. She embraced them both, as did Chris, then stood at one of the windows by the front door, watching as their taillights disappeared up the driveway. Chris slipped his arm around her shoulders and turned her toward the staircase.

"It's time for us to go to bed," he told her, leading her in that direction. "We have to get up early tomorrow."

"Are you nervous?" she asked as they climbed the stairs together.

Chris reached over and pressed a kiss against her head. "It will be a good report. If we need to do another round of chemo, we can, but I'm believing for a good report. We hit the cancer hard and fast. It's likely gone altogether."

Hannah nodded, but didn't say anything. She didn't want to tell her husband about the feeling she had grown surer of in the days since coming home. She had a feeling that the cancer wasn't gone.

Fourteen

Being back in the hospital, sitting in Dr. Hedgins office, felt all too familiar. As peaceful as she felt during the drive into the city and while the tests were being run, now her hands felt clammy, and her stomach was churning. Chris was holding her hand loosely between both of his, and his posture was relaxed; however, he was tapping his shoe on the floor to a very fast beat, a telltale sign that he was nervous.

After all the days of being sick, all of the exhaustion, nosebleeds, hair loss, days in the hospital, and being away from home, they were about to find out if it had been worthwhile.

When Dr. Hedgins walked into the room, Hannah couldn't read the expression on her face. Her heart jumped in fear, reasoning that if it were good news, Dr. Hedgins would be smiling. Taking a steadying breath, Hannah reminded herself that she didn't know the woman well, and the lack of emotion might mean nothing at all.

Dr. Hedgins sat down in her chair, laying Hannah's folder on the desk in front of her. Chris held Hannah's hand tighter. Dr. Hedgins looked down at the open folder as if reading, then brought her eyes up to meet theirs. She sighed, and in that instant Hannah knew they weren't going to get the news they were hoping for.

"There's no easy way to tell you this. The cancer didn't respond to treatment," Dr. Hedgins said, her expression now full of sympathy.

Chris moved to the edge of his seat. "It didn't respond to treatment? As in, not at all?"

Dr. Hedgins shook her head. "No. In fact, it's still

spreading. The number of cancerous cells is higher now than it was before we started treatment."

Chris looked completely shocked and at a loss for words. The disappointment and pain that showed on his face made Hannah's heart ache. Yet, something within her had been expecting this and, somewhere along the way, she had come to terms with it. "How long do I have?" she asked quietly. "How many years do I have left with my family?"

Chris looked at her as if he was hurt by her question. There was no doubt he felt betrayed. "Hannah, don't even say that. Surely there are other options…other treatments we can try! It's way too early to be making any assumptions or asking any questions like that…right, doctor?"

Dr. Hedgins pressed her lips together, then met Hannah's eyes. "As I've said from the beginning, you have a very aggressive form of cancer, Hannah. We could do another round of chemo and radiation, but I honestly don't know that it would do any good. There are a few experimental drugs that are out there right now that we could try, but I'm not confident in any of their abilities to help you. They just weren't created for your kind or stage of cancer."

"What are you saying?" Chris questioned fiercely. "Are you giving up on her?"

"Chris," Dr. Hedgins hesitated before going on. "Your wife is dying." She glanced back at Hannah. "I'm so sorry. Really, I am. If there was something else I could do, I would. Like I said, we can go ahead with chemo and radiation. We can try it again. Maybe it would help this time around, but if it doesn't, I'm afraid that's the grim reality we're looking at."

Hannah could tell Dr. Hedgins was trying to throw them a lifeline of hope in the midst of a hopeless situation. "In your professional opinion, do you think it would help?" Hannah asked, her voice calm. She felt a strange emotion that fell somewhere between numbness and peace.

Dr. Hedgins gave her another sympathetic look. "In

my professional opinion, no, I don't think it will."

"Okay," Hannah said. "Then, I'm done. I don't want another round. I want to go home and enjoy however much time I have instead of lying sick in a hospital bed."

"Hannah!" Chris' voice was angry now. He turned to the doctor. "Tell her she's wrong! Tell us what else we can do!"

Hannah felt tears prick her eyes, hurt by his harshness and anger. But, she also heard the pain in his voice, and knew his reaction was born of desperation. She reached out and took his hand. "It's okay, Chris."

He stood up, backing away from her as if her touch had burned him. "Okay? *Okay*?" he questioned. "This is not okay! There's nothing about this that's okay! There is more we can do. How long do we have to figure something out, doctor? Five years? Ten?"

"There's no way to put an exact time frame on it, but best case scenario, I think you're looking at a year. Probably less." Dr. Hedgin's gaze was level, her expression sympathetic, yet resigned.

Chris made a noise as if all the air had gone out of him. He looked from the doctor to Hannah and back. Then, he opened the door to Dr. Hedgins office and stalked out of it. Hannah shot the doctor an apologetic look and stood. "I'm sorry."

"Don't be. I don't blame him, Hannah. This is terrible news to hear. Not at all what you were hoping for today. I'm so sorry. I wish I had something else to offer you... some hope."

Hannah gave her a small smile. "I already have all the hope I need."

Dr. Hedgins met her eyes and nodded slowly. "Cling to that then."

"I should go after him."

Dr. Hedgins nodded. "I'll be in my office for the rest of the morning. When you've had a chance to process this, come on back."

Hannah slipped out the door, pulling it shut behind her before looking up and down the hall. It didn't take long to spot Chris; he hadn't gone far. He was standing at a tall window, his hand braced on the wall beside it, his eyes fixed on something outside. When she drew close, she could see that his expression was a mix of emotions. She could see pain, anger, fear, and desperation all etched into the tanned face that she loved, and her heart hurt for him.

"I'm not giving up on you. You better understand that right now," he told her, his face stormy.

She reached out and laid her hand on his arm. "Thank God," she breathed. "Because I couldn't handle it if you did! But know this – giving up on me and being realistic is not the same thing, Love!" She could tell he didn't under-stand what she was saying, and she grasped for a way to ex-plain what she had come to realize over the past week. "I believe that the LORD is no less likely to heal me now than He was yesterday, before we knew all of this, but we have to come to terms with the fact that He may not choose to. And to this point, He hasn't." Tears pooled in her eyes.

"How am I supposed to come to terms with that?" Chris asked, sounding miserable. "I can't! I love you!"

Too overcome with emotion, she couldn't utter an-other word. Instead, she wrapped her arms around him tightly. When his arms slid around her back in answer, she clung to him. He held her as if he was never going to let her go. "We serve a good God," she whispered to him, her face pressed against his shoulder.

"This doesn't feel good," he admitted brokenly.

"He is big, Chris, bigger and greater, more majestic and more powerful than we can comprehend...or even begin to."

"Big enough to heal cancer...even incurable cancer."

"And big enough not to," she answered. He pulled back and looked at her. Again, she grasped for a way to explain. "Who are we to tell Him what He should and should-n't do? Who are we to decide what is good and right?"

"What is good or right about you being sick? What would be good or right about you," he paused, unable to say the word. "About your life being cut short? What would be good or right about our kids living the rest of their lives without their mother, or our grandkids growing up without their grandma? What is good or right about that?" He demanded. "What was good or right about Kelsi dying when she was five-years-old? To what purpose, Hannah? What reason was there in that? What reason would there be in this?" His voice sounded tortured, and he pulled back from her, crossing his strong forearms across his chest.

Tears sprung to her eyes, and she shook her head, feeling his separation acutely. "I don't know, but I know that we only see in part, when He sees in full."

Chris's green eyes searched her face. "How are you so calm right now?"

"I don't know," she admitted. "All I know is that I'm sure that my Jesus is alive, and I'm sure that He is powerful enough to heal me today. I feel confident that if He does-n't...that He is still trustworthy and good. He has spent my entire lifetime revealing Himself to me, showing me who He is...His character. I cannot forget that now. I can't. Not even in the face of this. Even when I feel full of fear and despair, I cannot forget who He has been all these years... who I know Him to be."

She watched emotions play across Chris' face. He shifted his eyes off of her to something outside the window. He stayed quiet for a long time. Finally, he looked back at her. "You're right. I know you're right. But I am not okay with this."

She nodded, appreciating his honesty, thankful he was sharing his thoughts. "I don't know that I am either," she admitted. "Not when I think about the reality of saying goodbye...to you...to the kids. Not when I think about the things I'll miss and the people I love. But, so often I've been thinking about what you said about Kelsi." He shook his head, clearly confused. "Do you remember?"

Chris shook his head again. "You said that one day, if we asked her, she would never regret having been taken so soon. You said you thought she was rejoicing that she only had to spend five years separated from the physical presence of God. I've been thinking about that a lot. It's helped."

He stayed quiet, but he put his arm around her shoulders. They stood and looked out the window together.

It was quiet for awhile longer. Finally, he sighed. "Is what you said in there true?"

"Which part?"

"That you're done. Do you really want to give up on treatment? You really don't want to try anything else?"

Hannah switched from one foot to the other, thinking. Finally, she met his eyes. "Short of a miracle, Chris, I'm dying." She watched the hurt fill his face as she spoke the words aloud. "You heard Dr. Hedgins. I would rather hope and pray for a miracle at home than in a hospital bed. It feels more possible there. Hope feels easier to hold on to." She paused. "I want to spend time with my children and grandchildren and friends...I want to spend time with you. I want to feel the sun on my face, sleep in my own bed, putter around my kitchen, hold my grandbabies in my arms, cuddle with you during a movie, go out for dinner, worship with our church family...I want to *live* the rest of my life, however long it will be. If I am healed and live another fifty years, there will be nothing to regret. But if I'm not, I won't regret that I wasted the days I had left."

She watched Chris' emotions war for control. He didn't want to agree. Agreeing would be giving up, accepting death. Yet, he would not deny her wishes. She knew that and waited patiently for him to say so.

Finally, he blew out a breath and rubbed the back of his neck. "Are you sure?"

She nodded her head. There was no second-guessing within her. She had known from the time she left the hospital before Christmas that she would not come back for more chemo. She assumed then it was because she was better; now she knew otherwise. Still, every word she had spoken was true. The minute Dr. Hedgins said that additional treatment would likely not do any good, she knew she didn't want to go through it again. She had more hope that God would heal her than she did that chemo would. And His miracles were not confined to a hospital. "I'm sure. We have always believed in quality over quantity...I think it applies again here."

Chris watched her for a long moment. "Okay. Then let's go talk to Dr. Hedgins and get out of here."

Hannah couldn't agree more and held his hand tightly as they walked back to Dr. Hedgins' office. Rapping lightly on the door, they went in when summoned. Half an hour later, they were back in the truck and on their way home.

"It feels good to be done there," Hannah said, sighing in relief. Leaving the hospital for good had dissolved a heaviness she had felt since her cancer was first discovered. Come what may, at least it would happen at home. She felt peaceful, thankful that the days of trying everything they could were finally over. Now, things would play out as they would. The stress of trying to make herself get better had dissipated, leaving within her a new peace and joy. Things felt new and full of hope again.

"It does," Chris agreed with a sigh of his own. "You're right."

"Words I love to hear," she joked, and he couldn't hold back a grin.

"It's because you hear them so seldom," he told her, taking her hand. She was thankful that he was able to tease.

Her stomach growled, and she pressed a hand to it. That hadn't happened in a long while. "I'm hungry!" she announced happily.

He smiled at her announcement. "That's good to hear. What are you hungry for?"

She thought about all the options the city had to offer, but knew exactly what she wanted. "A taco."

Chris laughed, and it was like music to Hannah's ears. She had been afraid he would be like he was in the hospital all day, or longer. She was afraid his laugh would disappear with his grin, and sorrow would shadow their remaining days together. But, she shouldn't have worried. She should have remembered her husband's resiliency and determination to find the good in every situation.

"A taco it is." They drove until they found a taco joint, and Chris turned the truck into the parking lot. They did their best to set aside the news Dr. Hedgins had given them, and simply enjoy their lunch together.

Fifteen

Chris sat outside on the back patio, soaking in the sunshine on an unusually warm January day. Hannah was stretched out on the reclining lawn chair beside him. It wasn't everyday that they had seventy-five degree weather in the middle of winter, and they had decided it wasn't something they could pass up. Hannah fixed sandwiches, grabbed a bag of chips and glasses of sweet tea, and they had enjoyed a picnic out by the drained pool. Now, she had her eyes closed, and a faint smile was on her lips.

He watched her, his heart full of emotion. It had been two days since they returned home. Telling their children the news was almost as difficult as it had been to receive it. It was made even worse by the fact that the issue still wasn't settled in his heart. Hannah, on the other hand, seemed unwavering in her decision.

He understood her desire to be home, to be with her family, to enjoy her time. Yet, he could not give up on her. And, by letting her refuse further treatment, that's what he felt like he was doing. He was giving up on his wife, the love of his life.

He had stuck with her through thick and thin. Over the years, he had nursed her back to health when she was sick, dealt with her patiently when she was irritable, been gentle when she was impossible, overlooked her faults when they annoyed him, and put considerable effort into working out countless disagreements. He had worked hard to change imperfections in himself in hopes of being a better husband, all because he loved the blue-eyed, brown-haired woman beside him, and he knew without a shadow of a doubt that life was better with her than without her.

Sometimes, looking back, he realized that he barely remembered life without her. Sometimes, it felt as if his life had started when he looked across the college gymnasium and saw her in her white sweater and blue and white pleated skirt, standing with the other cheerleaders, getting ready for the game. In that instant, he knew she was different from the other girls and that he needed to be around her, a feeling he still had often. She was as drawing to him now as she was then. It was almost as if she possessed a magnetic pull that he could not escape, even if he wanted to.

She was full of life, caring and intelligent. She was interesting to be around, and he always found himself wondering what she would think about things, if she had any solutions to his problems, and longing for her intuition. She held great wisdom, and he trusted her more than he trusted anyone else on earth. She loved well and deeply, and he knew that she cared about him to a depth that no one else did. She had the most beautiful smile, and her laugh was like music. She was gentle and compassionate, and she had the innate ability to take the sting out of a painful situation. She always took the time to know their children, and she was an amazing mother. She encouraged him to enjoy their kids, and had a way of knowing all things, which still blew his mind. His gaze moved down to her full mouth, still as enticing as it ever had been. An amused smile played at the corners of his lips. One kiss from Hannah could still make everything right in the world, just as it always had.

Over the past thirty-four years, she had become more than just the girl he was infatuated with. She had become his life companion, his partner, his lover, his best friend, his everything. She had become so entwined in the fabric of who he was that his very existence felt dependent upon her.

Suddenly, like a rock in the pit of his stomach, he remembered that she was refusing further treatment. His smile faded, and he pressed his lips into a firm line. He had to change her mind. That was all there was to it. He had to insist that she go back for more chemo or perhaps one of the experimental drugs that was on the market. Something would help her. Something had to help her.

He thought about blurting out his thoughts right then and there. He thought about ordering her to continue with treatment, not relenting until she gave in. If he insisted, he knew she would do as he asked. He had never exercised great control over his wife, but he knew she respected him, and would continue with treatment if he really wanted her to. He opened his mouth to insist, but then shut it again.

He sat there for several moments listening intently, for in the moment he had prepared to speak, he heard a quiet voice above the turmoil in his heart. Suddenly, he pushed himself to his feet. At his movement, Hannah shaded her eyes and looked up at him. "I have a few projects that I want to get done today, and I need to go into the office this afternoon. Are you okay out here by yourself?"

"Yes. I'll probably go in and make some cookies in a bit, but for now, I can't leave this sunshine just yet." Her lazy smile warmed his heart, but was followed by what felt like a bucket of cold water being thrown on him. He nodded and left the patio, incapable of saying anything else.

Instead of going through the house, he walked around it. Upon reaching the driveway, he made a beeline for the barn. Lifting the latch, he swung open the wooden barn door and stepped inside, pulling the door shut behind him. The barn was dim and held the musty smell of dirt and animals. It had been years since there had been horses and cattle within the four walls, but the smell of them remained. Little slivers of sunlight streamed through cracks in the wooden siding where years of weather had shrunk the boards. Looking up, Chris could see particles of dust floating in the air, and it felt heavy in his lungs.

His eyes falling on what he sought, he made his way to the old dusty truck. It was a 1957 Chevy pickup – his dad's first truck. It hadn't run in years, but Chris kept it, thinking he would restore it one day. Perhaps one day he would. For now, it served as his getaway, his prayer closet, his place to meet with God. Joe had his Jesus tree; Chris had his Chevy.

Putting his hand on the old chrome door handle, he pushed in the button and pulled open the heavy door. Climbing inside, he shut it, and quiet settled around him.

Almost instantly, a reverence fell over him – a whisper of something supernatural that made his spirit take attention. He knew that the old truck was no temple, but he had a history of meeting God here. Leaving his wife and coming to sit in the truck had been the result of an invitation, blown across the surface of his heart. Now, he knew he was in the presence of God.

"God, I have to find a way to make her seek further treatment," he said into the dusty interior, feeling desperate and scared. "Doesn't she see that she's giving up on herself? Giving up on us? If she just continues treatment, it will work. She'll get better, won't she, Father? I just need to convince her that it will work."

His mind was set. He simply needed to put his foot down and tell Hannah that she was going to continue treatment. It wasn't like she would be on her own. He would be with her every step of the way. The kids would support her. They could video chat with the grandkids. Most importantly, she would get better. They would have countless years together to enjoy each other, retirement, and the family they had raised.

Suddenly a knowing, no more than a feeling, seemed to blow through the truck. *Hannah was dying.*

It wasn't audible, it wasn't even in words, but it was almost like a reality that settled over the cab. It felt like ice that instantly chilled him down to the bone. The hair on the back of his neck rose, and he tensed. A great hush fell over the dusty interior and Chris sat very still. Sorrow slammed against his chest, and he felt himself reeling. It wasn't true!

It couldn't be! God was supposed to heal her!

"No. That wasn't You. You are supposed to heal her," Chris pleaded, shaking inside.

Again the feeling came. It moved through the dusty truck almost like a wind and settled heavily on his heart. Chris sat very still for several long moments, fighting against his emotions. He didn't want to believe it. He couldn't.

"I can't lose her," he finally choked. All was still. "I can't lose her!" he said again, louder this time.

His wife was more precious to him than anything he possessed. He lived and breathed her. A day didn't feel complete if he hadn't spent it with her. Nothing felt significant, unless they experienced it together. To think of life without Hannah was inconceivable. He had not made her his idol, he felt confident of that, but after thirty-four years of marriage, good marriage, she was part of him. "You are the One who made the two of us one," he groaned, his throat aching. "How are we supposed to be separated now?"

He waited, but all was quiet, and in his humanness, Chris hoped his protest caused God to reconsider. He held his breath, hoping, praying.

But he knew. Deep down he knew that no matter how much he wanted to deny it, his wife was dying. Chris hit the steering wheel with the palm of his hand, knowing there had been no mistake, knowing the message was from the LORD. "Why?" he cried out in agony. "Why won't you save her?"

Conviction came swiftly and he belatedly realized his mistake. Hannah had already been saved in every way that really mattered. He had forgotten that the battle over Hannah's life had already been won. Not here in this moment in a fight against cancer, but in a Baltimore church, when she was twelve. Nothing would snatch her out of the hand of her Savior. There would be no sting in her death, only an incomprehensible sorrow and gaping hole in the hearts of those who mourned her. Whether the cancer claimed her life or not, the battle had already been won. Hannah was victorious. Jesus was victorious. Healing had already taken place, spiritually if not physically.

A grave understanding that God was God washed over Chris. In that moment, he knew that regardless of his begging and convincing, whether or not they did chemo, even if they tried every experimental drug on the market, it wasn't going to change the outcome.

The love of his life, the mother of his children, his lover, best friend, companion and helpmate, was dying. Tears came like a flood. His back shook.

For the first time, he let himself consider the possibility that God would not heal Hannah this side of heaven. Like scales being taken from his eyes, he realized that everyone died at some point. She would not live forever, nor would he. Fifty-four was decades away from the age he had thought either of them would pass away at, but he knew that even if she lived to be one hundred, it would never get any easier to say goodbye. She would be as much a part of him then as she was now, maybe more so.

She had lived a good life. She had lived a full life. She had loved and been loved. They had shared a romance that had spanned three decades. And she was saved. She had lived life abundantly. Even if she was never physically healed, he was confident that she would not taste death, but live for all eternity with the One she loved even more than him – the One who offered eternal life.

His head sunk down until his forehead rested against the old dusty steering wheel, and in the solitude of the barn, he came to terms with the fact that his wife was dying. His tears fell as fast as rain from the sky. She was his everything, and he had to find a way to let her go.

As sorrow and grief overwhelmed him, he cried out to God for help to make it down the road that lay before them, for strength for his kids, for courage for his wife, and for peace for his heart. He cried out for help, hurting and weak, broken and incapable of facing the coming storm alone.

With the situation in perspective, he knew he needed to make a change. He needed to switch his focus from pushing, planning, and making a way for the years ahead, to enjoying each and every day they had together. Hannah was not gone yet. He had her for today. Suddenly, he was filled with the understanding that he needed to rejoice in each day he had left with his wife. He needed to count each day as a gift from God and enjoy it as such. Determined to choose that path rather than grieving over the years they wouldn't have, he began to make a plan.

Two hours later, as he made his way back to the house, he knew two things to be true. Hannah was dying. Short of a miracle, which the LORD had never said wouldn't come, she was dying. While he would cling to the hope that the LORD would intervene, he would be practical and take the appropriate measures so that if the LORD didn't choose to heal her, he wouldn't be caught unprepared. Lastly, he would never tell Hannah about what had happened in the barn. Knowing she was dying was one thing. Telling her that he knew she was, was something altogether different.

~~~~~

Hannah was just pulling her first sheet of cookies out of the oven when she heard the front door open and close. It was a few minutes later when Chris came into the kitchen, a grin on his face as he sniffed the air. She held out a cookie with a laugh, and his eyes brightened. "I thought so! I can smell your monster cookies a mile away!"

"Did you get your project done?" she asked as she turned to finish transferring the cookies from the baking sheet onto a cooling rack.

"Yes," he said quietly. His response made her glance back at him, and she saw a peace in his face that hadn't been there before; a peace and a sadness. In that moment, she knew the projects he spoke of weren't physical. He had been in the barn. She smiled at him sadly, grateful that he had found peace, not brave enough to ask what had caused it. "I might take a few more of those cookies and go into the office for a couple hours," he told her, coming up behind her and laying his hand on her shoulder. "Is that okay?"

"That's fine," she agreed quickly. He had already missed so much because of her sickness. She was secure enough to know that he didn't mind, but she wanted his life to get back to normal as quickly as possible.

Over the past weeks, they often talked about how thankful they were that their residual income was more than enough to sustain them, but she knew that Chris missed his work as a realtor. She knew that he missed keeping a finger on the markets, as well as the going-ons of the town and church. He was a man who was deeply involved in his community, and to be yanked away from it so quickly and thoroughly, and immersed into the world of doctors, hospitals, and sickness, must have been difficult. She was thankful they were home again.

Chris snatched three more cookies from the cooling rack. "Don't make plans with anyone tonight, alright? And don't worry about making anything for dinner. You have a date."

Hannah glanced over at him, surprised. "I do?"

His grin accompanied his nod. He planted a lingering kiss on her lips, then turned, his cookies still in his hand. "I'll be home by six."

"Okay," she answered, feeling a schoolgirl excitement. They had been careful to maintain a weekly date night during the years their kids were home, but those nights had become less and less frequent as they navigated the years of being empty nesters. It seemed more important to be intentional about having dates when there were so many in the house, but now that it was just the two of them most of the time, they tended to forget.

Chris paused at the archway to the rest of the house. "I can't wait to spend tonight with you," he told her.

Her smile was bright and quick. "Likewise."

After Chris left, Hannah filled her pans with cookie dough and put them back in the oven. She had made a double batch, and it took awhile to get all of the cookies through the oven. When they had cooled, she put them in airtight containers so they wouldn't lose their softness. After she was done, she cleaned up her mess and put the kitchen back in order.

Feeling tired and seeing that she still had two hours until Chris came home, she climbed the stairs to her bedroom slowly, dragged a blanket off one of the wingchairs in the corner, and lay down, covering up with it. She set her alarm for five and closed her eyes. Her strength had slowly been returning since finishing chemo, but was not anywhere close to what it had been before her surgery.

When her alarm went off an hour later, Hannah forced herself to wake up. She felt tired and slightly confused. If it were up to her, she would have been perfectly happy to sleep for another hour or two. Yet, if Chris was going to the effort of planning a date for them, she could put forth the effort to look good for it. She took a shower, pulled her wig over the short stubble of her hair, applied her makeup, and then slipped into a blouse that she hadn't fit into in years, before pulling on a pair of jeans that Chris had once called her 'hot mama jeans.' Losing weight did have its advantages. She didn't know what he had planned, but she thought that whether they were staying in or going out, her outfit would be appropriate.

She was just fastening a necklace around her neck, when she heard Chris call for her downstairs. Stepping into her shoes on the way, she hurried out of her room and down the stairs. He was waiting for her at the base of the open staircase, and let out a whistle. "Look at you, Pretty Lady!" he said, his eyes shining.

Hannah couldn't help a grin, and twirled when he motioned for her to do so. He pulled her into his arms and kissed her firmly, then grinned impishly. "I've missed those jeans."

She laughed and pushed him back. "You promised me a date!"

"And a date you shall have," he told her, still grinning. He held out her jacket and helped her into it. Then, taking her hand, he led her farther into the house instead of out to the garage as she expected. He took her through the dark kitchen and out the sliding glass door. Seeing what he had done, her breath caught.

"Chris, it's beautiful!" she breathed. He had transformed their backyard into a thing of beauty. White lights were strung in the trees on the edge of the yard, as well as on the free-standing wood veranda that covered their patio furniture and barbeque grill. He had lit a fire in the outdoor fire pit, and it was burning brightly. He had pulled one of the wicker sofas close to the fire pit and had a blanket draped across the back of it. On the patio table was a bouquet of red roses positioned between two tall candles, which flickered in the darkness. The table was set with china, and a tossed salad sat on top of the dinner plates, with a long breadstick on the side. She caught the aroma of something heavenly, and she looked up at him, excited and surprised. "Did you get food from Bel Piatoo?"

He grinned. "Maybe."

Hannah's mouth watered at the thought of it. For Glendale being such a small town, their Italian restaurant was fantastic. It had been opened almost three decades ago by first-generation Italian immigrants, and could compete with any Italian kitchen in the city. It was one of Glendale's pride and joys.

Hannah shot a sideways glance at Chris as he led her to the table by her arm. Could he have...? Surely he hadn't gotten it... "Did you get the tiramisu?" she blurted, unable to keep the question at bay. It was a dessert she not only liked, but truly loved. She had been forced to go off it cold turkey a decade earlier when the authentic dish was single-handedly responsible for a ten pound increase on the scale. She had not enjoyed a bite of it since, knowing that it was like quicksand for her, but she had dreamed of it often.

He grinned as he pulled her chair out for her. "You'll have to wait and see." He sat down across from her, and they ate their salad while he filled her in on what had gone on at his office over the past few days. He told her which houses had sold, which houses had been listed, and discussed one in particular that he thought would make a great investment property.

He made no mention of purchasing it, though, which surprised her. She knew how he enjoyed buying up houses, remodeling them, then selling the properties for a hefty profit. At first, it had been a way to make money for their family. Now, it fell somewhere between an occupation and a hobby.

"Do you want to buy it?" she asked as he cleared away their salad plates.

"No," he answered simply as he opened the lid of the barbeque and took out two plates. Hers was full of chicken alfredo, his steak linguini in pesto sauce. He set hers in front of her, refilled her wine glass with sparkling grape juice, and took his seat again. He handed her the bread basket, and she took another breadstick.

As they started on their main course, she watched him. "Why not?" she finally asked.

"I'm not in the market right now," he answered casually.

She considered his answer as she enjoyed another bite of pasta. "I think you should buy it."

He shook his head. "There will be other houses."

"Why don't you want this one? Do we not have the money?" she questioned.

Chris sent her an amused smile and patted her hand. "We have enough, Love. It just isn't good timing."

Hannah let that settle. It wasn't good timing because of her – because of her sickness – she knew that was what he meant. But she wasn't going to let him put his life on hold. "I want you to buy it," she said firmly. He considered her across the table, and she could see a protest building. "We have a lot of extra expenses with all of my medical bills. Having the profit from flipping this house would be helpful."

"That money wouldn't come in for months."

"But it would come in," she reasoned.

He sat back in his chair and studied her. "You really want me to buy the house? Sight unseen? You haven't even looked at it. How do you know it would be a good investment?"

"Because you said it would be," she told him simply. "And I trust you."

"I'll need your help coming up with design ideas."

"I'm up for it," she answered. "I could use a project...something else to focus on."

He swirled his grape juice around in his wine glass, then took a drink before setting it down and looking up at her. "Alright, we'll go look at it tomorrow, and if we like it, we'll put in an offer."

She smiled, satisfied. Having won, she changed the subject. "This pasta is absolutely wonderful!"

"They sure haven't lost their touch," Chris agreed.

"Can I try yours?" she asked with a sweet smile. He grinned and handed her his fork wrapped with pasta with a piece of steak on the end. Pleased, she took the bite he offered, spun him some of her fettuccini, skewered a piece of chicken and returned his fork. "Wow, that really is good," she told him after she swallowed.

"Good enough to make you order something other than the alfredo next time?" he teased. She made a face at him, both of them already knowing the answer. If she hadn't ordered anything different in over a decade, why would she change now?

The rest of their meal passed in pleasant conversation, and when Chris' plate was clean and Hannah had eaten her fill, he came around to pull her chair out for her. He helped her to her feet and led her to the wicker sofa. He sat down first and pulled her down beside him, urging her to put her feet up. Then, he flipped the blanket over her and tucked it in around her shoulders. "Warm enough?" he asked.

She nodded, her face glowing in the firelight, her blue eyes reflecting the light of the dancing flames. Her smile was big and happy and she felt romanced and loved.

Their backyard was always a place of beauty, but the lights made it feel new and romantic. The fire pit was stylish and chased away the slight chill. The fact that they were enjoying a night outdoors in January made it feel special and rare. Hannah relaxed against her husband's side, wishing she could pause time and enjoy the moment for much longer than it would last.

"Would you rather travel by boat or by plane?" Chris asked, interrupting her thoughts.

She laughed. They hadn't played the simple game since college, when Chris had been pulling out all his tricks to get to know her. "It depends on if we were traveling for leisure or to get somewhere," she told him.

He shook his head, grinning. "There are no stipulations in this game."

"By plane then, because you get to your destination faster."

"Would you rather swing or go down a slide?"

She laughed again at his light-hearted question. "Swing. But you would rather go down a slide, wouldn't you? It's more adventurous. Swinging is too predictable for you," she told him, weaving her fingers between his.

"You know me well," he capitulated. "Alright, would

you rather read by lamplight or by firelight?"

"I'm too old to read by firelight," she told him. "I think I would need reading glasses to attempt that."

He chuckled. "Agreed. You know, this game was a lot easier before we spent thirty-four years together. It's hard to think up questions that I don't already know your answer to."

"Oh, you think you know me so well?" she questioned, her eyes laughing.

He looked down into her face, his eyes locked on hers, his mood changing slightly. "Not nearly as much as I want to," he told her quietly, then slowly lowered his lips to hers and kissed her softly.

She caught her breath like a schoolgirl, and pressed her hand to butterflies that sprang up in her belly. His kiss was soft and restrained, and even after he pulled back, she could feel the warmth of it spreading through her. She stared up at him adoringly, full of wonder that even after all their years of marriage, he could still make a kiss feel new and exciting.

"Would you rather go to Hawaii or Europe?" he asked.

She contemplated that one for awhile before answering. She had never been to either, although she had always wanted to go. She glanced around the backyard, and snuggled a little deeper into her blanket. The unusually warm day made her anxious for more sunshine. "A beach sounds really nice right now," she answered. "So, I'm going to go with Hawaii."

He laughed. "You're going to stake your entire answer on what sounds good right now?"

"Yes," she told him, smiling. "You choose Hawaii, too, right?" She was the one who wanted to go to Europe. He had never been overly interested. Hawaii was the place they had always dreamed of going together.

"Definitely."

Acting like college kids again, their game went on as

they asked each other questions, some of which they didn't know the answer to prior to asking, most of which they did. Finally, Chris reached down and tweaked her nose. She batted his hand away. "Last question," he said.

She smiled up at him expectantly. "Okay. Shoot."

"Would you rather kiss me or have a piece of tiramisu?" His eyes sparkled at her, and she knew what he expected her to say. Instead, she reached up and pressed her lips against his. She could tell she had surprised him, but after the initial surprise, he responded, catching her up against him and holding her close, deepening the kiss.

"I choose this any day," she murmured, drawing back just a little. He followed her back into her space and kissed her again, his kiss lingering. His fingers splayed out across her back, pressing her tighter against his chest, and she reached up and ran her fingers through his hair. Warmth spread from her lips through her entire body, setting her on fire. She felt like she was twenty again, and it was the first time Chris had ever held her. His hands on her back were big and strong, and his lips were exploratory.

She pulled back, breathless, feeling things she hadn't felt in what seemed like years. He watched her, his eyes almost caressing her face. She wondered if he knew the fire he had started within her with his first kiss of the evening.

Grinning, he disentangled himself and stood. She started to protest, but bit her tongue, not wanting to ruin his plans for the evening. She waited while he jogged back to the house and came back a moment later with two cups of steaming coffee. He handed one to her, and she wrapped her hands around the china cup, enjoying its warmth. Going to the barbeque, he took a paper sack that sat behind it, and put it up on the table. Reaching in, he pulled out two disposable containers. Opening one and tearing the lid off, he handed it to her, his face stretched in a grin.

She couldn't hide her delight to see the dessert she had denied herself of for years. Wearing a top that had been pushed to the recesses of her closet for more than a decade because it didn't fit, while it now hung loose, she didn't feel the least amount of guilt for eating the treat her husband had brought her. Her mouth watered, and she broke off the corner and ate it while she waited for Chris to sit down with his own coffee and dessert, unable to wait any longer for a taste.

When Chris was settled, he watched in amusement as she took her first full bite, savoring the flavors. "There is truly nothing like this," she told him, pointing at the dessert with her fork. "Thank you for getting it." She paused. "And for dinner, and for the lights, and for the date."

He leaned over and pressed his lips against hers briefly. "Thank you for going on this date with me. I'm remembering all over again why I fell in love with you."

She smiled up into his face, soaking in his words, the sound of his voice, the love she saw shining in his eyes. He planted a soft kiss on her forehead and settled into the cushions before taking a sip of coffee. She followed suit, and they finished their dessert in warm silence. When they were done, Hannah took their cups and empty containers to the patio table where she added them to the other dirty dishes. When she turned back around, Chris had stretched out on his side on the sofa, and he held the blanket out, beckoning for her to join him. She did, stretching out beside him, fitting in against his body, her face toward the warm fire.

She watched the flames jumping upward toward the velvety dark sky, and followed them up until she became distracted by the glory of the stars in the heavens. They were so small and far away, yet they shone so brightly. There seemed to be thousands of them, sprinkled across the vastness of the night sky, and something in the pit of her stomach stirred. It wasn't fear so much as an uncomfortable knowing accompanied by wonder. Somewhere out there was heaven. A place she would soon go.

Chris' warm lips pressed against the curve of her neck,

bringing her back from her thoughts. She snuggled back against him, enjoying his warmth. She might be fatally ill, but tonight she was wrapped in the loving arms of her husband, her stomach was comfortably full, the fire was warming her face, the taste of her favorite dessert was still on her tongue, she could smell Chris' cologne, and she could see his expression of love all around them from the pretty lights to the table set with china. Life was good.

"Why haven't we done this before?" she asked, that being her one regret of the night. Why had they waited thirty-four years to discover how wonderful a night in their backyard could be?

"I have been wondering the same thing," Chris admitted. After a short silence, he asked, "Have you had a good time tonight?" She could hear the smile in his voice. It was one of those questions he asked, even though he already knew the answer.

"Yes," she answered, her voice full of emotion. Turning slightly, so that she could see his face, she met his eyes. "Thank you. Thank you for tonight." Reaching up, she tugged his head down until she could reach his lips. When he pulled back, his grin was mischievous.

"Thank you for wearing these jeans," he told her, tugging lightly on her belt loop. She laughed, and curled her hand in the front of his shirt, pulling him back down for another kiss, then another and another, taking joy in fanning the flame they had started in one another over three decades earlier that, even after five children, ten grandchildren, an ugly bout with cancer, and a myriad of heartache and joy throughout the years, had never gone out.

~~~~~

Hannah walked quietly alongside Chris as they made their way through the foreclosed house. The floor plan was nice, as was the location right on the edge of town. The dining area had French doors that opened out to a backyard that faded into the forest. The house was new enough, having been built less than a decade before, but the previous owners had done a number on it, no doubt incensed over being foreclosed on. It was a shame. Hannah knew the couple and wouldn't have thought them capable of the damage that had been done; then again, she had never experienced the frustration or heartbreak of losing her home.

"You would need new drywall, new cupboards, and new appliances," she observed.

"The floors would need to be redone," he continued. "Or maybe you could buff these scratches out of the hardwood. Then they would only need to be refinished and the carpet replaced."

"It looks like there's some electrical work to be done," Hannah added, carefully holding up a wire that had been snipped. Chris nodded.

"You still think it's something we should buy?" he asked, smiling wryly. They had been through the entire house now, and there was not one room that wouldn't need repairs.

Hannah thought about his question as she turned in a full circle, looking around the open dining room, living room and kitchen area. "The roof is good, the floor plan has a nice, open concept, nothing structural would need to be done, and it has a great location. The problems are mostly cosmetic, and it would be a great house when you were finished with it. It's a nice size, and has a good feel to it."

Chris nodded slowly. "That's all true enough. What changes would you make?"

"Besides drywall, carpet and paint?" He grinned. "I would finish the walkout basement by putting in two more bedrooms, a laundry room and a great room with a small minibar on the southeast wall. Then, up here I would take out the wall between the laundry room and the master suite, using half of the added space to enlarge the master closet and the other half to enlarge the master bathroom. That would give room to add a freestanding tile shower to the master bath, and you could take out the preexisting shower unit and replace it with a Jacuzzi tub. Then, come in here and rework the kitchen, adding an island here for extra counter space and move the stove top over to it, giving you room for double ovens there, with a nice hood over the island to add separation between the kitchen and dining room. With new countertops, a new backsplash and the new arrangement, it would look a lot better."

"That would take a lot of money," Chris said, rubbing the back of his neck.

"You know kitchens and master suites sell a house, Hon," she reminded, knowing she was right. "Then, out here," she started, opening the French doors, "I think you should add on a big covered porch with thirty inch high stone walls to serve as railings. If it's a long, rustic concept, it will go with the log and stone exterior and play up the charm of the location right here along the edge of the trees." She glanced back at her husband, hoping he could envision the picture she was painting. "It would be a lovely place to drink tea."

"A covered porch?" Chris questioned, crossing his arms and setting his chin in one hand. She nodded. "That would be a huge extra expense."

She shoved him gently. "Stop focusing on that. You bring me with you to dream like this because you know I have good ideas, and they always increase the value of the house in the end."

He rubbed his chin and didn't respond, but turned back toward the house. "How wide do you think the island should be? How long?"

They went through the house again, talking about specific plans, and Chris jotted down notes. Hannah knew he would take his notes home where he would sit down and work out exactly how much the improvements to the house would cost, then think through how much a house like that could be listed for. He would then compare those numbers with the current asking price and the profit he would like to make on the property, and put together an offer to submit to the bank.

When they were done at the house, they drove over to Justin and Kara's, arriving at six, just as Kara had requested. Hannah couldn't keep herself from gushing over Kara's swollen abdomen that seemed bigger than it had even the last time she saw her, and Kara showed her a few things she had picked up for the baby since Hannah had been there last. They stood in the nursery and dreamed about how to decorate it, talking about different ideas until the oven timer went off in the kitchen.

Hannah joined the men at the table, while Kara carried in a baking dish full of chicken enchiladas. After setting it in the middle of the table, Justin led them in saying grace, and they ate. When they were finished, Justin and Chris cleared the table, insisting that both women stayed seated. When the leftovers were put away and the dishwasher loaded, they came back to the table with a deck of cards and bowls of brownies and ice cream.

When the grandfather clock in the living room struck ten o'clock, Chris nodded to Hannah and they stood. No matter how bright-eyed and bushy-tailed the couple looked now, both Justin and Kara had to work in the morning, and especially Kara needed her rest. Justin and Kara walked them to the door.

"You'll come over again this weekend?" Kara questioned. "We can pick colors for the nursery, then the guys can paint."

Hannah looked to Chris, and he nodded. "Sure. We can do that. I don't think we have anything planned."

"Good!" Kara said, looking happy. Justin stepped forward to shake Chris' hand and Kara reached out and gave Hannah a long hug. When she pulled back, Hannah saw the tears in her daughter's eyes. Kara tried to blink them away, but Hannah had already noticed. She didn't say anything, but squeezed her daughter's hand, patted her baby bump affectionately, embraced Justin and walked out to the truck holding Chris' hand.

Hannah was thankful for the cover of darkness as they drove home that kept Chris from seeing the tears that rolled down her cheeks. For all the joy and laughter the evening had held, she knew the reason her daughter was so eager to have them come over every couple of days was because she knew a goodbye was coming. A goodbye that neither mother nor daughter was ready for.

Sixteen

That weekend the nursery was painted a pale lavender. Hannah and Kara spent the better part of the following weekend stenciling a gigantic tree on the wall where the crib would go, which they painted a darker purple the following week. They used purple, teal and brown as accent colors throughout the room from the teal of the lamp that sat on the espresso-colored dresser to the purple fabric-covered lamp-shade. Dark brown picture frames were hung in a collection on the western wall, waiting for pictures of baby.

January flew by.

In February, the elders of their church came to Chris and Hannah's house and prayed over Hannah, anointing her head with oil, and calling upon the mercy of God, asking for healing. She talked to each of her kids on the phone count-less times every week, as well as her mom, Jessi and Carla. Kaitlynn filled her in on how training for the marathon was going, Kim relayed all the news of the boys, and Joe talked about flying back to see her. During each phone call, her kids urged her to reconsider her decision not to seek further treatment. She reminded them all that Dr. Hedgins did not think it would do any good, and reiterated that she wanted to be home and as healthy as she could be, rather than lying in a hospital bed, sick.

Every morning, the first thing Chris said when she opened her eyes and saw him was, "I can't wait to spend this day with you." Every morning his words were like a blanket of love that he wrapped snugly around her. She kept them with her for the rest of the day, drawing them close around her when sadness crept in, when she had episodes of intense pain, or when little moments of fear came. She spent increasing time in the Word and simply sitting with the LORD.

The increase in her intentional time with Him was not the scurrying of a woman who knew the end was coming and was afraid, but instead, the peaceful realization that she wanted to be very intentional about living and loving well during the next several months, and knew that she needed God-given wisdom and understanding to do so. She felt no fear when she looked ahead, but felt sorrow at the end of each day as another twenty-four hours slipped away from her – twenty-four hours that she would never get back.

Now, she found herself sitting on the floor in the living room in a patch of winter sunshine that was filtering in through the window, soaking in its warmth. An episode of great pain had just ended, with the aide of prescription pain medicine, and now she sat very still, exhausted from the episode and relieved that it was over. She heard a text message come through and reached for her phone. It was a text from Chris saying that he was taking her on a date and to be ready by five. She smiled, instantly feeling excited for the night ahead, and was tapping out a reply when her phone started ringing. The face of a woman she loved dearly filled her screen.

"Hi Jari!" she answered brightly. Jari Cordel, who was Jessi's stepmother and married to Carla's ex-husband Bill, had become one of Hannah's dear friends in the years since Joe and Jessi were married. They had met during the year leading up to Joe and Jessica's wedding and instantly connected, finding common ground in their love for Joe, Jessi and the girls, their common faith, and their tender hearts. When Hannah needed encouragement, someone to cry with, or someone who would understand her, she called Jari.

Their friendship had been a gift over the years, as Hannah felt so connected to the younger woman emotionally and spiritually, yet Jari was removed enough from her life that she could see Hannah's issues within the church, the community or her family with a fresh perspective. Hannah knew the feeling was mutual when Jari asked her to mentor her just a few months after meeting. Jari had needed a friend who was also motherly, and Hannah pulled her right into her inner circle. Jari wasn't the kind of peer friend that Carla was, but almost more like a beloved younger sister.

Over the past several years, Hannah had walked with Jari through both heartbreak and joy in the younger woman's life. From wanting children, a miscarriage, finding reconciliation with her parents, the birth of her first son, the wedding of her divorced parents, another miscarriage and the birth of her second son, Jari's last several years had been full of ups and downs. Most recently, Jari's time had been consumed by the hectic campaign trail Bill had embarked upon as his sights were set on the White House. The election wasn't for almost two years, but already they were traveling, raising support and thinking about primaries.

At Jari's bright greeting, and as she launched into sharing a verse she felt the LORD had just given her for Hannah, Hannah lay down in the sunshine, curled on her side, thankful beyond words that Jari had called. It was just the encouragement she needed, just the perfect reminder that there was still a plan for her life, that God had not forgotten her and not all hope was lost. Tears filled Hannah's eyes, and she wiped them away, glad that they were tears of joy and encouragement rather than sadness this time.

When the phone call ended an hour later after promises to talk again soon, Hannah released a deep breath and repositioned to follow the moving sunlight. "My eye has not seen, my ear has not heard, nor has my mind conceived the things God has prepared for me," she whispered into the stillness of her empty living room. "There is a time for everything, a season for every activity under heaven. Teach me, God, to number my days, that I might gain a heart of wisdom. Help me to be wise and intentional with the days I have here on earth, that I leave nothing undone, nor that I would believe that my work here is done until it truly is. Remind me that You have a plan for my life, and that You have a plan for this world that I am merely a small part of. I want to bring You glory until the last of my breaths. You are worthy of the highest praise, the greatest sacrifice, the most extravagant love."

Speaking and praying the words aloud encouraged her heart, knowing they were true and right. The One she spoke to was not far off, but in the living room with her, rejoicing over her as she proclaimed truth. She laid on the floor, smiling up at the unseen God who she was sure was smiling back at her. In a moment of simple revelation, she realized that therein lay the reason that only sadness and longing filled her in the moments she remembered her days on the earth were numbered, and not fear. She was confident that she was the beloved of the King of Kings, and His thoughts toward her were not disapproving, but instead, He rejoiced over her with joy and gladness.

Whatever was coming, it would not, could not snatch her out of His hands. She would be safe and loved, whole and healthy, hidden away under the shadow of His wings. She fell asleep in the warm patch of Sonlight.

When Hannah woke, there was no more sunshine streaming through the windows. Sitting up, confused, she glanced out the window and saw that the sun was low over the bare trees. The memory of Chris' text hit her, and she grabbed her phone to check the time. It was ten past four, and she was supposed to be ready for their date in fifty minutes. Standing up, she took a moment to let the dizziness pass, then hurried upstairs to take a shower. She was just finishing fixing the hair of her wig when Chris walked purposefully into their bedroom.

"Hi, Honey!" she said happily.

He stepped close and kissed her cheek. "Hi! Are you ready to go?"

"Where are we going?" she asked, her eyes sparkling. As she prepared for their date, her anticipation had steadily grown. After their backyard escape, pizza and a movie at the theatre, sledding and hot cocoa after a January snowstorm, a cold picnic out on the lake in a canoe, and a number of other sweetly unforgettable dates, she couldn't wait to see what he had planned.

"You'll have to wait and see," he told her. He looked like he knew some great secret, and she studied him suspiciously. "Are you ready?" he asked again.

Feeling his rush, she stepped into her shoes and grabbed her purse. "Ready."

He took her hand and hurried her down the steps and out to the garage, where the garage door was up, and the truck was running. "Why the rush?" she asked as he opened her door for her.

He didn't answer until he was seated and backing down the drive. "You'll see."

She shot him another suspicious look and noticed how his face was nearly glowing. Whatever he had planned, she could tell he thought it was pretty amazing and that she was going to love it. That knowledge made her smile. She loved his confidence, and even his smugness. She loved that he knew her well and wasn't shy about it. "How come I get all these great surprise dates?" she questioned.

"Because you're a great date," he answered.

His cheesy answer drew a smile, but failed to give her any kind of a clue as to where they were going. She contemplated different things she thought they could be doing on the short drive to town. Once they pulled into town, his pace slowed until it almost felt like he was stalling. With as big of a rush as he had been in to leave the house, now she couldn't make any sense out of the slow pace.

He stopped to fuel up the truck, then convinced her to go in with him to see if she wanted any snacks. They finally decided on a candy bar and some cheese crackers. Tucking them away in his pocket, he told her they would be for later. Then he gave her a choice between the two fast-food joints in town, and they went through the drive-thru, which took a ridiculously long time because Chris couldn't decide what he wanted.

Finally, they had their sack of food, and Chris announced that he needed to stop by the office to pick up a few things he had forgotten. He disappeared inside, and Hannah was left in the truck by herself, puzzled by his behavior. It was now almost six, and they had gotten nowhere. She munched on a few fries, engrossed in trying to figure out what was going on. A rap on her window startled her.

Seeing Kara's beaming face, she opened the door quickly. "I saw Daddy's truck, so I thought I would stop and see what you guys are up to tonight," Kara said, leaning into the warm interior of the truck to give Hannah a hug. The movement was awkward, as her baby bump was growing. She had less than two months to go until she delivered.

"I wish I knew what to tell you! I don't have a clue what we're doing. Your Dad said he was taking me on a date, but so far we've been to the gas station, picked up a hamburger and now are here."

"Fun date," Kara laughed.

Hannah shrugged. "It's been a fine evening, I guess I just expected...something more eventful."

"Like in weeks past?" Kara asked, referring to Chris' impressive date record over the past couple of months.

"Yes, something more like that."

"Well, you know Daddy. He can have a lot up his sleeve."

Hannah caught the merry twinkle in Kara's eyes. "Do you know what he has planned?" she asked, surprised.

Kara held up her hands with a grin. "I came to town to get groceries! Oh look, here's Daddy now! Have fun on your date! Love you!" Kara gave Hannah another hug and stepped back to shut the door before Hannah could respond.

Chris jumped in the driver's seat, waved to Kara and put the truck in reverse.

"Sorry to keep you waiting, Love," was the only explanation he offered.

"Odd that Kara happened to drive by," Hannah observed.

"Yeah, but Glendale is a small town. Oh, Hon, you didn't eat yet? You should before it gets cold."

She studied his face out of squinted eyes. He was acting funny. "What's going on?" she asked.

He grinned. "You'll find out," he told her. When she realized they had left town and were headed away from home, she asked again, only to get the same answer. Finally, she accepted the fact that she wasn't going to know until they arrived at their destination. She fell quiet as she ate her hamburger and fries. Chris ate his too, and they chatted about their day, Hannah's conversation with Jari, and Chris running into Chuck Perry, whom Chris hadn't seen since Chuck moved to Phoenix five years ago.

They drove for over an hour, and when Chris took the airport exit off the interstate, Hannah glanced at him in surprise. "Are we going to the airport?"

"It would seem that way," he answered with a grin. He didn't tell her anything else, no matter how many times she asked, but that was okay – she was fairly certain she had the surprise figured out. Joe and Jessi and the kids must be waiting for them at the airport. Her heart soared. However, when Chris pulled into the long-term parking, she realized they were actually flying somewhere rather than picking someone up.

"I didn't bring anything with me!" she protested as he opened her door for her. She followed him as he went to the back of the truck and lifted two big suitcases over the tailgate, beaming. Her mouth fell open, surprised. "Where did those come from?"

"Come on," he told her, as he locked the truck and

started walking. She hurried to follow him. "Chris, you can't possibly have what I need in there, because everything was in its place when I was getting ready. I know you're a man, so you may not understand this, but I can't just go without or get replacements of all my cosmetics wherever we're going," she rattled on.

He stopped and looked over at her, his face still stretched in a grin. "Hannah, I have everything you need. Stop worrying and enjoy the suspense."

Shutting her mouth abruptly to keep any other protests at bay, she followed him to the shuttle stop and waited as he maneuvered both suitcases onto the shuttle, then reached back to help her up the stairs. They took their seats, and the shuttle took off for the main terminal of the airport. The realization sinking in that their bags were packed, they were at the airport and they were about to fly somewhere, Hannah turned shining eyes toward Chris. "Where are we going?"

"Guess," he told her smugly.

"Minnesota," she answered confidently. They had talked often about going out to see Joe, Jessi and the kids. She was glad they were finally going to do it.

He made a sound like a buzzer. "Wrong."

Her brows drew together, perplexed. She had felt confident they were flying to Minnesota. A second option entered her mind. "Baltimore?" It would make sense that he was taking her home to see her family.

"Guess again."

"DC?" It was a long shot, but it was the only other destination she could think of. Chris knew how much she enjoyed Carla and Jari. Perhaps they were going to see them. Was that why Jari had thought to call? Because she knew they were coming?

"Three strikes and you're out," he said, looking quite pleased with himself.

She narrowed her eyes at him, trying to figure out the surprise. "Fine. Give me a hint." He didn't respond. "Come on, Chris!" she urged.

He grinned as the shuttle pulled up at the departure door. When the suitcases were on the ground, and she was standing beside him once again, he asked, "Would you rather go to Europe or Hawaii?"

Her mouth fell open as understanding dawned on her. "Are you serious?" Chris just grinned, his eyes never leaving her face. "Are you serious?" she cried again, excitement shooting through her like lightening. He nodded, and despite her cancer, despite her ever weakening state and the pain that never completely went away, she bounced to him like a little girl. She threw her arms around his neck, jumping up and down as she shrieked in delight.

He laughed and drew back enough to press a kiss against her lips. "Are you excited? Was this a good surprise?" he asked, grinning.

"Yes!" she told him emphatically, smiling so big that her cheeks hurt.

"Good! Then let's check in and get through security. We fly out in an hour and a half."

"How did you plan this?" she asked incredulously as she followed him through the automatic door toward the ticketing counter. "How did you get our bags packed without me noticing?"

"I had help," he told her, still beaming.

"Kara! That little tease! She knew all along, didn't she? I knew she didn't stop by accidentally! Your office isn't even on her way to the grocery store! Did she rush in and pack our bags after we left, then bring them to you at the office? That's why you were dinking around so much, isn't it? That's why you've been spending so much time at the office this week, making sure you have everything squared away on this house deal, isn't it? Because we're going to be out of town for awhile!"

Chris laughed. "Alright, Detective. Since you have everything all figured out, pause for a few minutes while we check in, will ya?"

"Okay," she agreed, grinning from ear to ear. He turned toward the ticketing counter, then paused and turned back toward her for a brief moment.

"I can't wait to spend the next two weeks with you in Hawaii." She heard the excitement in his voice and smiled.

"Neither can I, Love!" While she stayed at the entrance to the line, and he went on ahead to check their luggage, all she could think about was the fact that he had said 'two weeks.' They were going to Hawaii for two weeks!

She wanted to jump up and down, but the reality was that her body was not at full strength. Already, she could feel herself tiring from the walk to the shuttle, her episode of energy outside and now standing and waiting for Chris. There was still security to get through and the walk through the airport to their plane. Choosing to be wise, Hannah looked around until she spotted some chairs, then walked over and sat down. She saw Chris look back for her, and she waved her hand to get his attention. Seeing her, he nodded and smiled. When he had checked their luggage, he came to join her, and she stood and met him halfway. She may have taken a moment to rest, but it had not calmed her excitement in any way. She chattered like a magpie all the way through security and to their gate.

While they waited for their plane, Chris showed her the website for the resort they were staying at on the Hawaiian island of Maui. From the pictures, it looked breathtakingly beautiful, but the next day when they stepped out of the shuttle and saw it with their own eyes, Hannah could barely breathe for a moment.

The resort itself was gorgeous, but through its open doors she could see the serenity pool, the beach and the ocean, a sight even more beautiful. As soon as they had checked in and settled their things in their ocean-front room, they changed into clothes better suited for the beach, and headed downstairs.

"Look at that view!" she exclaimed as soon as they stepped outside into the Hawaiian sunshine.

They passed the serenity pool, where Hannah knew she would be spending a lot of time during the next two weeks, and walked down the few stairs to the beach. Golden sand spilled over the landscape until it met with the greenish -blue water, which rolled in over it in white-fringed waves. What the shuttle driver identified as the trade winds were blowing, and Hannah wrapped her arms around herself, tilting her face up toward the sun, breathing deeply of the salt-tinged air mixed with the fragrance of flowers.

When she opened her eyes, she realized that Chris was watching her. He smiled, but the warmth didn't reach his eyes. "What is it?" she asked, frowning slightly. They were standing on a beach in Maui. What could possibly be wrong?

He shook his head. "Nothing. I just keep wondering why I waited so long to do this."

Understanding, Hannah stepped close to him and wrapped her arms around his waist. "This is perfect timing, Chris Colby. Perfect timing."

He wrapped his arms around her and held her close, both of them looking out at the breaking waves and birds that soared above the water, looking for their dinner.

Hannah had expected this moment to be full of awe and excitement, but instead, it felt sad. In the distance, they could see surfers trying to ride the waves. She knew that Hawaii was a surfer's paradise, but she was too sick to surf. It was a great place to snorkel or scuba dive, but she knew she didn't have the energy for either. She was wasting away. Every day she felt weaker, tired more quickly. Her cancer was no longer an undetectable force. She could feel it now, sapping her strength and riddling her with pain that sometimes brought tears to her eyes.

"This place is truly beautiful," she said, forcing a bright smile. "We can walk the sand beaches, swim in the pool and put our feet in the ocean," she said bravely. Enough of focusing on what she couldn't do. They were in Hawaii – what could there possibly be to feel sad about?

"That's right! And I have more planned that you don't even know about yet!" Chris told her, excitement jumping back into his voice.

The sadness faded, and joy and excitement returned. They spent the afternoon sitting on the beach, watching the waves roll in and talking about everything they wanted to do while on the island. When they grew hungry, they went upstairs to change for dinner, then went back to the beach to dine in the open-air restaurant. They sat with the sand between their toes, the island breezes ruffling their hair, and the sun on their backs. They watched the sun go down together, the sunset unlike anything they had ever seen, then turned in early, wanting to make up for the sleep they had lost the night before during their flights.

The next morning, Hannah woke up to kisses being sprinkled over her face. When she opened her eyes, she saw the beloved face of her husband. "I am so excited for today!" he told her. "I'm so excited to spend it with you."

She smiled and kissed him sleepily, then closed her eyes and dozed off and on for another half an hour. After breakfast, they spent a couple of hours at the serenity pool, going back and forth between stretching out on the lounge chairs and cooling off in the water. After lunch, they walked the beach, their sandals in hand. Chris insisted they go upstairs to take a nap after their walk, and then they attended a traditional Hawaiian luau for dinner.

The next day, they took a tour of one of the island's prized pineapple plantations. The tour guide cut pineapples directly out of the field, giving them tastes and explaining the growing process. It was a tantalizing taste of Maui's history and culture, and Hannah was thrilled with Chris' choice for the day. She talked about it all the way back to the resort, and they both agreed that the pineapples they thought they had enjoyed back home were something altogether different than the fruit they ate that day. The flavor and juiciness of a freshly-picked pineapple simply did not compare to the ones they bought off the grocery store shelves.

Their third full day on the island was another relaxing one, which they spent the majority of at the pool and the beach. It was restful, it was warm, and it was tropical. That evening, Chris ordered two Mai Tais from the poolside bar, and they tried the traditional Hawaiian drink together while watching the sun set over the ocean. It was a sight Hannah felt confident she could watch daily for the rest of her life and never tire of. Watching the sun sink into the ocean was absolutely stunning.

Over the next several days, they went on whale watching trips, took a tour to see the island's waterfalls, and took a day trip to the big island to visit the volcanoes. In between every tour day, they spent at least one day simply enjoying the resort, resting, and soaking in the sunshine.

They shared romantic dinners, played together in the surf, saw scenery that took their breath away, spent hours in conversation as they walked the beach, and laughed so hard that they cried. Regardless of the activities they couldn't do, it was the best vacation they had ever taken. They both enjoyed every moment of it, focusing on enjoying it to the fullest and making memories that would last.

On their last day on the island, Chris woke early with an overwhelming sadness filling his chest. He turned on his side and watched his wife sleep, trying to memorize every detail of her face, the subtle scent of flowers that encompassed her, the way her breathing sounded while she slept.

He was losing her. He had been trying to deny it ever since finding out about her cancer, but he couldn't hide from the terrifying fact any longer. She was slipping away from him. He could feel it. She was getting weaker every day. He knew that she knew it, too, but they didn't talk about it. He didn't know how, nor did he think he was strong enough to hear her vocalize what he saw. He had tried to keep from thinking about it during their vacation, not wanting it to taint their time together, but it had proven to be impossible. She tired easily and he was only too aware of how important it was to make sure she was getting enough rest. He found himself always on the lookout for anyone who sneezed or coughed, making sure they gave the individual a wide berth in case they were sick, instinctively knew when it was two o'clock and Hannah should take a nap, fussed over if she was getting enough to eat, and was constantly watching her face for signs of pain or weariness.

Even knowing what he did, it had been the most wonderful vacation. The scenery, the food, the fun they had, Hannah – all of it had been absolutely perfect.

But now, their vacation was over. Their last vacation together. Chris felt hot tears slipping down his face, and could feel the coldness of his wet pillow against his skin.

He had made time to take Hannah on little getaways over the years, both with their kids and just as a couple, but now, at the end of the last vacation he would ever take with his wife, he knew he hadn't taken her on nearly enough. He wanted to grasp after the years of the past, go back and re-live them over. He didn't have regrets, he simply didn't know how to accept that they were over.

Nothing had changed in the sense that he couldn't fathom living life without Hannah. He didn't know how; didn't know if he could. Yet here he was, with that reality staring him in the face.

Today, they would go on their last walk on the beach, go for their last swim in the pool, stand in the ocean together for the last time. His breath caught in his throat, and he pressed his fist against his aching heart. The pain had not subsided by the time Hannah's eyes fluttered open close to twenty minutes later.

"Good morning, Beautiful," he told her softly. "I cannot wait to spend this day with you," he finished, his voice breaking.

He had not been able to stop the tears, and he knew that she saw them, for compassion filled her sleepy eyes. Tears welled up in hers as well, and he knew that she could read his thoughts as easily as she ever had. He wanted to deny them, wanted to change the subject to something light and happy, but felt incapable of doing so. As painful as it would be, he knew they were about to have a conversation that needed to take place.

~~~~~

Hannah studied her husband's face, watching, waiting, wondering. She had been waiting for an opportunity to talk to him, but the moment had never felt right. Now, she wondered if this was it. He was quiet, watching her as well. Fear and dread filled her, knowing the words she needed to speak. Finally, she took a shaky breath, swallowed back the lump in her throat, and started.

"I'm dying, Chris." She watched as the tears poured from his eyes. She wanted him to deny it, wanted it not to be true, but she could see that he knew the truth as much as she did. Knowing that made something within her hurt. It was as if her last hope had gone out. For a moment, she didn't know how to go on. How did she have this conversation with the man she loved and had hoped to spend another forty to fifty years with?

"Thank you for bringing me here…for giving us this time together. I have so enjoyed the sunshine, the beach, the ocean, the romantic dinners, the tours and…just having this uninterrupted time with you."

"So have I," he told her, his voice strained. "I will never forget a moment of this." There was something comforting about the fact that they were finally talking openly about the reality they were facing.

"Neither will I." It was quiet for a long moment. "I'm not afraid, Chris, not of dying."

He wove his fingers between hers. "I'm glad, Love."

"I'm only sad that I'm going to miss out on so many years with you and the kids. There were so many things I thought I would get to do here on earth before going to heaven, but I know, Chris, that I'm the lucky one. What I miss out on here on earth is going to pale in comparison to what I will experience in heaven."

"That's right," he agreed, choking on his words.

"I need you to know that I'm okay," she told him, her smile pure. "And I need to know that you're going to be okay, too." He didn't answer and she could see he wasn't ready. "Are you afraid?" she asked after a moment.

"I'm afraid of living life without you," he admitted. "I'm afraid of waking up without you in the mornings and going to bed without you at night. I'm afraid of you not being a phone call away while I'm at the office, and of you not being there when I get home at night." Chris took a steadying breath, dragging his hand over his face, not able to watch how his words made her cry. They were saying goodbye, at least starting to. It was something they had both been running from and avoiding, but it needed to be done. Their time together was short, and they both knew it.

"You have been the best wife I could have ever dreamed of, Hannah. I truly did not know how blessed I was the day you married me. I thought you were the nicest, prettiest girl I had ever met, and I knew that I wanted to spend my life with you, but nothing could have prepared me for the gift God gave me that day. You have not only been the best mother I could have imagined for my kids, but you have been the kindest, most patient and loving wife I could have asked for. You have become my best friend."

"If I could go back I wouldn't do one thing differently," she told him. "Not one thing. Marrying you was the best decision of my life." Hannah's heart was breaking and she didn't know if she could bear the pain of it. "With that being said, there are a few things that I want you to do for me in the days ahead."

"What are they?" Chris asked, careful not to promise anything, afraid of the heartbreak her requests might bring.

"First of all, I will have letters for each of the kids, grandkids and you in the drawer of my nightstand. The morning of my funeral, I want you to hand them out for me. I know that will be a hard day, and I want to be able to help all of you say goodbye."

"Oh Hannah, always taking care of us," he said softly, swiping at his tears and then carefully catching hers on his fingertips and wiping them away. "You have always done such a good job of it."

She smiled and pressed a kiss against his hand that was still wet from their tears. "Secondly, I want 'Great is Thy Faithfulness' sung at the graveside service." She couldn't believe she was having this conversation.

"Done."

She covered her face for a moment before finding the courage to speak her next request, but then forced the lump in her throat down and forced the words out. "Next, I want you to move out of our house and into the one you just bought."

That drew a fierce reaction from him, just as she knew it would. "I won't move! I can't! I can't leave the home we shared together."

"That's why you have to move. You can't move on in that house, Love. I'll be everywhere," she explained sadly.

He shook his head, tears brimming in his eyes once again. "That's why I want to stay! Hannah, I don't want to move on," he told her, pressing a salty kiss against her lips. "I don't. I want to stay as close to you as I can."

"I know, but that's not healthy. You know it's not. Stay for awhile, for a few months, while you grieve, and then move. Please."

Chris shook his head. He couldn't promise her that he would. She laid her hand against his cheek. "At least remember this conversation in six months."

"In six months you'll still be here with me," he protested through watery eyes.

She shook her head sadly. "No. I don't have that long."

"Don't say that," he told her, his face crumpling.

Closing her eyes for a brief moment, she let it go and moved on. "The last thing I want you to do, and I know you don't want to hear this right now, but after time passes, I want you to move on and be happy again. And if that means another woman who is good and kind comes into your life, then I want you to embrace her wholeheartedly."

He pressed his finger against her lips. "Please stop," he begged.

But she had to go on. She had to finish. "Chris, the selfish part of me never wants you to love anyone but me, but deep down, I know that I want you to be happy. I want you to have love in your life. I don't want you living the rest of your life alone. I don't. I really don't." He shook his head. "Please, just remember this conversation down the road and know that it's okay with me if it happens," she told him. "I am releasing you now from any feelings of guilt or betrayal that you might have then. I want you to be happy, so know that."

"I can't handle any more of this," he told her. "Please stop."

She did. More would come later, but for now, they had both had all they could stand.

They laid side by side, tears running down both of their faces. Finally, Chris turned to her, and drew her close, cradling her against him. She clung to him, burying her face in his neck. Eventually their tears subsided, and the heartache ebbed into a lasting ache.

"I am going to be fine, Chris," she told him, her voice soft. "I am going to be dancing on the streets of gold, worshipping the God of glory." He studied her face and she smiled. "And you're going to be okay, too. You are. You have to be – the kids are going to need you more than ever. They're going to look to you for leadership, just as they always have. You're going to need to lead them through a time of mourning and then back out the other side into the land of joy. I'm depending on you."

He studied her a little longer and then nodded. He didn't say anything, but that was okay.

After awhile, Hannah lifted herself up on one elbow and glanced out their sliding glass doors. Looking back down at him, she propped up a brave smile. "Whatever tomorrow holds, we're in Hawaii together today! Let's enjoy every moment of our time here."

And they did. They spent the day walking the beaches, lying together in the sun, splashing in the surf, eating good food, and talking about everything and anything. Despite the painful conversation they had that morning, that day was the sweetest of their entire vacation. They had discussed the elephant in the room, had faced their future head on, and enjoyed each other even more because of it.

That night, they ate at the open-air restaurant where they had eaten the first night of their stay. Hannah's smile was bright as she sat down in her chair, dropping her sandals beside her. "I will never get tired of feeling the sand between my toes," she told Chris.

He grinned back at her. "Me neither. This beach is amazing."

After leafing through the menu, she studied him across the table. "Do you remember our wedding night?"

Chris met her eyes, his smile lazy. "How could I ever forget?"

She knew he was referring to the romance, but she was referring to something else. "Remember how we broke the bed?"

Chris' hearty laugh rang out across the beach and mixed with the sound of the ocean. "I'd forgotten about that." He had carried her across the threshold into their hotel room and dropped her playfully on the bed. They had heard the immediate crack of wood splitting, and she had rolled onto the floor as the entire bed collapsed. "How you broke the bed at a hundred and fifteen pounds, I'll never know."

"Talk about embarrassing, trying to explain that to the hotel manager," Hannah added, blushing even now. Chris chuckled.

"If I remember right, *I'm* the one that had to try to explain it. You hid in the car like a chicken." Now it was Hannah's turn to laugh.

"Very true."

"That wasn't the only bed we broke, though, remember?" he asked.

Hannah thought of the bed they had shared for their first five years of marriage. One day she had ran and jumped onto the bed in a silly attempt to wake him up on a Saturday morning. Both of the legs on his side of the bed had broken and they had both wound up on the floor, confused and disoriented. When they realized what had happened, they both laughed so hard they cried.

"No it wasn't, was it?" Hannah mused with a smile. "It seems like it was always my fault. I must have been packing more pounds than I remember."

Chris chuckled. "Remember how we put that mattress on the floor and grabbed Kaitlynn and Kimmy – Kelsi was just a baby then – and all four of us jumped on the bed together? We told them that was the only time they were ever allowed to jump on a bed."

"I think they thought we had gone crazy," Hannah agreed with a laugh.

"What was it we made for brunch that morning? I remember it was good and the girls loved it."

Hannah tried to remember while the waitress came to take their order. "I think that was the first time we made strawberry crepes," Hannah said once the waitress left, thinking back through the years.

"That was it! Man, you haven't made those in forever!"

"No I haven't. I should do that." Chris nodded his agreement. There was a slight pause. "That was a good Saturday wasn't it?" she asked, smiling again at the precious memory.

"It sure was."

"Do you remember the first Saturday the kids decided they were going to make us breakfast in bed?" Hannah asked, one memory leading to another.

"Oh, I never thought we would get the smoke smell out of the house," Chris answered, grimacing.

"What I remember most was waking up, smelling smoke and being terrified that the house was on fire," Hannah told him.

"If I remember right, you were so terrified that you forgot to put your robe on before running out of the room," Chris mused.

Even after so many years, Hannah blushed. "I had forgotten all about that."

"That was a sad morning," Chris continued. "Not only did everything in our house smell like charred bacon for weeks, but it was the last time you ever slept in the—"

"Shhh!" Hannah hushed him fiercely as the waitress approached with their drinks. She plastered on a smile, accepting her glass of freshly-squeezed strawberry lemonade, hoping and praying the waitress hadn't overheard their conversation.

Chris grinned at her as he settled back in his seat, taking a sip of his mango-flavored iced tea. Flustered, Hannah turned to gaze out at the ocean. The waves rolled in faithfully, the surf calmer than it had been all day. Sea gulls dipped and soared above it, ready for their dinner, too. A breeze ruffled the sheer pink fabric of her ankle-length skirt that had a split up to her knee. Chris had bought it for her at one of the beach shops and it was perfect for their last dinner on the sand. She had paired it with a white sleeveless blouse, and tucked a pink flower into her wig.

"Remember how badly Kaitlynn burned her hand on the griddle, trying to get the bacon off? That took awhile to heal," Chris went on after a few minutes.

"It wasn't Kait, it was Kimmy," Hannah corrected.

Chris tipped his head, his expression doubtful. "Are you sure? I think it was Kaitlynn."

Hannah shook her head. She was the one who had changed the bandages for weeks, having to watch Kim cry every time, knowing she was hurting her daughter, but having to do it anyway. It had been gut-wrenching – much worse than trying to air the smoke out of the house in January. "I'm positive."

Chris shrugged. "Alright then." He was quiet for awhile, looking out at the ocean. "How old were they then?"

"I think Kaitlynn was maybe seven, which would have made Kim five and Kelsi three. Joe was still in his crib, because I remember being thankful that he was trapped in there rather than in the kitchen with the girls." Chris smiled.

The waitress brought Hannah's lobster and Chris' steak. The food was delicious and Hannah felt happy and peaceful as they ate. They spent the evening reminiscing about days passed, vacations they had taken, and funny moments they had shared. When the sun began to set, Chris pulled his chair around the table to sit beside Hannah, and they watched in awe as the sky was transformed into the brightest shades of pink and purple that they had ever seen in nature. Reflecting the colors, the ocean turned a dark pinkish-red. Surrounded by palm trees with a faint mist from the water cooling their faces, they both sat in awe-struck wonder as the sun slipped below the horizon, looking as if it slipped right into the sea itself. Once it had disappeared, Hannah realized with a laugh that she had been holding her breath. She had never seen anything so beautiful, and she couldn't help but wonder if there would be a sunset like that every night in heaven. If so, she would never tire of watching it.

They stayed at their table, talking and laughing, as twilight settled over the beach. As darkness fell, tiki torches were lit and a band began to play. Grabbing her hand, Chris pulled her onto the sandy dance floor, which was sectioned off by white lights. Hannah rested her head against his shoulder, and wrapped her arms loosely around his neck as they danced. She reveled in the feel of the sand under her bare feet, the sound of the breeze playing in the palm trees, and the feel of her husband's strong arms around her waist. It felt like a little bit of heaven on earth.

When they went to bed that night, Chris knew they could never have another day or evening that would compare to the one they had just shared. It had been perfect in every way.

The next morning, they boarded a plane back to the continental United States, and that night they slept in their own bed again. Their getaway to Hawaii was over. Their last vacation together had come to an end.

Seventeen

When Chris saw the text message from Joe, asking him to call first thing in the morning, he thought something was wrong. It had been three days since they had returned from Hawaii, and it was the first either of them had heard from their son.

Chris glanced at Hannah, who was already sleeping. Looking at the clock on the bedside table, he saw that it was just past ten. He had been reading, but now he carefully crawled out of bed and went downstairs. He dialed Joe's number as he shut the door to his home office.

"Dad," Joe answered, sounding agitated.

"Hi, Son. What's going on? Is everything okay?"

"Is everything okay?" Joe repeated, incredulously. "No, everything is not okay!"

Chris sat down in his office chair, puzzled. Joe sounded angry, not sad, confrontational rather than afraid. He had only heard his son truly angry a handful of times, and he couldn't begin to guess at the reason for it now.

He didn't have to guess for long. "I can't believe you're giving up on her! I cannot believe that you're just going to let her die without putting up a fight! She has cancer and you let her quit treatment, then take her away to Hawaii for one last vacation before she dies? That's it, isn't it? That's why you went? Because you think she's dying? You're accepting it? What about prayer, Dad? Where's your faith that God is going to heal her? You have given up on her!" Joe accused.

Chris felt taken aback by his son's passionate onslaught, but his surprise quickly faded. "You stop right there, Son," Chris interrupted, his voice low. "I will pray and ask the LORD to heal your mother every moment of every day, and I will hope beyond all hope that He will until she takes her very last breath, and maybe even beyond that, so don't you dare accuse me of giving up on her." Chris took a moment to take a deep breath and stabilize his shaking voice. "Joe, your mother is dying."

"Don't say that!"

"Son, if you were here, you would know. She is getting weaker by the day. Her clothes hang on her, no matter how many calories she eats. She takes prescription medicine to control the pain. Short of a miracle, she is dying."

"Then help her," Joe pleaded, his voice changing. Chris knew Joe's anger came from a grown man who felt as helpless as a child in the face of suffering. He knew that anger well.

"Modern medicine cannot help your mom. If we subject her to further treatment, her condition will not improve, her quality of life will only diminish. Right now, she's home. She gets to go to church. She has helped your sister paint her nursery. She walked the beach with me. She is making cookies." Chris didn't add that Hannah was filling their deep freeze with homemade meals, a fact that had made his heart break all over again when he had realized she was making things for him to eat once she was gone.

"You have seen God heal cancer," Joe said, fiercely.

"Yes, I have," Chris responded after taking a moment to stabilize his voice. "I have seen God heal people from cancer many times." It was something he was having a hard time comprehending himself. He had prayed for people with cancer, and they had come back with clean bills of health. They had come back, praising God, cancer-free. And yet, here his wife was, dying of the disease.

"Then why isn't she getting healed?" Joe demanded.

"Are you insinuating that I'm not praying enough? Or that my faith isn't strong enough?" Chris asked, incredulously. "Because if you are, you need to check your theology, Son."

"No, I didn't mean that," Joe answered, his voice sounding smaller than it had.

Chris let the silence stretch for several moments, formulating his answer. He needed to put into words something that he only had a vague concept of. Joe was asking questions that he himself was still wrestling with, yet he needed to be a father and help his son understand. "Joe, the Bible tells us that it is not God's will that any should perish, right?"

"Yes."

"So, it's fair to deduct that it is His will for all to be healed, right?"

"Yes."

"But is everyone healed?"

"No," Joe answered, sounding miserable.

"No," Chris echoed. "I have prayed for a lot of people who have not been healed. In fact, I've seen people who I've prayed for die. I've seen people that other people pray for, die."

"But lots of people do get healed," Joe cut in. "Why not her? *Why not her?*"

Chris was quiet. He looked to heaven, trying to form some kind of an answer to a question that had been echoing around his own heart for the past several months. "You need to ask God that question, but when you do, Son, remember that He is not on trial. You can ask God questions, but don't play the prosecutor. Questions and accusations are very different things. You take your inquiries to Him in hopes of gaining understanding, but don't ever question Him with the intent of laying blame."

Joe cleared his throat. "I just don't understand why God isn't healing her."

"Here's what I think," Chris started carefully. Whether his theology was solid or not, he wasn't sure, but it was the conclusion he had come to over the past several months of asking the same questions his son was asking now. For months he had struggled to line up the character of God that he knew to be true, with the situation going on before him. "I think that it is always God's will for someone to be healed, but it's not always His plan to heal someone. This is earth, not heaven. While God is in control, His will is not always done on earth because we live in a fallen world and He continues, day after day, to give humans freewill. He is a good God, but bad things happen sometimes because we live in a world that is full of sin."

"Are you saying Mom is dying because of sin in her life?" Joe questioned, defensively.

"No, I'm saying that we live in a fallen world, and there are natural consequences of sin all around us. Death and disease are two of those consequences. I believe that it is God's will to heal your mother, but I'm not sure it's His plan. I will ask God to change His plan every day from now until the end. I will ask him to heal my wife. I'll ask for His will to be done in her life. But I think we can live out a dual reality. We can entreat the LORD to change His plan while living practically."

"That's not living in faith, Dad," Joe countered.

"But where's wisdom, Joe? There is both. They can coincide. I absolutely believe God can heal your mother, my faith is not lacking, but wisdom says not to presume that you know the thoughts and plans of God. Wisdom says to number your days and be prepared." Chris sighed, hoping it was all coming out right, knowing it probably wasn't. "Short of a miracle, we have a funeral that needs to be planned, and your mother can't do it alone while I stand be-hind my badge of faith. I'll keep believing for healing, but I also want to be prepared in case His ways aren't mine."

It was quiet for a long time, and Chris could almost feel his son wrestling against what he was saying. Joe didn't want to accept it. He couldn't. It felt easier, better, to be-lieve that the LORD would heal Hannah, and that all of this would simply feel like a bad dream. Chris understood. Finally, the young man put voice to his thoughts. "I keep begging Him to heal her, Dad, but—"

"Don't, beg, Joe," Chris interrupted. "You are not a begger, but an heir, grafted into the family of God." He paused, then continued. "I recently heard a pastor say that to beg God to heal someone is to presume that we possess more mercy than He does."

Joe didn't answer, and Chris went on, gentling his voice. He hadn't meant to be harsh. The reality of Hannah's condition was difficult for them all. His children would deal with it in different ways. He wanted to help them through their grief, not chastise them for it. "Asking and begging are different things, separated by the position of the one who inquires. A starving man doesn't ask a stranger with confidence, and a beloved son doesn't beg," Chris explained. He let out a deep breath. "You better believe that I'm asking, too. Joe, I will hope beyond hope that the LORD will heal your mother, and I expect you to do the same, but we also need to be practical. I don't want either of us to have regrets. We need to say our goodbyes," Chris finished softly.

"I don't know how," Joe admitted, his voice broken.

"I don't either," Chris told him honestly. "But try to imagine yourself ten years down the road, when most of the pain from this time has gone, and your memories of your mother are only beautiful, sweet, and dear to your heart. Try to imagine what you would say to her then, and say it to her now. Try to imagine what you would go back and change then, if you can, and change it now."

"I would spend more time with her, despite the distance," Joe answered immediately. "I would make sure my kids have time with her."

"Then you had better come home."

~~~~~

Joe, Jessi and their kids did come. They came once at the very end of February, and then again toward the end of

March. They stayed for a couple of weeks each time. Hannah spent long afternoons sitting and visiting with her only son. She played games with Joe, Jessi and the girls. She rocked Joshua during his afternoon naps. She colored with the girls. She enjoyed conversations with her lively daughter -in-law.

When they came in March, Jessi helped Kimberly throw a baby shower for Kara. Hannah helped as much as she could, but her strength was quickly waning.

Chris saw it and felt dismayed at how quickly she was slipping away from them. At the beginning of January, he had thought it inconceivable that they only had a year left together. In February, she shocked him by saying six months was optimistic. Now, he was hoping she could hang on until Kara's baby came in April.

The day of the baby shower, Hannah sat on a chair and supervised Kelsi and Kamryn's coloring, while Kimberly and Jessi decorated the fellowship hall at the church with purple and lavender streamers. Chris and Joe had Joshua and Kim's boys at the park, but the girls had begged to stay for the shower. Watching them, which took very little effort at their age, gave Hannah something to do.

The food table was set up with purple-frosted cupcakes as the main table decoration. A bowl of pink punch, a platter of cheese and crackers, a pan of homemade mini quiches and two large vases filled with balls of colorful melons finished off the spread. The table skirt was a cascading array of long tuffs of dark purple and lavender tulle.

A decorated table for the gifts was set up next to the food table, along with a third table that was full of ribbons and hot glue guns. The bow table was Jessi's idea, and one that Hannah loved. She could only imagine how dolled up Kara's daughter would be, and thought giving shower guests the opportunity to make bows for the baby was a great idea. It would be fun for the women and helpful for Kara. Kim had started making bows to sell as a little side business a few months earlier, and volunteered to be stationed at the bow table throughout the party to instruct guests on different kinds of hair bows to make.

Chairs for the guests were set up and decorated, as was a large whiteboard where they would play baby shower Pictionary. After sitting with the girls, conserving her energy for the shower itself, Hannah stood up right before Kara was set to arrive. Checking her appearance, she straightened her wig, making sure the hair was hanging naturally. Her own hair was starting to grow back, but it was still short and patchy, making the wig a continued necessity.

Hannah moved around the room, admiring the food and the decorations. She praised Kim and Jessi's efforts, and gave them both hugs. A few minutes later, Kara arrived in a wave of hugs and laughter. Shortly after, the guests began to arrive.

During the baby shower, Hannah sat in the seat beside Kara at Kara's insistence, and watched her youngest daughter. She was so beautiful and full of life. She seemed to be nearly glowing, the joy of her pregnancy lighting up her small face. She was sweet, gracious, and well-liked, as was evident by the large turnout. Hannah's heart swelled with pride. She offered a quick prayer up to heaven, asking again if she could please be around for the birth of her granddaughter. She wanted to meet the new baby, but even more than that, she knew how important it was to her daughter.

After watching Kara, her attention turned to Kimberly. She was as full of joy as her sister, with her laughter always bubbling right below the surface. She too was beautiful and exuberant, finding it easy to connect with Kara's friends, most of whom she had never met. Hannah was so proud of the woman she had become, and her heart felt full and heavy with love.

Jessi moved on the opposite side of the room, ladling punch for guests at the food table, drawing Hannah's attention. A smile filled her face. She could not think of a better wife for her son. Over the years, the one thing that stood out most clearly about Jessica was how deeply and unselfishly she loved Joe. She was always trying to do what was best for him, even if it meant sacrificing her own comfort. Hannah loved her for that, loved her fierce loyalty and feisty charm. The love she felt for the beautiful brunette was every bit as equal to that which she felt for her own daughters.

Her thoughts moved to Kaitlynn, who she knew was in Texas wishing she could be at the shower with them. She had planned to come until Ava came down with the flu. Without feeling right about leaving her daughter, and not wanting to expose Hannah by bringing the little girl with her, Kaitlynn made the difficult decision to stay home and miss the shower. While it caused a few tears on Hannah's part, as she had been looking forward to having all of her kids home again, she was proud of Kaitlynn's decision. She was a wonderful mom – a legacy she hoped she had been responsible for passing on.

Automatically, Hannah's thoughts moved to her last daughter. For a brief moment, she saw Kelsi's freckled face as it was before the cancer ravaged her. The sadness that usually came when she thought of her daughter, who had been taken so young, didn't come. She would be with her again soon.

Turning her thoughts back to the party at hand, Hannah reached over and laid her hand against Kara's belly. The baby moved under her hand, and she beamed.

She was still in the land of the living, surrounded by her girls, her granddaughters, relatives, and friends. Life was good.

~~~~~

"I was so sure that she would be healed," Joe said softly, sounding confused.

Chris looked away from the movie in time to see Jessi take his son's hand in both of hers and hold it tightly. It was almost nine o'clock, and Hannah had gone to bed at the same time as the kids, worn out after the excitement of the baby shower earlier that day. Now only Chris, Joe and Jessi were still awake to watch a movie. "So did I," Chris admitted.

"Do you still think she will be?" Joe questioned.

Chris held his steady gaze. "I still hope."

"Me too," Joe answered.

Jessi squeezed his hand and stood. "I promised Kara I would call her tonight to talk about plans for tomorrow," she said, excusing herself. Joe nodded and let her go. Chris watched the young woman until she left the room. He turned back to his son.

"It feels like your mom and I were you and Jessi's age not long ago. We often recognize how fast the time goes when we think about our children, but not always when we think about our spouse." He paused and met Joe's eyes, a fierceness in his voice when he continued. "You love that girl well, Son! Don't you ever forget to open a door for her, pray with her at night or kiss her in the morning! You get up with the kids when they're sick, put them to bed at night so she can take a bubble bath, and steal her away for romantic weekends. I don't care what a disagreement is about, it is never important enough to let it come between you, not even for five minutes. I know that you're young and healthy now, but don't you ever take her for granted!"

Joe shook his head, and his eyes shone with moisture. "How are you doing it, Dad? How are you letting go? I cannot imagine losing Jessica. I honestly don't know if I would survive."

Chris drug his hand over his face. "I know that my God is good. And I have to remind myself over and over every day to be thankful for the years I have had with your mother. I have already received a gift greater than any man has a right to. Without remembering that, I don't know that I would make it through the day," he answered raggedly. There was a long silence. "Unless the LORD intervenes,

Joe, we're going to lose her."

"I know," Joe answered quietly.

"And I don't know how – it seems inconceivable to me now – but we're going to survive it, and we're going to be okay. Do you know why?"

Joe shook his head, unable to speak.

"Because we have our faith and we have our family, and that is all we need, Son, to weather any storm and to overcome any trial."

"That's what Mom always says," Joe said quietly.

"She's one smart lady."

Eighteen

During the end of February and the month of March, Chris and Hannah had constant company. Everyone came to enjoy as much time with her as they could. Kaitlynn, Kimberly, and Joe were home more than they had been in years. The big house was full of children and laughter. Kara was over every day. Jimmy and Kostya came and stayed for several weeks. Tim and Carla came, Bill, Jari and their boys came, Hannah's siblings came. Hannah's heart was full – she felt exceedingly loved.

In early April, hospice was called. Hannah had grown so weak that she could no longer get out of bed. Chris was carrying her everywhere she needed to go, but she felt that her care was more than she wanted him to have to handle.

Even with hospice in her home, she felt total peace. Despite the weakened state of her physical body, she was on the brink of true life. Additionally, she had been given wonderful and adequate time with her family and friends. It hadn't felt rushed. There was nothing left unsaid. She was sure that each of them knew how she felt about them, and how she felt about what was coming. Hannah felt confident that nothing had been left unspoken or undone. The only thing that didn't feel complete was that she had yet to meet her unborn granddaughter. She prayed unceasingly that she would hang on until Kara's baby came.

Two weeks before Kara's due date, Hannah came down with a cold. She could see the fear in Chris' eyes every time she coughed and knew that it was founded.

That night, her youngest daughter burst into the house, calling for her. Chris called out to Kara from the living room where he and Hannah were watching a movie together. Kara came and dropped to her knees in front of Hannah. Her eyes were brimming with tears, and Hannah reached out and pressed her hand against the side of Kara's face. "What's wrong, Honey?"

"Daddy told me you're sick."

"It's just a cold," Hannah told her gently.

"I'm going to call the doctor in the morning and have him induce me," Kara said firmly.

Hannah shook her head weakly. They had had this conversation before. "That wouldn't be best for the baby. She needs to stay inside of you until *she's* ready to come out."

"I want her to meet you," Kara cried. The young woman glanced up at Chris, then back to Hannah. "Daddy told me it's been a rough day." Kara reached out and impulsively pressed a kiss to her mother's palm. "I want this baby to meet her grandma."

"She will, Kara, don't worry," Hannah said gently.

Kara didn't look convinced. "Mama, I'm getting induced."

Hannah shook her head weakly. "Don't do that. Please. Promise me you won't. Labor is going to be hard enough on you and this little one. Don't make it happen before you're both ready."

Kara turned pleading eyes up to Chris, looking for his support, but he only shrugged.

"The LORD is kind, Kara," Hannah started.

"Mama, you're dying! What is kind about that?" Kara questioned miserably, tears running down her pale cheeks.

Hannah smiled. "But I'm going to get to meet my granddaughter! That is His kindness. I will hold on until this baby comes, you wait and see. I may not get to see her turn one, start to walk, go off to her first day of school, or get married," Hannah paused to blink back tears, "but I will get to meet her. I promise you."

Kara's head sank forward against the couch, and she

cried. Hannah ran her hand through Kara's hair, comforting her, even that small, repetitive movement taking all the strength she had. She wished she could comfort her daughter more, wished she could simply get better and make all the pain and heartbreak her family was experiencing go away.

She wasn't worried about herself, but she worried about them. She hurt for them. She cried for them. She had lived a good life. She had enjoyed her days. She had loved and been loved. She had no regrets. But saying goodbye was still difficult, especially knowing that she was leaving them behind to deal with her absence. That was the hardest part of all.

She glanced up at Chris and saw that he, too, had tears in his eyes. He reached down and put his hand on Kara's head in a comforting gesture. They stayed like that for a long time.

Kara didn't get induced, and the baby didn't come. Her due date came and went, and yet the baby showed no signs of coming.

The cold Hannah had caught settled in her lungs and became pneumonia. She was hospitalized. Kara reasoned again that she should be induced, but Hannah wouldn't let her. She assured her again, as she had so many times in the past, that she was going to meet her granddaughter.

Finally, two weeks and a day after her due date, Kara went into labor. Hannah convinced Chris to put her in a wheelchair and wheel her into Kara's delivery room. Wearing a mask to protect her daughter and the newborn from her pneumonia and using all the strength she had, she stayed at her daughter's side, serving as her labor coach until a beautiful baby girl made her appearance at one in the morning. Hannah was the first person to hold her, and she watched in rapt adoration as the infant stared up into her face, as if she knew how precious little time they would have together. Hannah felt the tears running down her cheeks.

Hannah counted her ten little fingers and ten little toes. She laughed at how the baby's bottom lip was sucked in to the point that Hannah wasn't even sure she had a bottom jaw. With a fingertip to the tiny mouth, she pulled open the lip to make sure that there was one and laughed in delight as the baby tried to eat her finger. The infant's eyes never left her face.

"She is absolutely beautiful, Kara! A perfect little girl!" she exclaimed, her voice unsteady with emotion. "Have you decided on a name?"

Kara nodded, her face shining despite her exhaustion. Her makeup had been washed away, and her blonde hair was slicked back by Justin's tender strokes, but Hannah thought she had never looked more beautiful.

Hannah's heart sang, praising the LORD as she reflected on the fact that her daughter, who was supposedly unable to have children of her own from birth, had just delivered a healthy, beautiful baby girl. And, she had lived long enough to meet her. The LORD was kind indeed.

"Her name is Hosanna Kostya," Kara said softly, watching her mom cradle her daughter.

"Hosanna Kostya," Hannah repeated, her eyes shining. "It's beautiful."

"We're naming her after you, Mom," Kara said.

Hannah nodded, tears slipping down her cheeks again. She was too overcome with emotion to say anything.

"We hope she becomes the kind of woman that you are," Justin added, still holding Kara's hand.

Hannah nodded again, smiling through her tears. She felt Chris' hand on her shoulder, and felt the gentle pressure he applied. He knew how deeply their words touched her, just as he knew everything about her.

"Baby, get some pictures," Kara said, giving Justin a gentle push toward their camera. Time was running short, and they all knew it. He retrieved the camera and did as

Kara asked, snapping what seemed like a couple dozen pictures of Hannah and Hosanna, then added Chris to the small group and snapped some more.

Hosanna continued to stare up into Hannah's face, quiet and serene, and Hannah smiled beneath her mask. She ran her fingertips lovingly over her granddaughter's face.

"Hosanna, I bless you in the name of our LORD Jesus Christ with knowing that you are loved, cherished, accepted, delighted in, and enjoyed. I bless you with loving the LORD all the days of your life, listening to His voice and looking to Him for your strength and counsel. May He bless you and keep you and cause His face to shine upon you," Hannah said, putting all her hopes and dreams for her tiny granddaughter into that one blessing. She knew it would be her only.

Hannah cradled the sweet infant until her body shook with fatigue and pain, and she no longer trusted herself to hold her. Then, she reluctantly gave her to Justin, who handed the baby to her mother for the first time. Hannah watched the new little family, tears gathering in her eyes. Finally, she embraced Kara and then Justin, telling them how much she loved them and how proud of them she was. Then, she let Chris push her back to her room and lift her into her hospital bed.

When she was settled, she took Chris' hand and pulled him down to sit on the bed beside her. Looking up into his eyes, she saw that he wanted to ask her not to speak. He knew what was coming and didn't want her to say it. Even knowing that, she knew that she had to. "I don't have much longer, Love. You need to call the kids. They need to come. Call Jari and Carla and my mom, too. I want them all here."

He stared down at her, tears running down his face. "I don't want this to be it," he admitted.

She pressed her lips against his hand, feeling tears on her own cheeks. "We know He works all things for the good of those who love Him," she quoted in a whisper. "I have lived a full and wonderful life with you. I just saw my granddaughter be born. Please, Chris, call the kids."

Chris nodded and stood to leave the room. She stopped him. "Wait. Before you leave, can you give me a paper and pen?"

"Why?" he asked, even as he looked for the items she requested.

"I want to write a letter to Hosanna." She thought of all the other letters she had written and stowed away in the drawer of her nightstand. There was one for Chris, each of their children and each of their grandchildren. Hosanna would not be left out.

Chris gave her a pen and paper, then left the room to do as she had asked. She barely had enough strength left to write a few words, and she concentrated on making her handwriting neat and legible.

Hosanna,

Meeting you was worth hanging on. You are beautiful, and I love you so much even this soon. Your birth has brought so much joy! Meeting you was one of the sweetest gifts I have been given. Know this, the LORD is good, and His kindness endures forever. Wrap that around your mind and bind it to your heart, precious girl.

All my love,

Grandma

Exhausted, she set aside the pen and paper, knowing Chris would fold it up and put it in a safe place when he was done with his phone calls. She fell asleep in his absence, but roused when he came back into the room. "Will you lie with me?"

He smiled faintly. "Will I hurt you?"

She shook her head. He climbed carefully up onto the bed beside her and laid down, wrapping her tenderly in his arms. He kissed her face, and she studied him. He was still vibrant and strong. He was handsome and full of life. The fifties looked good on him. She studied his strong chin, tanned skin, and green eyes. She looked at every laugh line in his face and remembered all the good times they had together that had put them there.

"I wish I could have had longer with you," Hannah whispered, feeling sadness and longing fill her. She didn't know how to say goodbye to this man she loved.

Chris kissed her face again and rested his forehead against her sallow cheek. He smiled sadly. "Love, forever would not have been long enough."

By the next morning, the fluid in her lungs had increased to the point that the doctors had to hook her up to machines in order to keep her alive until all the kids could arrive. Chris could feel her fading away, and he stayed by her side, holding her hand as she slipped in and out of consciousness.

She awakened around eight o'clock. Her eyes settled on his face and she smiled weakly. She reached for his hand and he held hers tightly. "Don't be sad, Love. I'm ready to go home. I'm ready to meet Jesus face to face. I'm ready to see Kelsi," she said. "But someday you'll come home too – to our home that we'll share. When the time comes, don't be scared. I will be waiting for you."

He leaned forward, his face close to hers. With tears in his eyes, he said the only thing he could think of to say. "Hannah, I can't wait. I can't wait until I see you again. I can't wait to see your face, to feel your embrace." He ran his fingertips over her face and pressed his lips softly against hers in a final kiss. She smiled. "I can't wait, Love," he finished in a whisper, even as he watched her eyes close. For the last time, she slipped into unconsciousness.

Two hours later, Chris sat on the edge of her hospital

bed as Justin wheeled Kara into the room in a wheelchair, baby Hosanna cradled in her arms. Joe and Jessi, Kelsi, Kamryn and Joshua, Greg and Kimberly, Carson, Samuel, Clinton and Caiden, Jake and Kimberly, Austin, Adam and Ava, Jim and Kostya, Tim and Carla, and Bill and Jari all crowded into the room behind them. Chris looked at the crowded semicircle of people he loved, people Hannah loved, people who loved her, and felt his breath catch. It was time. It was what she wanted.

Doctor Thorlo was there and at a nod from Chris, he turned off the machines and unhooked them from her quietly before stepping back out of the way. Without the aid of the machines, Hannah's breathing slowed and grew shallow. "Please heal her now, God!" Chris cried out within. Suddenly, her breathing picked up speed until her eyes flew open and her face lit up in a brilliant smile, as she focused on something near the ceiling.

"Oh, Beloved! Beloved, You're beautiful!" she exclaimed, almost glowing. Laughter bubbled from her lips as she stretched her hands upward. Then, suddenly, Chris realized she wasn't breathing at all anymore, and the heart machine plateaued as she coded, her arms falling limply to her sides.

He could hear his daughters crying all around him, could hear a confused little one asking what had happened. Yet his gaze was fixed on Hannah's smiling face. He reached out and gently closed her eyes. "So are you, my Love, so are you. And you're home with the One you love." In that knowledge there was comfort.

In that moment, even as his heart broke and pain overwhelmed him at the realization that the love of his life was gone, he knew that the LORD had healed her after all. She no longer had cancer or pain – she was healed, happy and whole. Though he could not see the proof of it, he knew his prayers had been answered. Cancer had not claimed another victim – the LORD Jesus Christ had the victory. Through

Him, Hannah had overcome death. Her healing was complete. She lived!

Chris lifted his eyes to his family and good friends and said the one thing that filled his heart and mind.

"God is kind. Though he slay me, yet will I trust Him. We will overcome by the blood of the Lamb, we are reconciled because of His great love."

Behind him, he heard his only son say, "Amen," and Chris knew that no matter how hard the following hours, days, weeks, months and years might be, they were all going to be okay. Their faith would sustain.

A NOTE FROM ANN

Dear Reader,

Tears fill my eyes as I finish this book. Saying good-bye to Hannah Colby was like losing a good friend. And yet, her story of victory through Jesus has done something inside my heart.

A few weeks into starting this book, I was stuck. I knew the storyline, knew what was going to happen, but I did not know how to write it. How do you write about the early death of a beautiful Christian woman with a praying family? How do you justify or attempt to understand why she was not healed? I believe in the power of prayer. I believe in a big God who is able to heal, who is able to work healing miracles even in those diagnosed with fatal illnesses. I have seen it happen. A year ago, a doctor was in the process of calling time of death over my eleven-month-old niece. Last month, she celebrated her second birthday with pink-frosted cupcakes and pigtails in her blonde hair. The only explanation? Jesus. A year and a half ago, my mom was told that she had cervical cancer and immediate treatment was ordered. However, when they ran their pre-surgery tests, there was no cancer to be found. The only explanation? Jesus. Healing does happen. But, not everyone is healed.

I wrestled with this question, knowing that it was a foundational issue in this book, and here I am at the end of the book without ever having received any answers. Here's what I know to be true, though – God is good. He is kind. He is able. And His ways are higher. Sometimes, He heals people or situations, but sometimes He doesn't. Sometimes, we walk through a trial and do not find the victory we expect, but know this – with Jesus, we always have the victory, whether we can see it now or not. In this life or the next, those who are in Christ Jesus will emerge victorious. Through the uncertainty, faith sustains.

When the healing comes this side of heaven, we rejoice and praise Him with thanksgiving! How we deal with those diagnoses that shatter our world, that news that stops our heart, or a loss that we cannot fathom ever recovering from, I do not know, aside from this – we run, walk or crawl to the feet of Jesus and stay close to Him, taking shelter in the shadow of His wings, knowing that whatever happens, He is God, and He is good.

With all that being said, this book wasn't just about saying goodbye to Hannah Colby – it was also about saying goodbye to all of the characters in the Glendale novels. This is the last book in the series. It's a journey I've been on for several years, and I have enjoyed it immensely. When I started writing "Glendale" at the age of sixteen, I started dreaming that this series would serve to answer questions, give a bigger perspective, bring healing or lead to an encounter with the very real God for even just one reader. At its conclusion, my heart has been blessed by the stories that have flooded in, explaining how those very things have happened. I hope and pray that continues in the months and years ahead. That is my one desire for these books – that the one true God would meet readers in these pages filled with fiction.

Despite the fact that it feels sad and strange to be done with this series, it's time to move on to new things, new characters and new stories. And I will! I am certainly not going to stop writing, so, Lord willing, expect to see more books coming soon! Although I don't have any release dates yet, you can check in with me on facebook to see updates on what's coming and when it will be released.

I am so grateful and humbled that you have followed me on this journey over the last six books, and I hope and pray that you have enjoyed getting to know these characters and reading their stories. I know that the Mothers of Glendale series was more for a select audience, and I thank you for wading through those times with me. I hope you have found inspiration in the pages of these books and that somehow, someway they have touched your heart. I know they have mine.

Again, thank you so much for reading the Glendale novels! I am truly honored that you have taken the time out of your busy life to read my books. I pray that they have been worth your time.

As always, although I love to write, I write for my readers. With that constantly in mind, I would love to hear from you. I enjoy having people stop by my website, getting emails, hearing from you on facebook and getting to know you, so please, always feel free to drop me a note!

Until next time, may Jesus Christ, whose hair is white as wool, whose eyes are like flames of fire and whose voice is like that of many waters, strengthen you to rise up and join Him as an overcomer, tasting victory and going forward confidently, knowing His great affection toward you!

Ann

www.anngoering.com
ann@anngoering.com
www.facebook.com/AuthorAnnGoering
Twitter @Ann_Goering

GLENDALE SERIES

The Glendale Series wrestles with the age-old dilemmas of love, faith, family, forgiveness and growing up in a fresh story format. With relationships that grip readers' hearts as they reflect raw realities plentiful in our society and an ending that will keep readers on the edge of their seats right up until the end, The Glendale Series is one girl's unforgettable journey to health, wholeness and joy.

MOTHERS OF GLENDALE

The Mothers of Glendale Series tells the personal, emotional, and sometimes painful stories of three special women introduced in The Glendale Series. Glendale mother figures Jari, Carla, and Hannah are each on their own journey, with their paths weaving together with one another to create a beautiful tapestry of faith, hope, and unconditional love. With raw realities that women face every day, covered by the grace of a very big God, Mothers of Glendale takes readers a step further than new love to the weathered and deeply beautiful land of seasoned marriages, motherhood and saying goodbye to a full life, well-lived.

AWARD-WINNING AUTHOR ANN GOERING

Ann Goering is a four-time award-winning journalist who has worked as a senior editor/writer of magazines, newspapers and online publications since 2005. A theatrical production she wrote was performed on stage in 2005, and she was asked to co-write a screenplay for a Hollywood film in 2009.

She works for an international Christian ministry that specializes in relationships and evangelism to children, youth and families around the world. Her involvement in that has given her a heart for the broken, hurting and lost and a desire to see individuals and families operate in healthy relationships.

She has her degree in communications and enjoys writing Christian fiction and speaking to groups of women about the love of Jesus. She resides in the Ozark Mountains with her husband, whom she's terribly in love with, their baby girl, Alija, and their fluffy white dog, Sheesha.

Made in the USA
San Bernardino, CA
05 July 2015